DISCARD

The

Bloom

Girls

D1173362

The Bloom Girls

A Novel

EMILY CAVANAGH

LAKE UNION
PUBLISHING

Text copyright © 2017 by Emily Cavanagh
All rights reserved.

No part of this book may be reproduced, or stored in a retrieval system, or transmitted in any form or by any means, electronic, mechanical, photocopying, recording, or otherwise, without express written permission of the publisher.

Published by Lake Union Publishing, Seattle

www.apub.com

Amazon, the Amazon logo, and Lake Union are trademarks of Amazon.com, Inc., or its affiliates.

ISBN-13: 9781503942530
ISBN-10: 1503942538

Cover design by Kimberly Glyder

Printed in the United States of America

To Reuben—my partner in everything

Chapter One

Suzy

When Suzy Bloom first heard about her father's death, she was making a cheese soufflé. In the stainless-steel test kitchen of the *FoodArt* offices, Suzy cracked egg after egg, straining the whites into one bowl and the sunny-yellow yolks into another. Her fingers were slippery when she picked up the pencil to record in her notebook the exact measurements for this recipe.

She'd been at work since seven, partly because this was a new job and she was still getting comfortable, and partly because she'd been having trouble sleeping lately. By the time she rose at five, she'd been staring at the ceiling for an hour. This was her third soufflé today, and it was only a little after eight. The first had come out too dry, the second tasted wet with cheese, and the third was too eggy. Suzy hoped she'd finally gotten the proportions right.

When Suzy came to work at *FoodArt*, just two months earlier, she'd been told by the magazine editors that they believed in the science of cooking. Since she'd been forced to unexpectedly quit her restaurant job, Suzy had nodded enthusiastically at the hiring committee, agreeing that she too believed in the importance of specificity, the value in tinkering with a recipe until it was just right.

She hadn't fully understood what this philosophy of exactness would mean on a day-to-day basis. She hadn't realized she'd be expected to spend an *entire* day on a single recipe, trying endless variations, offering up tastes to her overfed colleagues, until finally, *finally*, she got the science just right. Even on those rare occasions when she perfected a recipe the very first time, Suzy was required to try out at least two more versions to confirm it. It was unlike cooking in a restaurant where you got one chance to make a dish right. The kitchen at *FoodArt* was more like a lab with rows of individual stations set up for the test editors. It was quiet too, unlike the bustling kitchen at Ciao where the noise from the dining room overflowed into the crowded space where Suzy and the rest of the staff worked hip-to-hip.

Suzy finished pouring the soufflés into the white ramekins and closed the oven door, assessing what needed to be cleaned up. She'd been tweaking the soufflé recipe since yesterday. Her colleagues would start to come in soon, and Suzy was hoping she could run out for a quick cup of coffee and then start her first batch of granola. The March issue would have a featured section on brunch.

She didn't have much interest in eating lately. Last week, the morning sickness had started, and she spent the workday trying not to gag as she mixed up each dish. Her purse was now filled with miniature bags of oyster crackers that she surreptitiously snacked on throughout the day between sips of ginger ale.

The pregnancy was ridiculously ironic on so many levels. First of all, she'd recently declared herself a lesbian, though she and Lani broke up a few months later. The breakup resulted in a moment of self-pitying weakness and a one-night stand with her ex-boyfriend, Ian. They'd fumbled awkwardly in the dark of Suzy's bedroom, and after an unsatisfying fifteen minutes, Suzy looked down at the torn condom Ian had pulled off. That was nearly two months ago, and she hadn't called him or returned his calls since. She hadn't told him about the pregnancy—or the abortion scheduled for tomorrow morning.

Since she'd made the appointment, Suzy had tried not to think about it. She hadn't told either of her sisters, partly because she didn't know how to explain the pregnancy and abortion so soon after she'd told them she was a lesbian, but mostly because she couldn't face Cal, who had struggled for years to get pregnant before finally finding success with in vitro. Suzy could picture the wounded look on her oldest sister's face, as if her not wanting to have the baby was a rebuke of Cal's choices and an intentional act of depriving Maisy and Sadie from having a cousin.

Suzy was washing dishes when the head of the department came in. Marie was a tall, slender woman who wore her spotless white apron cinched tightly around her tiny frame. Though she'd been nothing but kind, Marie's formal and imperious manner always unnerved Suzy. Marie's polished leather shoes clicked across the 1950s black-and-white linoleum floor.

"You have a phone call."

"I do?" Suzy was elbow deep in hot water and suds, washing the bowls out for the fourth time, in case she needed to redo the recipe again. She didn't know who'd be calling her here. Her phone was in her bag, though she hadn't looked at it since arriving at work.

"Jane tried to send it to voicemail, but they said it's important." Marie came to the sink and handed Suzy a striped dish towel for her hands. "I'll finish up here for you. You can use my office."

Suzy nodded, unsettled by Marie's gentleness, by the assumption that bad news was about to be delivered. She checked to make sure the timer for the soufflés was set, then hurried down the hall to Marie's spacious office. Only the senior editors got their own offices; the test-kitchen editors had cubicles instead. Suzy sat down at Marie's long black desk, leaning back in the plush leather chair. A red light flashed on the phone, patiently waiting. She stared at it for a moment before picking up. She hoped it was Violet. How often had Violet called in tears over a bad date or a rejection letter from a literary journal? With Violet, everything was a crisis.

"Hello?"

"Is this Suzy Bloom?" It was an unfamiliar male voice.

"Yes."

"This is Barry Wentworth." The name meant nothing to her. "I work with your father at Veg."

"Oh." Suzy tried to conjure up Barry's face but couldn't picture him. She'd been to her father's restaurant only a handful of times and not in over a year. "Is everything okay?"

"No." There was a strained silence. "Your father didn't come in to work this morning. So I went by his house. He was collapsed by his treadmill." Another long silence. "I'm very sorry, Suzy."

"What do you mean?" Suzy held the phone to her ear so tightly that her head started to ache. She loosened her grip.

"The doctors think it was a brain aneurysm. He was already dead by the time I got there." Suzy opened her mouth, but no sound came out. Barry kept talking. "I'm sorry to have to be the one to call you. I tried calling Cal, but her phone went right to voicemail. I found your number in your dad's phone."

Suzy finally found her voice. "I have to go. I'm sorry, but I have to go." She fumbled with the phone and slammed it back into the receiver. Her breath was coming in short, shallow pants. How could this be happening? She needed to call Cal. And Violet. She needed her sisters.

Chapter Two

Cal

Cal Bloom measured out some Infants' Tylenol and stuck the plastic syringe in Sadie's mouth. Sadie sucked down the sweet medicine and let out a hoarse cough, nuzzling into her mother's shoulder and leaving a sticky pink smear on Cal's white blouse. Across the hall, Maisy was whining about a purple skirt. Hoisting Sadie in her arms, Cal walked back to her bedroom where Howard was still trying to sleep. His eyes were closed, an arm thrown over his head. She stood above him, waiting for him to open his eyes. She knew he couldn't possibly be sleeping, with Maisy having a fit in the other room and Sadie fussing only a few feet away.

"Sadie has a fever," Cal said when it became clear that Howard was going to hold on to the last few moments of sleep before the onslaught of the day. Howard groaned, finally pushing himself up to sitting and propping a pillow behind his head.

"How high?" Howard's sandy hair stuck up in tufts. He yawned.

Heat radiated from Sadie's body through the thin fabric of Cal's now-ruined shirt. "A hundred. I think it's just teething, but she can't go to day care." Cal kissed the side of Sadie's warm head, rubbing circles along the baby's back. "I have a meeting this morning," she added quickly.

Howard sighed. He always looked like a little boy in the morning, eyes puffy and cheeks pink. While Cal seemed to spend half the night in and out of consciousness, Howard slept heavy and deep, which meant she was usually the one up in the middle of the night when one of the girls needed something. "I stayed home last time," he said.

Cal sat down on the bed and unbuttoned her blouse to nurse. Dread coursed through her at the idea of calling in sick again. It would be her sixth sick day since she went back to work five months ago. Sadie was only eight months old, and she was spending up to nine hours a day in the germ farm that was day care. Despite the best intentions of the teachers, who scrubbed the toys down with bleach at the end of each day, it seemed that every time Cal picked Sadie up, all the children had unwiped runny noses and sticky fingers.

"Is there anyone else?" Howard asked.

"Like who?" Cal shot back. She didn't mean to snap at him, although that seemed to be the way they communicated lately.

"I don't know. Your sisters?"

"Yeah, right." It wasn't fair to dismiss them entirely. Suzy would have stayed with Sadie if she hadn't just started a new job. Until just a few months ago, Suzy worked at a restaurant at night, and she'd stayed home with Maisy several times. But Suzy kept regular hours now, and it wasn't fair to ask. And Violet. Violet's schedule was erratic, and while Cal might have trusted Violet with four-year-old Maisy, she didn't trust her with Sadie. When Sadie was older, Violet would be the fun aunt. But you didn't leave your baby with the fun aunt.

"Jonathan will understand," Howard said.

Jonathan would *not* understand. Jonathan Fitch, her boss at the law firm Fitch, Lowe, and Dunn, was fifty years old. His children were in their teens, and Cal somehow doubted he'd been the one to stay home with them when they were sick.

Howard was also a lawyer, though at a different firm. But because Howard was a man, he'd already made partner. When Howard called in sick, she doubted his colleagues rolled their eyes and sighed as they struggled to cover his cases. Cal had done the same thing before she had kids. Most of the other women in her office were single or childless, and many of them left after their first child was born. The rules were different for Howard.

He palmed Sadie's head. "Poor babe."

Maisy burst into their bedroom, eyes stormy. "Where's my purple skirt?"

"It's in the wash," Cal said. She'd forgotten to turn the dryer on last night and could picture the damp load sitting in the machine, growing mildewed.

"You said you'd wash it," Maisy said, crying. Her curly dark hair was wild and unkempt. Getting the girl in the tub was a battle, much less getting a comb through all that hair. Maisy looked at Cal accusingly, her mouth drawn in a pout.

"I forgot. Go pick something else." At her breast, Sadie sucked greedily away, the fever clearly not affecting her appetite.

"You *always* forget," Maisy said, which wasn't true. "I need it. Get it for me," she demanded.

"Don't talk to me like that," Cal said automatically. She turned back to Howard. "Can you do it?"

"Do what?" Maisy asked.

"It's your turn," he repeated.

Cal looked down at Sadie, who ate contentedly, eyes closed, long dark lashes brushing her cheeks. Cal hated to leave her. Howard would try to work from home, propping Sadie in her bouncy seat while he checked e-mail and did paperwork, and he'd forget what time Sadie needed more Tylenol. Cal wanted to stay home with her, to be the one to rub Sadie's back and feed her applesauce, but she could picture Jonathan's stern red face, the way he would ignore her when she came into work on Monday.

Outside the window, the sky was a stony gray. It was supposed to snow later in the afternoon. Cal hated February, the bleakest month in Boston, a purgatory between the frenetic bustle of the holidays and the distant promise of spring. The guy who plowed their parking spots had moved out of town last year, and she hadn't had a chance to look for anyone else. A pulsing ache began behind Cal's left eye.

"Please?" She hated that she was reduced to begging Howard, but she was willing to do it if it meant not having to leave a message with Jonathan's receptionist.

"Do what?" Maisy asked again.

Howard sighed. "Okay. But it's your turn next time. I can't keep missing work either."

"I know. Thank you." Relief rushed through Cal.

"Do *what?*" Maisy yelled.

"Stay home with Sadie," Howard said. "She's sick."

"Again," Cal added.

"I want to stay home with Mommy and Sadie too." Maisy jumped on the bed, jostling Sadie in Cal's arms. Sadie let out a whine and then latched back on. "Can I?"

"Stop jumping, Maisy. I'm not staying home. Daddy is." The morning would need to be recalibrated. Cal would have to drop off Maisy at preschool, which was in the opposite direction of her office, so they'd need to leave early. She'd gotten home late last night and hadn't had a chance to pack Maisy's lunch. She'd need to do that before they left too. "Maisy, go get dressed."

"I can't find my purple skirt," Maisy reminded them, as if this were the most pressing matter for everyone.

"Find something else," Cal ordered. Maisy frowned, her solemn brown eyes narrowing at her mother. "Maisy, I'm serious." Maisy stomped dramatically back to her bedroom, hands on her hips. "Four going on fourteen," Cal said under her breath to Howard, her mood a little lighter now that he'd agreed to stay home.

"I'm going to shower before you guys leave." Howard threw the blankets off. Seeing him in just his boxer shorts, Cal wondered if he'd put on a little weight. Though he tried to get to the gym a few days a week, dinner often came from the freezer or a takeout box. She'd have to look up some quick, healthy dinner recipes. Maybe during her lunch hour.

Cal picked up her phone to check the time and noticed a missed call, though she didn't recognize the number and there was no message. Probably a wrong number. No one called this early. She and Maisy needed to be on the road in less than an hour.

"Thank you," she said again.

"You're welcome. But I mean it, Cal. Next time, you have to stay home. Or we have to figure something else out." Her relief was replaced with anxiety over the next time someone would be sick. It *was* winter. Any one of them could be home sick on Monday.

She and Howard had been married for eight years. He knew her better than anyone, even Suzy and Violet. But these days they spoke in sentences peppered with the interruptions of two children. When Maisy and Sadie weren't interrupting them, the logistics of caring for the children included doctor's appointments with Maisy's allergist, after-school activities, and the coordination of dropping off and picking up two children. Even during the rare moments of quiet in the evening after the kids were asleep, Cal had trouble slowing the endless loop of chores and reminders in order to have a normal conversation with her husband. They tended to watch television instead. No need to talk or think.

"You should probably call the doctor today," Cal said. "I think it's just teething, but they'll be closed for the weekend." Howard nodded and went into the bathroom. Sadie had nearly fallen back to sleep, and Cal carried her back to her bedroom, placing her gently in the crib and then pulling the blankets up over her shoulders. She stood for a moment above Sadie, watching the rise and fall of her chest, chubby fingers clenched in a fist.

Back in her own bedroom, Cal unbuttoned the stained shirt and stood in her skirt and bra in front of the open closet. The bathroom door opened and Howard emerged, steam leaking from the bathroom as he dribbled water all over the bedroom floor.

"You're dripping everywhere. Can't you dry off in the shower?"

"God, Cal. Anything else?" Howard rarely got angry, but she was pushing the limits of his patience. She didn't mean to. She was just on edge all the time. Howard smelled of soap and shaving cream, and Cal placed her hand on his arm to stop him as he passed.

"Sorry." She leaned in and kissed him on the cheek, letting herself relax for a moment.

He slipped a hand around her waist, cupping a breast over her bra. Cal twisted away from his grasp. "Maisy's right outside."

"I know. I'm just saying hello." He smiled at her, his gray eyes crinkling in the corners.

"I've got to get ready. We're running late." She found another shirt and slipped into it, pulling away from Howard. His hand dropped to his side, and he turned to his own dresser to find clothes.

Maisy came back into the bedroom, wearing only a pair of Cinderella underpants. "I want my purple skirt," she whined.

"I swear to God, Maisy, if you don't get some clothes on this minute, you're going to be in so much trouble," Cal threatened, though she didn't know what actually lay on the other side of the threat. "Get yourself dressed right now."

"Take it easy," Howard said after Maisy had sulked back to her room.

"How many times do I have to ask?" Cal buttoned her shirt, making a mental list of what she needed to do. Maisy had swim class after school today. She'd need to pack a bag before they left. And her EpiPen. Always her EpiPen.

Outside the window, flakes had begun to fall, tiny flecks of white whirling through the air. Traffic would be terrible. Beside the bed, Cal's phone rang.

"It's early. Who's that?" Howard asked. Later, Cal would want to burrow into the moment, her last few seconds of not knowing, when her biggest concern was being late to work. Cal walked to the nightstand and picked up the phone. It was Suzy.

"Hi. What's up?" There was a noise on the other end, a soft snuffling, a whimper. "Suzy? Are you okay? What's wrong?"

When Suzy spoke, her voice was soft. "I just got a call from a friend of Dad's. Barry Wentworth."

"Is everything okay? Is Dad all right?" Cal was suddenly hot, her whole body flushed. She wondered if she was coming down with Sadie's fever. Howard frowned questioningly, taking a step closer.

"No." Now Cal could hear the tears in her little sister's voice. "He's dead, Callie. Dad is dead."

She didn't realize she'd dropped the phone until she heard the crack of it on the wood floor. Down the hall, Sadie began to cry.

.

Chapter Three

Violet

Violet opened her eyes to the light of another gray morning streaming through the windows of the living room. She blinked in the unfiltered light, her cheek damp from the small patch of drool on the couch cushion. She pushed herself to a sitting position, her neck and back already showing signs of the aches that would be there all day after another night on the overstuffed sofa. In the kitchen Annie made breakfast, slamming cabinets and rifling through the silverware drawer. Dishes clattered in the sink.

Annie didn't make any effort to be quiet in the mornings, though the digital clock on the DVD player showed it was past ten. Violet had been living on Annie's couch for over a month, and she'd long worn out her welcome.

Violet pushed herself up and made her way to the kitchen. Annie was pouring coffee into a metallic thermal mug the length of her arm. Her white overalls were stained with crusty splatters of clay, and her short hair was pulled back in a dusty-pink bandana. Annie was a potter and spent most of the day hunched over a wheel in her studio. The apartment was cluttered with Annie's chunky mugs and vases in the shape of naked women. While Annie managed to support herself from her work, Violet didn't think it was all that good. Maybe it was easier to support yourself as a potter than as a poet.

"Morning," Violet said.

"Is it?" They'd been friends for over ten years, since college, but Violet knew the friendship was buckling under the weight of her presence. She didn't want to stay—the apartment was a small one-bedroom in Brighton, and the musky scent of curry from the Indian restaurant downstairs permeated the building. Violet would have loved to move out, but she had no place to go.

She and Luka had broken up in late December, and since she was the one doing the breaking up, it didn't seem fair that he should have to leave their airy apartment in Somerville. She couldn't afford the rent on her own anyway. So here she was, alone, without any place to live besides Annie's thrift-store couch. If Violet thought too deeply about the history of that couch, she'd demote herself to the mangy carpeted floor.

"There's coffee," Annie said, gesturing to the half-full pot.

Violet fixed herself a cup and sat down at the kitchen table. She took a sip and winced. Annie always bought the cheap store brand. Even cream and sugar couldn't mask its acrid tang.

"What do you have going on for today?" Annie asked. She foraged in the fridge, which always seemed to be bare, and withdrew a container of garlic hummus and some baby carrots. Both looked like they'd seen better days. Violet leaned back a little so as not to get hit with the whiff of hummus.

"I have a class at two and another at four."

Violet was an adjunct professor in the creative writing department at Boston University. She taught a graduate poetry seminar and a freshman poetry workshop, and she hated both for different reasons. The graduate students were all good poets, but they were pretentious and competitive, marking up each other's poems in slashes of red ink and making obscure allusions Violet often missed. The freshmen weren't pretentious, but their poems were usually awful—Hallmark card meets fortune cookie meets Dr. Seuss. On the other days, she taught a poetry workshop to high school students in a cafeteria that smelled of hot dogs and sour milk. She was surprised these were the days she most enjoyed.

"I won't be home till later," Violet said. "Luka and I are meeting for a drink tonight." Annie raised an eyebrow. "No, it's just the post-breakup meeting. For closure, blah, blah, blah." Annie nodded, unsuccessfully trying to mask her disappointment. "I'm looking for an apartment, though," Violet continued. "I promise, I'll be out of here soon."

"It's no problem," Annie lied, throwing the now-empty bag of carrots and hummus into the garbage. "I'm headed to the studio." She tucked a granola bar into the pocket of her jacket. "Give the bathroom a clean today if you get a chance."

Cleaning the toilet was Violet's least favorite chore, especially in Annie's bathroom. The toilet seemed to retain the urine stains from the last hundred tenants who'd lived in this run-down little apartment. The last time she cleaned it, she actually gagged, dry heaving into the filthy bowl before spraying the room with Lysol and fleeing. "No problem," Violet said.

Annie bent to pick up her bag from the floor. "I'll see you tonight. Good luck with Luka." The heavy door slammed behind her, the chain lock rattling after she was gone. Violet placed the still-full cup of coffee in the sink. She'd stop at Starbucks on her way to class. She headed for the bathroom to get ready.

As she stepped into the shower, her cell phone rang in the kitchen. Ignoring it, Violet rubbed Annie's rosemary shampoo into her hair, the sharp, earthy scent washing away the curry smell that filled the mildewed bathroom. Violet carefully shaved her legs and lathered her body in soap, noting that Annie always had expensive bath products though the apartment was a dump.

It wasn't until Violet was dressed and making breakfast that she checked her phone. There were four missed calls from Suzy and a text saying, *Call me as soon as you get this.* There was a voicemail from her too. Nestling the phone into the curve of her neck, Violet slathered butter on an English muffin and listened.

It was short, just telling Violet to call her back, though her voice was tight and strained, more like the messages Cal left. Cal was always tight and strained about something. She'd been this way for as long as Violet could remember, but it was far worse since Cal had children. Violet sympathized with how difficult it was to work full-time and take care of two little kids, but it all seemed rather self-inflicted to her. Cal didn't even particularly *like* kids, as far as Violet could tell; it just seemed like another goal she'd set for herself, like getting into Yale or finishing law school at the top of her class. Actually being happy was the one thing she couldn't do purely by working harder.

Suzy had recently broken up with her girlfriend, and while Violet thought Lani had been kind of a bitch, Suzy was uncharacteristically emotional about the whole thing. Usually, Suzy was the calmest of the three of them, the third-born child, left to her own devices and remarkably self-sufficient. But the whole relationship with Lani had left Suzy surprisingly fragile, and she'd been calling Violet almost every day as she questioned her identity. Violet ate breakfast quickly without calling her back.

Putting on makeup, Violet thought ahead to drinks with Luka that evening. Despite what she'd told Annie, she was looking forward to it. Part of her desperately regretted breaking up with him and hoped he'd be willing to have her back, but she worried her feelings were influenced by her desire to get the hell out of Annie's apartment.

She was just settling back onto the couch to grade a stack of papers on experimental poetry in the twentieth century when there was a knock on the front door. The apartment building had a locked exterior door, and guests were expected to use the call box and intercom to request admittance, unless someone unknowingly held the front door open.

Violet felt a little ripple of fear, which was out of place for an ordinary Friday morning. The neighborhood wasn't great, but it wasn't *that* bad.

Squinting through the tiny peephole, Violet saw Suzy. She looked disheveled, her frizzy hair unruly and her eyes puffy. Even through the greasy glass Violet could tell that Suzy was on the verge of tears, probably not for the first time today. Violet unlocked the door, the relief at not being confronted by a burglar quickly replaced by fear over her little sister's appearance. Something was wrong.

Violet opened the door and Suzy fell into her arms. "Suzy?" Suzy didn't answer, but she began to cry, her slender body trembling against Violet. "What's wrong, Suzy Q?" Their mother's nickname for her slipped out, unbidden. There was something about this raw edge of emotion that made Violet wish for her mother, though they always seemed to argue when she was around.

"It's Dad," Suzy croaked, finally peeling herself from Violet. Her voice was hoarse, and Violet was gripped by a whole new wave of terror. "He's dead."

Chapter Four

Cal

Cal was not a crier. Anyone who knew her would agree. She wasn't hard or unsentimental, but it took a lot to bring Cal to tears, and she'd never been the type to cry in front of others. Even as a child, Cal would run into the bathroom and lock the door if she felt the telltale prickle behind her eyes that signaled imminent tears.

Most people would cry upon learning their father was dead. There was nothing unusual about this. But for Cal, the sudden flood of tears and convulsive sobs that overtook her that morning was shocking both for her and those around her. Howard stood by helplessly as Cal crumpled to the floor at his feet. She lay there, her cheek pressed against the soft carpeting, all rational thought wiped away as the tears just kept coming. It was like when she gave birth to Maisy and took a crap on the bed while she was pushing. In a normal moment, this would have caused Cal incredible humiliation, but given the circumstances of Maisy's twenty-hour labor and the fading epidural, Cal really didn't care. But both then and now, she knew Howard had worked hard to conceal the alarm and horror he actually felt.

Howard had picked the phone up off the floor and finished talking to Suzy while Cal crawled into bed. She'd been there ever since. The tears eventually subsided, but she couldn't catch her breath. Maisy kept hovering around the bedroom door, her eyes wide in fear and fascination. She'd never seen her mother cry and wasn't sure whether to be scared or thrilled.

"Just deal with the girls," Cal begged. "Please. Just keep them out of here." Howard brought Maisy into the living room to watch a cartoon, and Cal pulled the covers over her head, willing herself to be released into a sleep she knew would never come. She was surprised when she fell into a fitful doze. When she woke up several hours later, she was damp with sweat and wrung out, her body and mind empty and numb.

It wasn't until late morning that Cal emerged from bed. She splashed cold water on her face and pulled her hair back into a severe ponytail. She was the oldest. She needed to pull herself together. She was still in her work clothes, a now-rumpled silk blouse, pencil skirt, and stockings. She stripped those off and found a pair of cotton yoga pants and an old Yale sweatshirt and then returned to bed with her phone.

Cal called Violet first and wasn't sure if she was relieved or upset when it went straight to voicemail. She knew Howard was listening from down the hall where he was likely giving Sadie a bottle. Though her breasts ached, she hadn't been able to work up the energy to nurse. There was something far too intimate about her daughter's lips hungrily latched onto her. She'd pump later instead.

When Suzy answered, Cal began a fresh round of tears at the sound of her sister's voice.

"Did you call Barry? Do you know anything more about what happened?" Suzy asked.

"No. I don't know anything." And who cared? What did details matter? Her father was dead. Anything else was just extraneous information.

"What should we do now? I'm with Violet. Do you want us to come over?"

"No," Cal said, more sharply than she intended. The idea of Suzy and Violet coming to her house in the hopes that she could comfort them was too much to bear. Suzy and Violet had never been close with their father after the divorce, alienating and isolating him with their selfish anger. Cal needed to be alone. She mumbled something about speaking later in the day and then hung up. She turned off her phone.

Cal lay back down in bed and buried her head under the pillow. There was an autistic boy in Maisy's class who was prone to tantrums. During these moments, the teachers would guide him to a beanbag chair and cover him with a weighted blanket. Cal wished she had a blanket like that now, a hundred-pound quilt that could press her into the earth, crushing everything out of her heart. She squeezed her eyes shut.

From down the hall she heard the thin peal of Sadie's cry and dimly wondered if her fever was higher. Cal pulled the pillow tighter. With her head safely cocooned under the darkness of bedding, she let the silent sobs overtake her once again.

Chapter Five

Violet

After calling to say she wouldn't be able to teach her classes for the next week, Violet spent the day in a strange dreamlike state. For most of the afternoon she was at Suzy's apartment, where they called their mother in London to break the news. Though their parents rarely spoke, Violet's mother had wept quietly on the phone, and Violet wished more than anything that she was nearby to carry the three of them through the coming days. Cal's phone, which was never more than two feet away from her, kept going straight to voicemail, and when they called Howard, he said she was sleeping.

Violet and Suzy were able to get in touch with Barry again, and eventually it was agreed the three of them would drive up to Maine the following morning. The idea of staying in their father's house didn't feel right, but Barry had an empty rental cottage they could use for as long as they needed. Cal finally called back later that afternoon, but she didn't say much. Her voice was thick with tears, and her words blended together like she was still half-asleep. For a moment, Violet wondered if Cal *was* still asleep.

As a child, Cal had been a sleepwalker. Their mother would joke that Cal could never turn off her mind, not even at night. Cal never remembered it in the morning, and someone would fill her in on what she'd done the previous night—foraging in the fridge for a snack of mayonnaise and mustard, brushing her hair in the dark bathroom, and once, watching a whole episode of *Law & Order* before their father heard the TV and guided her back to bed.

Violet remembered a night from high school, soon after their father had moved out. It was Christmas vacation, and Violet awoke to the sound of talking. Suzy was snoring softly in her bed, and the door to their mother's room was closed tight. When Violet peered into Cal's dark room, her unmade bed was empty.

Violet tiptoed downstairs and into the living room. Someone had forgotten to unplug the lights on the Christmas tree, and the prickly fingers of the evergreen were cast in colored shadows on the wall. Cal sat on the couch in her sweatpants and T-shirt, her legs pulled into her chest, rocking slowly back and forth and crying softly. Her face was damp with tears and perspiration. Violet knew that trying to wake a person up from a night terror did no good. Sometimes it made things worse. Instead, she sat down on the couch and put her hand on Cal's back, rubbing in slow circles.

She wondered what the dream was about. What could make Cal cry? Getting a B? Not getting into Yale? Going to a state school? It was hard to imagine.

Violet reached for Cal's hand, and Cal unfolded her body and stood up. Though she was still whimpering quietly, she let Violet lead her upstairs. In Cal's bedroom, Violet pulled back the comforter and tucked Cal in like a small child before sliding in beside her.

"Shh," Violet whispered into Cal's hair. Slowly, Cal's noises stopped, and after a few minutes she drifted off to sleep. Cal's face was just a few inches away, close enough that in the dim light from the hall Violet could see the faint sprinkling of acne on her chin that Cal always covered with makeup, close enough to smell Cal's warm, sour breath.

Violet lay awake for a long while, trying to remember the last time she'd slept beside her big sister and wondering why it was only in her dreams that Cal could cry. She finally drifted off to sleep herself. When she woke the next morning, Cal was already gone.

Back at Annie's that evening, Violet sat down on the fusty couch. She knew there were things that needed to be taken care of, but as the middle child, she also knew Cal would end up taking care of everything. Annie would be getting home from the studio soon, and Violet couldn't deal with her right now. Though she knew it was ridiculous, she worried Annie would be annoyed that she hadn't cleaned the bathroom, but the idea of taking a toilet brush to the smelly bowl nearly brought her to tears all over again.

It was almost six o'clock, somehow still the same day her father had been alive, when Violet remembered Luka. She was supposed to meet him in ten minutes. She pulled out her phone to cancel, but then hung up without leaving a message. She was wrung out from crying and needed to get out of the claustrophobic apartment before Annie returned. With only a quick look in the mirror and a mechanical brush of her hair, Violet left the building, walking the twelve blocks to the bar where they'd planned to meet.

She arrived fifteen minutes late, but she was always late, and Luka would wait. It was a Friday, but the bar was still quiet. Luka sat in the corner, and he raised his eyes at Violet when she came in. He'd already finished most of his beer, so Violet ordered a round for them, taking a thirsty gulp at the bar before walking over to the booth.

On the seat beside Luka was a black garbage bag and a shoe box, filled, Violet imagined, with the odds and ends she'd left behind—a favorite lip gloss, a sweater swept under the bed, a bottle of lotion, an old hairbrush, dog-eared books of poetry. She hadn't cried in nearly an hour, but the sight of the forlorn trash bag and shoe box started a fresh wave of tears.

"Violet?" Luka looked at her in confusion, rising to hold her in his arms. She leaned against him, breathing in his achingly familiar scent. Violet let her body go, let the loss sweep over her, *her* loss, which was different from Cal's and Suzy's. Whether Luka thought she was crying over their breakup, or if he realized something much bigger had happened, he didn't try to talk, and he didn't ask for explanations. He just let her cry, stroking her hair with his hand, his body sheltering her.

After several minutes, Violet lifted her head from his chest, and they sat down at the table. She began to sputter out the story, wiping her nose with a soggy cocktail napkin.

"Violet, I'm so sorry," Luka muttered every few minutes. "I just can't believe it." His voice was soothing, the clipped syllables of his accent like a steady hand on her back.

Luka had only met her father once, right before they broke up. He knew little about Violet's father, other than he lived in Maine and that they weren't close. It was too difficult to try to explain more. But now she wished she'd told Luka the full story, explained the complexities of the distance between them. It would have made her convoluted grief easier to understand.

Luka was a bartender, and they'd met two years earlier when Violet became a regular at the bar where he worked. He was a tall and striking man, nearly six three with the slenderness of a teenager. Originally from the Czech Republic, he'd been living in the United States for more than ten years, ever since he came over on a travel visa and never left. He'd made Boston his home, yet he still wasn't legal.

His immigration status was a constant source of friction between them, a problem that could have been solved easily by a trip to the courthouse. And not just for the paperwork that would allow him to stay in the country legally, not just so he could return home to see his own country and family after so long. He wanted to marry *her*. He wanted babies and a house with a yard and a few dogs. He wanted a life with Violet.

Violet tried to talk to her mother about Luka. Violet wished she were here to help them through this, but she was in London for the year with her husband, accompanying him on his sabbatical. She had sublet their childhood home for the year to a visiting professor from Harvard and his family. Last summer, Violet had gone over to the Cambridge house to salvage a few things from her old bedroom before they were put into storage for the year her mother and Walter would be away. Walter was upstairs in the office (which had once belonged to Violet's father), and her mother was surrounded by cardboard boxes, haphazardly stuffing them full of old tablecloths and chipped mugs. Violet sat on a stool with a cup of iced coffee, telling her mother about the most recent conversation she'd had with Luka about their future.

The day was hot and muggy, and her mother's face was damp with perspiration, her arms and chest shining despite the table fan that blew warm air in their direction. She held a stack of dish towels and let out a sigh of exasperation. It took Violet a moment to realize the sigh was directed at her, not the pile of junk.

"Do you love him?" her mother asked, throwing the towels into an overflowing box.

"Well, yeah." Violet took a sip of coffee. The ice had all melted.

"So what's the problem?"

"That's not always enough, is it? You should know that. You and Dad once loved each other." Violet waited for her mother's response. They rarely discussed her father and never the divorce.

"It's not the same thing at all, Vi," she said, unwilling to take the bait. "If you love him, if you really love him, I don't see why you don't marry him. And if you don't, then let him go. Move on."

"I know." Violet sulked and stirred the watery coffee with a straw.

Her mother pointed at Violet with a handful of wooden spoons. "I know it's probably not worth much, but I like Luka. And you have dated a lot of jerks over the years, honey. No offense, but it's true. Luka's a keeper." Violet hated that expression. Were all the other guys in her past merely trash, junk that wasn't worth keeping, like her mother's ancient collection of utensils and linens? Deep down, Violet knew her mother was right; of all the men she'd been with, Luka was the only one worth hanging on to, yet he was the one she pushed away the hardest.

The reasons that made her hesitant to commit were hard for Violet to articulate, aloud or to herself. She knew they were shallow and reflected poorly on her. What she told other people was that she and Luka wanted different things. Violet wanted to get tenure at the university, to publish another book of poems, to receive more recognition for her work. She wanted to be untethered enough to live the life of an artist. She didn't want to be dragged down by a mortgage or changing diapers or having to make enough money to fix the roof.

But more than that, and more difficult to confess, was that she never expected to end up with someone like Luka. She had pictured herself with someone creative or intellectual, an artist or a fellow writer, a professor or musician. Not a bartender, an illegal immigrant who hadn't gone to college. To voice such thoughts would be to admit to all sorts of "isms" she'd been raised to denounce—classism, elitism, as well as a few more she couldn't think of. So Violet told people, including Luka, that they wanted different things. It was easier that way.

But sitting with Luka now, her father's body already growing cold, Violet realized how stupid and shortsighted she'd been. Even before this morning, Violet's life had become foreign. It was like wearing a coat that didn't fit, the shoulders and arms too tight, yet being unable to take it off and find the old comfortable one she'd dropped in the donation box. For the first time since she'd broken up with Luka, she realized the magnitude of her mistake. *I want to come home,* she longed to tell him, but stubborn pride kept her from saying the words.

"Can I come home with you tonight?" she asked instead.

"Vi." His brown eyes were filled with sadness. "It's not a good idea. Not tonight."

"Please," she said, and the word held so much that he agreed.

It had snowed a few inches earlier in the day, and the sidewalks crunched beneath their feet as the snow froze to ice. Already it had been a hard winter, and the new snow dusted the top of the dirty frozen piles, a fresh coat of makeup that would fade by the morning. Luka held her hand the whole way back to his car.

In the apartment that had recently belonged to both of them, Violet walked through the living room and kitchen, trying not to look around the warm familiarity of her old home. She led him straight to the bedroom. She undressed Luka, pushing off his canvas jacket, yanking at the belt of his jeans, all the while standing by the bed. She wanted to bury herself inside him. Never had she felt more vulnerable, more depleted. All she wanted was to climb inside Luka's sturdy body and let him keep the outside world at bay. He watched her without speaking.

She kissed his face, inhaling the scent of his shaving cream, brushing her cheek against the black stubble of his chin. He was so tall he had to hunch over to reach her, Violet on her tippy-toes. His lips parted for her and she found his mouth, a sudden and overpowering desire rearing up inside her. She stripped off her own clothes quickly, stepping out of her skirt and wool tights, shedding her thin sweater and bra, not caring that her underwear was plain cotton. For once, she hadn't thought to wear something nicer.

She stood before him, naked, her skin glowing white in the shadowy room. In all the time they'd been together, Violet couldn't recall ever presenting herself to him so openly. He lifted her heavy red hair and pushed it behind her shoulders, and she inhaled quickly, eyes closed, as his thumbs brushed against her nipples. Fluttering behind her lids was her father facedown on the spinning treadmill, so Violet quickly opened her eyes, grabbing Luka more forcefully, pulling him down onto the bed. She arched her back, aching for him to fill the terrible emptiness that pervaded her body. It was like a storm cloud, damp and cold, and she felt it in her stomach and chest, even in her groin. She needed him to make her warm again.

"Please," she moaned, and Luka entered her, though when she looked at him, he was still watching her, measuring her, handling her like something that might crack. This was his gift, his only way of giving comfort. Ordinarily this would have enraged Violet, his cautious manner, as if she might burst into flames and engulf him. Not tonight though. Tonight she was greedy and desperate for whatever he had to offer.

Chapter Six

Suzy

When Suzy graduated from culinary school, she knew her father hoped she'd come work with him at Veg. He'd taken pride in Suzy's work, as if she were following in his footsteps, despite the fact that his career as a chef had only begun when his career as a father was waning.

Aside from not wanting to work for him or move to Maine, Suzy had no interest in working solely with vegetables. She was a carnivore, drawn to the succulence of rich beef dishes steeped in their own juices. She took a job as a sous chef at Ciao, a high-end restaurant in the South End. She'd been there for a year when she met Lani.

Lani was hired after the head chef was fired for assaulting one of the servers in a cocaine-infused rage. Lani came in as Marty's replacement, a tiny tattooed force of energy and nerve. Suzy arrived at work one evening and there was Lani, all five feet two of her, short black hair trimmed in a pixie cut, arms inked with flowers and stars, her black apron knotted tightly around her boyish hips.

"You must be my sous chef." Lani laid out an expensive set of knives on a plastic cutting board.

Suzy bent over the sink to wash her hands. "Who are you?"

"Your new boss." Lani's brown eyes twinkled wickedly.

"Where's Marty?" Suzy dried her hands, found a clean apron in the linen closet, and buttoned up a chef's coat. Lani wasn't wearing a jacket, just a tight black T-shirt with the sleeves cut off.

"Got fired. You're stuck with me now. Suzy, right?"

Suzy nodded, surprised and a little pleased Lani already knew her name. She hadn't liked Marty all that much, but he'd never given her a hard time. He saved that for the waitstaff. Already Suzy worried Lani might be a more serpentine boss. In her experience, women usually were. And it didn't help that Suzy's eyes kept being drawn back to Lani's sculpted biceps and small breasts. Marty had a giant beer belly and smelled of stale Marlboros.

"Grab a menu. There's a few things I want to go over," Lani ordered. Reaching for a menu, Suzy breathed in Lani's citrusy perfume. Lemons and grapefruit.

In high school, Suzy had been lab partners with a girl named Caroline Parker. Caroline had wispy blond hair and freckles that covered every inch of her face, even her lips. Suzy spent junior-year chemistry class staring at Caroline's mouth over the flame of the Bunsen burner, imagining how smooth those lips would feel against her thumb. At the time, Suzy thought she just liked looking at Caroline. She didn't realize all that staring was attraction until later.

In college, Suzy fooled around with a few girls, but she'd gone to school in western Massachusetts, a place where everyone experimented. There was even a name for girls whose experimenting had an expiration date—LUG, lesbian until graduation. When Suzy finished school and moved back to Boston, she quickly returned to heterosexuality. She'd even had a serious boyfriend for a while, Ian—a kind, bland-faced young man she still kept in touch with. After a year, they'd gone their separate ways in a breakup so amicable it clarified the lack of intensity between them.

But despite the absence of sexual energy, Suzy hadn't been ready to consider the possibility that the problem was men in general. Her family wouldn't object to Suzy as a lesbian. They were all liberal, though her father was Catholic, and for several years Suzy had accompanied him to church every Sunday. It didn't take much to conjure up the spicy, woodsy scent of St. Theresa's church and the way the light shone through the stained-glass windows on a winter's day. Even now, Suzy felt a kind of warm serenity in her chest when she remembered the sign of peace, when she and her father would turn to their neighbors in the pews in front of and behind them, clasping their hands and softly saying, "Peace be with you."

But it wasn't religion that kept Suzy from coming out as a lesbian either. She knew it wasn't politically correct, but she had an image in her head of a lesbian—a squat, short-haired woman in mannish clothes, with heavy breasts masked under a men's button-down shirt or tufts of unshaven hair sprouting from spicy-smelling armpits, who listened to angry, folksy musicians and wanted to be called "womyn." She knew it was a ridiculous stereotype, but she'd also known women like this in college. Suzy wasn't like *that*.

But neither was Lani. Lani was sexy and feminine without being the standard definition of sexy and feminine. She wasn't masculine, but there was a coy boyishness in her compact frame. She didn't dress like a man, but she didn't dress like the girls Suzy knew either. If Lani was a lesbian, then maybe Suzy was too.

Suzy had never been good at identifying the line between friend and something more, but when Lani pressed up beside her at the stainless-steel counter, there was no doubt that she was flirting. By the end of the shift, they were sharing a drink at the bar. By the end of the week, they were sleeping together. And by the end of the month, Suzy had told her mother and sisters about Lani and declared herself a lesbian.

The end happened just as quickly as the beginning. Lani was hot-tempered, prone to her own type of rages, though she didn't physically lash out like Marty. Instead, she'd tear Suzy to shreds in front of whoever happened to be in the kitchen. Or else she'd freeze her out in the privacy of the bedroom, Lani's curved back a wall of silence that Suzy couldn't overcome.

Suzy hated the drama of it, the screaming fights in the middle of the night, the tears and dramatic makeups, the way she'd come to feel like a caricature of a woman in love. But when the breakup finally happened, Suzy wasn't ready. She'd turned her whole identity upside down for Lani. She'd told her family she was gay. More importantly, she'd told *herself* she was gay. Without Lani, Suzy wasn't sure what she was.

The day after they broke up, Suzy called Violet in tears. "But I came out for her. I decided I was gay. And now I'm not sure if I am, or if I just wanted to be with her."

"Who cares what you are?" Violet asked. "Why do you need to put yourself into a neat little box with a label? Can't you just like girls sometimes and guys other times? Does everything have to have a name?" Suzy knew Lani would have said exactly the same thing, *if* they'd been speaking.

But Suzy needed a label. She needed to sit in one box or the other. Trying to move back and forth between both was just too confusing. She needed things neat and orderly, like in her kitchen, all the ingredients laid out before she even preheated the oven.

So Suzy tried the box labeled "straight" one last time. She went with some friends to listen to a band and bumped into her ex-boyfriend. She was already drunk by the time she saw Ian, but so was he, and in the moment it seemed like a good idea for her to go home with him. By the time he'd stripped down to his boxers, the smell of stale beer hovering in the air between them, Suzy realized it was probably a bad idea, but this was Ian, not a stranger. Being with Ian did nothing to clarify which box she sat in. However, it turned out there were some fast-swimming sperm determined to find their target.

Even though Suzy had been at Ciao longer than Lani, Suzy was the one to leave. She volunteered and Lani agreed, which probably said a lot about Lani. Suzy regretted it almost immediately when she realized she had no job and that Lani was still an up-and-coming culinary star, but by then it was too late. A friend from culinary school helped Suzy get the job at the magazine. It was totally different from any other kind of cooking job Suzy had ever known. She'd only been there a few months, and she wasn't yet sure if she hated it or loved it.

The last time Suzy had spoken to her father was after the breakup. She hadn't told him about Lani or that she was a lesbian. It didn't seem to be any of his business, and she couldn't imagine it was information he'd really want. He'd mellowed out a lot since moving to Maine, but he was still an uptight Irish Catholic New Englander at his core.

It was hard to believe he was dead. When Suzy opened her eyes the morning after her father's death, she lay in bed, staring at the water stain on her ceiling and remembering waking up in the Cambridge house where she and her sisters grew up. On Saturday mornings before the divorce, Suzy and her father would make a huge batch of pancakes for everyone. Cal and Violet were teenagers and liked to sleep late, and their mother was never a morning person, so it was usually just the two of them doing the cooking. Suzy would sit at the high counter and sieve the flour, whisking in milk and eggs, dropping in a cup of fat Maine blueberries. Her father would fry up some bacon and let Suzy help flip the pancakes. The rest of the family would slowly drift into the kitchen, the smell of frying bacon and butter rousing them from the depths of sleep. They'd all sit around the table, in various states of rumpled, pajamaed disarray. There was never any focused conversation, more a disjointed frenzy of plans for the day, arrangements for rides, please-pass-the-syrup, and good-natured teasing. But it was one of Suzy's strongest and fondest memories of them as a family.

When her parents announced their father was moving out, Suzy had been stunned. Cal and Violet had been upset, but they didn't seem as shocked as Suzy. Their parents kept saying how much they loved the three of them, and the next morning their father packed up his old Toyota Camry and was gone.

Suzy had never forgiven him for leaving. As a child, she remembered being told over and over again it wasn't her fault. They still loved her; it had nothing to do with anything she had or hadn't done. *It wasn't her fault.* But Suzy had never thought it was her fault. It was *his* fault. *He* had abandoned her. One day they were a family; the next day he was gone. And then, as if it weren't bad enough, he moved to Portland, Maine. Suzy was left behind, with Cal already at Yale, Violet a teenager who had no time for Suzy, and her mother wrapped up in her own grief and survival as a single parent. Suzy was alone, and for that she couldn't forgive him. And now she would never have the chance to try.

Suzy forced herself out of bed. She tied an apron around her waist, trying hard not to look to see if her stomach was any larger than the day before. In the small kitchen of her studio apartment, she mixed up a miniature batch of pancake batter. Blueberries weren't in season, so she sliced in a banana and added a few shakes of cinnamon. The smell of butter in the pan filled the kitchen, and Suzy waited for bubbles to form on the circles of batter. She flipped them one at a time, a perfectly golden skin on each disk. She slathered butter and syrup over the pancakes, a feast for one. She wasn't sure if it was grief or morning sickness, but when she sat down at the table, she found she couldn't even eat a bite.

Chapter Seven

Cal

The next day, Cal awoke before dawn. She left Howard sleeping in their bed and tiptoed downstairs. Miraculously, both girls had slept through the night and were sleeping still. She brewed coffee and then brought her mug into the living room, pulling the heavy wool afghan over her on the couch, not bothering to turn on the light. Outside it was still dark; the digital light on the DVD player read 4:52.

Yesterday's hibernation in bed needed to be a onetime thing. Cal knew her sisters would be little help with any of the details that needed to be taken care of. She'd already begun a mental to-do list—calling people to tell them the news, meeting with the funeral home, picking out the casket, and planning the service. Her laptop sat on the coffee table, charged and waiting for her.

Cal had seen less of her sisters this past year since their mother had gone to London. They'd grown up in a big house in Cambridge, just a short walk from Harvard Square, and the house had always been a weekly gathering spot. Her parents had bought it before Cambridge was trendy and expensive. Though the house was still a fixer-upper, a teacher and social worker would never be able to afford it now. There was a large backyard that their mother filled with flower beds soon after they bought the house. When the girls were born, their free-spirited mother somehow convinced their father that with a last name like Bloom, they should name the girls after the flowers she carefully tended—calla lilies, violets, and black-eyed Susans.

Now their mother preferred vegetables to flowers in her garden. The house was in constant need of repair, and for these last years it had been just Cal's mother and Walter, her second husband, living in it. It was only a matter of time before her mother would decide to sell the house and buy something smaller with Walter. It was strange not gathering there every few weeks for dinner. Easter was coming up, and Cal knew her sisters were expecting her to host, waiting for the invitation she hadn't yet issued. She would eventually.

With their mother away this year, Cal was more aware of how their mother and the house in Cambridge were the glue that held Cal and her sisters together. Cal and Suzy still saw each other every other week, but Cal hadn't seen Violet in nearly a month. They talked on the phone regularly, but physical distance between her and Violet was a good thing. The energy between them could border on combustible.

Cal sipped the hot coffee, black and bitter, just the way she liked it. Their father had always been a contentious subject between them, and Cal wasn't looking forward to watching Violet struggle with her grief. Violet had chosen to alienate herself from him, and Cal had no interest in easing her guilt.

"Hey. You okay?"

Cal looked up from the depths of her coffee mug to see Howard coming down the stairs. He wore an old plaid flannel shirt over sweatpants, and he settled beside her on the couch, pulling her legs into his lap. "Not really." Cal shrugged, focusing on her mug. It was her favorite, heavy porcelain with red-and-white stripes. She noticed a tiny hairline fracture from the lip extending halfway to the base. It would crack soon. "There's coffee," she told him.

"In a minute." He looked at Cal, his eyes scanning her face, as if he were reading a secret code, trying to discover what was really there.

Cal looked away, took a sip of coffee just to protect her face from his probing eyes. "When are you leaving?" he asked. They had decided Cal would go up today, and Howard would bring the girls for the service once it had been arranged.

"Soon." Howard nodded. "I'll have to do some shopping on the way," she continued. "Suzy will want to cook and Violet's a picky eater." She was overcome with a wave of fatigue and closed her eyes for a moment.

"I'm sure they're not expecting anything," Howard said gently.

"Yes, they are," she said without opening her eyes. Howard sighed, but didn't say anything more. He yawned, lifting her legs back up, and stood.

"It's still early. Come back to bed for a little while?" His voice was so tender, so loving. *I don't deserve you,* Cal thought to herself, *and one of these days you'll leave me.* The thought came to her so sharply and suddenly that her eyes filled with tears. She pressed her lips to the edge of the coffee cup and blinked so he wouldn't see.

"I'm not tired," she lied. The truth was she was beyond tired, but she knew she wouldn't sleep and lying in bed wouldn't help. Howard stood over her for another moment, waiting. When she didn't say anything or change her mind, he bent down and kissed the top of her head. Cal watched him climb the stairs slowly, his shoulders hunched in a defeat she had caused.

Cal poured more coffee and returned to the couch. She opened up her laptop and pulled up a fresh page. "To Do," she typed in bold letters at the top. She stared at the blank page for a long time.

Chapter Eight

Violet

Violet's head rested on Luka's warm chest. She didn't want to get out of the safety of his arms and start the process of burying her father. Being here felt natural, as if she'd never left. The room was the same, though neater than when she lived here. Her clothes always seemed to end up in piles on the floor or chair. She didn't recognize the navy-blue sheets or gray bedspread, and it seemed strange that Luka would have gone shopping for new bedding, but then again, maybe he hadn't wanted to sleep in the same sheets they'd shared.

"Do you want me to come?" Luka asked. "I could, you know. If it would help."

"No way," Violet said absently. "You don't want to deal with this. The whole thing's going to be a mess."

"Okay." Luka threw off the blanket and she was hit with cold air, the warm cocoon ripped open. She'd hurt him. Again. Even when she wasn't trying to, even when she wanted him back, she kept hurting him. Luka threw a towel around his waist and went into the bathroom. Violet heard the whoosh of the shower and rolled over, shutting her eyes against everything. He returned a few minutes later, the sharp scent of deodorant and body wash following him into the room.

"I'll probably be up there for a week or so," Violet said, sitting up in bed. "Can I see you when I get back?" She shivered and pulled the blanket up. The heating in the apartment had always been temperamental, but when Violet lived here, she cranked the heat high despite Luka's objections and the exorbitant bill they received each month. It was cold in the apartment now.

Luka dropped the towel unceremoniously and stepped into a pair of boxer shorts. He found jeans and a shirt, not answering until he was zipping up his faded blue sweatshirt.

"I don't know." He stood above Violet, looking down at her. Her clothes were in a pile beside the bed, and she wished she'd gotten dressed while he was in the shower. The air in the bedroom had changed.

"Why not?"

Luka looked away. "I just started seeing someone," he said.

"What? Who?" Violet asked, genuinely surprised. It had only been two months.

"It doesn't matter." He didn't say, *You don't know her,* she noticed.

"Who is it?" Violet pressed, sitting forward to snap on the bedside lamp. She winced at the brightness that filled the room.

"It doesn't matter," Luka said, his voice louder this time. "It's none of your business."

"None of my business?" she cried. "You just spent the night with me."

"You wanted that. I tried to tell you it wasn't a good idea . . ." He raked his fingers through his damp hair.

"Oh, I'm sorry." Violet's voice was ripe with sarcasm. "I really had to twist your arm." Luka shook his head and sat down on the edge of the bed. "Well, where is she now? What is this?" She swept her hand around the room, toward him, herself, still naked beneath the sheets.

"I don't know. It's not serious yet, but . . ." He raised his hand at Violet, palm up. "I wasn't planning on this."

"Yeah, me neither," Violet snapped, anger rising up in her. "Sorry my dad's death was so inconvenient for you." At the word *death,* her voice caught, but she threw off the covers and began pulling on yesterday's clothes. Her toenail snagged on her tights, and she cursed inwardly but didn't slow down. "I didn't mean to mess up your new relationship."

"*No!*" Luka said. His voice was an octave louder than usual, and it stilled her. Violet paused where she was, her skirt unzipped. "No," he said again. "You don't get to do this." He shook his head. His whole body was nearly trembling with fury. "You had your chance. You don't get to make me feel bad now." His face, usually so ready to break into a smile, was tense and stern.

Violet had never seen him this angry, this ready to draw blood. Yet she knew she had brought him here. They stared at each other for a moment, neither saying a word until Violet shivered in the chilled room.

Luka finally dropped his gaze, and Violet zipped up her skirt and pulled on her sweater and boots. She found her purse where she'd left it on the chair and scanned through the missed calls on her phone so she wouldn't have to look at him. It was 6:20 in the morning, still dark, and she didn't have a car.

"When are you leaving?" Luka asked, but his tone had lost its edge.

"Eight. I'm supposed to pick Suzy up."

"Do you want me to drop you at your place?" This *was her place,* she wanted to say. But he meant Annie's.

"That's okay." She avoided his eyes, noticing instead that Cal hadn't called. Which was odd.

Luka shook his head, endlessly exasperated with her. She was always exasperating someone. "Let's just go so we don't hit traffic."

In the car, Violet gave him directions to Annie's apartment and then neither of them spoke. Like the apartment, the car was cold, and Violet pulled her coat around her tightly while she waited for the heat to kick in. Luka kept the radio on a morning talk show, the DJs' voices brash and loud, though Violet couldn't focus on the words. She was trying to figure out whom Luka was seeing now. In the back of her mind was her father, the trip to Maine, the pain of the upcoming week, but this worry—this mystery girl—was here now to fill her mind, a distraction.

She figured it out a few blocks from Annie's. "It's Elena, isn't it?"

"What?" Luka tightened his grip on the steering wheel. Violet didn't believe his feigned confusion.

"That's who you're seeing."

Elena was the younger sister of one of Luka's friends. She'd arrived in the country just a few months earlier. She was young, in the States from the Czech Republic on a student visa, thin and pretty with long black hair that hung to her waist and too much eye makeup. She'd always seemed surly and moody to Violet.

Luka ignored Violet's gaze, confirming her guess. "God, she's ten years younger than you. She's a baby," Violet whispered, her throat thick with tears.

He turned down Annie's street. "This one?" he asked, passing a garbage truck that was stopped to load trash. Violet nodded, and he pulled over in front of Annie's dingy gray duplex. He put the car in park but left the engine idling. The sun crept higher in the sky, a beautiful pink-and-gold sunrise that mocked the dreadfulness of the upcoming day. The bushes and trees glittered with frost. Luka picked up her hand where it lay in her lap and held it gently between both of his.

"Violet. I'm very sorry about your father." He wasn't even going to acknowledge she'd been right about Elena. There was a tiny patch of black stubble on his cheek that the razor had missed. Violet longed to feel the roughness against her thumb, but she kept her hand still in his. She nodded, biting her lip to hold back the tears. "I don't think we should see each other when you get back," he said, and Violet nodded again miserably. She imagined him having a drink later tonight with Elena, pretending last night had never happened. They were early in the relationship—he could easily omit his unfaithfulness and pick up where they'd left off.

He released Violet's hand, looking in the rearview mirror. The garbage truck was getting closer, just a few buildings behind them. She hadn't cleaned the bathroom yesterday, and she was supposed to take out the trash. She hoped her father's death was enough of an excuse for Annie, though she suspected it might not be at this point in their tenuous roommate situation. Violet opened the car door, one foot on the sidewalk.

"I forgot your stuff," Luka said.

"What stuff?"

"The bag I brought—with your stuff from the apartment." The black trash bag he'd brought to the bar last night.

"Forget it. You can throw it out." There was no way either of them could bear to do this again. Luka nodded.

"Good luck this week." His hand was on the gearshift, waiting for her to leave. The garbage truck was behind them now, its engine loud and grinding.

"Thanks." Violet climbed out of the car, then bent down one last time to look inside. Why had it taken her till now to realize how much she loved him? Or was it the fact he wasn't hers anymore that made her love him more? She hated herself either way. "Bye."

"Bye, Violet." She held his eyes for another moment before closing the car door. The air smelled of rotting fruit and old fish, and Luka's car pulled away as the garbage truck pulled up. Violet headed toward Annie's apartment.

Chapter Nine

Suzy

Suzy was fully packed and flipping through a cooking magazine when the buzzer finally rang. The time on her phone read 8:38, typical Violet. Suzy rose from the futon and pressed the intercom button.

"Vi?"

"I'm here. Hurry up, I'm in a loading zone," Violet's voice crackled through the speaker. Suzy picked up her suitcase, suppressing irritation. There was no point in getting annoyed with her sister; it didn't do any good.

Violet's battered Honda Civic was double-parked, and Suzy threw her tiny suitcase into the trunk, on top of Violet's enormous one, before getting into the passenger side. Violet wore dark sunglasses, her long red hair twisted into an elaborate fishtail braid. Despite the early hour and the long ride ahead of them, Violet wore a blue wraparound dress and knee-high leather boots, a shimmery purple scarf wrapped loosely around her neck. Violet had never grown out of the dress-up stage. Though she was always broke, Violet was an incredible thrift-store shopper, and when it came to clothes, she was always able to cull the treasure from the trash. Suzy was more comfortable in her own uniform of jeans and sweaters, but she admired Violet's style.

"You're late." Suzy buckled her seat belt.

"Give me a break, my dad just died." Violet pulled out into traffic, narrowly missing a biker. "I had a rough night."

"Yeah?" Violet was a terrible driver, but defensive about it. Suzy settled into her seat, trying to relax.

"I saw Luka." Violet dug in her pocket for lip gloss. She put it on one-handed, checking herself in the mirror. Suzy gripped the seat.

"How was that?" Suzy liked Luka and was surprised when they broke up. He was down-to-earth and unpretentious compared to other guys Violet had dated. He seemed to actually get her.

"Great. And then terrible." Violet fiddled with the radio. Finding nothing, she turned it off and then back on, scanning some more.

"Let me," Suzy said, reaching forward. Violet put her hand back on the steering wheel.

"He's already seeing someone," Violet continued.

"Oh yeah?" Suzy found the classical station and hoped Violet would leave it alone. Violet's car was filthy as usual. Empty wrappers and old coffee cups littered the floor of the passenger side. Suzy shifted her feet amid the trash, hoping none of the cups were full.

"The little sister of a friend of his. She's, like, twelve." Suzy raised her eyebrows. "Or twenty-two. Either way, she's much too young for him." Violet took the exit for the highway and for the first time seemed to fully focus on the road as she merged into the lane of speeding cars. Suzy let out the breath she'd been holding.

"Have you talked to Cal?" Suzy asked Violet.

"No. Do you want me to call her and tell her we're on the road?" Violet's hand was already rummaging around in the purse perched between them.

"I will," Suzy said quickly, pulling her own phone out of her coat pocket. She held it in her palm without making the call. "This is going to be terrible for her."

"I know." Violet pushed her sunglasses up onto her head. Her eyes were a little bloodshot, but not bad. "When did you last talk to him?"

"I don't know," Suzy said, thinking back. "A few weeks ago? He called to see how my new job was. He left a message last week, but I hadn't had a chance to call him back." Her father had called to invite her up to Portland for its annual food festival in March, and she hadn't come up with an excuse yet. She'd avoided returning the call.

Suzy dialed Cal's number. Straight to voicemail. "She's not answering. I think she's actually turned off her phone."

"She's acting weird," Violet agreed. "I mean, weird even under the circumstances."

"How do you think Mom is?" Suzy took a sip from Violet's mug and then put it back quickly, making a face. She'd forgotten how much cream and sugar Violet liked in her coffee.

"I don't know. In shock, probably. I don't think they've seen each other since he moved to Maine."

"That was what . . ." Suzy tallied the years on her fingers. "Fourteen years ago?"

"Something like that."

Suzy leaned back in the seat and closed her eyes. She wished she'd had more than just a slice of toast for breakfast. She wished she'd eaten the pancakes. Her stomach was quivering. In the chaos of yesterday, she hadn't canceled the abortion scheduled for this morning. The phone lines didn't open till nine, but Suzy was supposed to arrive at eight thirty.

"I have to make a phone call," she told Violet. She dialed the number of the clinic and looked out the window at the barren stretch of I-95. "I have a nine o'clock appointment I'm going to have to cancel," Suzy said to the woman who answered. She tried to lower her voice, but the car was small. There was no way for Violet not to hear.

"Name?"

"Susan Bloom." She heard the clicking of keys over the line.

"The room is already prepped and ready. The doctor's waiting for you," the woman said, accusingly.

"I'm sorry. There's been a death in the family. My father." Violet glanced over at her, and Suzy returned her focus to the scrubby evergreen trees outside.

"Oh. I'm very sorry," the woman said more gently. "When would you like to reschedule?"

"I'm not sure when I'll be back in town. I'll call to reschedule another time," Suzy said.

"How many weeks along are you?" the woman asked.

Suzy swallowed, keeping her face toward the window. "About eight, I think," she said quietly, though Violet was less than a foot away.

"I just want to remind you it's best to do it as early as possible. If you've made your decision, you shouldn't wait too long."

"Okay, thank you," Suzy said, anxious to get off the phone. "Bye."

"What was that?" Violet asked.

"Nothing. Dentist appointment." She was glad Violet had to watch the road. She couldn't see the tears in the corners of Suzy's eyes.

Chapter Ten

Cal

Cal arrived at Barry's rental cottage before eleven. She'd intended to stop for groceries, but once on the highway, she just kept driving. The idea of entering the fluorescent-lit Stop & Shop was more than she could manage. Even the soothing bamboo floors and softly lit aisles of Whole Foods would have been too overwhelming.

The house was small but cozy, right on the water. The downstairs was sunny and light-filled, every window facing the bay. She and Howard used to bring Maisy up to Maine for long weekends to visit her father. As she dragged her small suitcase inside, it felt like the beginning of a vacation, except for the pall of sorrow that clung to her. The idea of coming here on vacation now was preposterous. Her father's house and the whole town would now be covered in a foggy mist of grief. Cal couldn't imagine coming up here ever again. They would have to sell her father's house and his business. She closed her eyes for a moment, taking a breath, though for once there was no one here to see her mounting anxiety. She really should go to the grocery store.

The truth was that Cal wasn't ready to deal with any of it. She wanted to wrap her grief around herself like a cloak and be subsumed by it. She didn't have her usual energy to be strong for everyone else. Her sisters' presence would force her to rise up, but for now she just wanted to lie down and close her eyes. For once, she wanted someone else to take charge, for someone else to do all of the endless things that needed doing.

There were three small bedrooms upstairs, and Cal chose the smallest. She didn't want to share this week. There was only room for a twin bed, a dresser and nightstand, and a bookcase lined with tattered paperbacks. The room was all white—white wainscoting and white furniture—bathed clean in sunlight. Cal stood at the window and stared out at the deep gray ocean. The beach was empty, the sand bleached colorless, and the ragged dunes a muted greenish brown. Cal and Howard usually came up here during the summer or fall, and she'd never seen the coast so barren. She was glad the landscape matched the bleakness of her mood. She didn't think she could bear it if there were tourists drinking cans of beer and sunbathing outside her window. She let the curtain drop.

Peeling back the stiff white comforter, Cal crawled into the narrow bed as the springs creaked beneath her. She pulled a pillow over her head to block out the relentless light pouring through the sheer curtains, and she burrowed deeper under the blankets, seeking the refuge of darkness, just as she had yesterday.

She hadn't left instructions for Howard. Likely Maisy would end up missing gymnastics class this week because Howard would forget about it. And he wouldn't know what to pack for lunch, so Maisy would pick at whatever he sent, then come home and gorge on crackers and pretzels. Cal hadn't even pumped any milk for Sadie. She'd been taking a bottle for several months now, but she didn't drink much formula. Sadie would be weaned overnight, without Cal there to help her through the transition. It was unlike her, such a careful planner, a constant maker of lists, but she supposed grief had a way of knocking things loose.

She'd been having trouble sleeping the past few months. During the day she'd find herself dazed with weariness, her eyes grainy and tired. But at night, lying beside Howard, an alertness would settle over her. Her legs would get twitchy and restless, and her mind wandered to dark caverns she couldn't help peering into. At two o'clock in the morning, she'd find herself scripting what she'd say at the next day's meeting or planning out meals for the following week. On bad nights, she'd imagine Maisy accidentally eating a peanut at preschool and going into anaphylactic shock. She'd lie still and try to get her heart rate to return to normal. At some point Sadie would need to nurse. Cal never seemed to sleep well anymore.

Recently, she'd bought a book on meditation, something she'd already known she'd be terrible at, and her few attempts had confirmed it. One of the techniques to combat insomnia was to imagine a beautiful place and to settle your body there. It was one of the few tips she'd taken away from the book.

She'd lie in bed and picture herself on a beach somewhere warm—Greece, or Hawaii, someplace tropical. They'd gone to Kauai on their honeymoon, and Cal remembered the turquoise water and brightly colored fish, the soft breeze that floated around her shoulders like a cape. Cal would close her eyes and re-create the white sand and the sound of waves crashing. She could almost feel the nubby terry-cloth towel beneath her, at last her mind blank and uncluttered by thoughts of lunches to pack, doctors' appointments, or the upcoming client meeting that conflicted with Maisy's dance recital.

Cal wasn't sure where Howard and the girls were in these fantasies. Sometimes she imagined they were back in their spacious hotel room or swimming in the ocean. But more often, she knew they hadn't boarded the plane with her. She'd fled, empty and unencumbered, free of everything she held dear.

She would get up soon. She had to, she thought to herself as the dark relief of sleep finally came. When her sisters arrived, she would be back to herself.

Chapter Eleven

Violet

Violet focused on the endless ribbon of highway. Something was up with Suzy, though she wasn't sure what. Suzy was preoccupied, though on a day like this, on a trip like this, she could have just been lost in her own sadness.

"Do you want to stop for lunch?" Violet asked when they crossed the border into New Hampshire.

"No. Let's just get there." Suzy rested her head on the window. "I'm sure Cal brought food."

They drove a few more minutes without talking. The snow up here was deeper, the piles ugly and gray. Violet was getting fidgety in the silence. "Are you all right?" she asked.

"Yeah, just tired." Suzy didn't elaborate.

"Have you talked to Lani?"

Suzy shook her head. "It's over. For real." Violet thought that was for the best. The one time they'd met, Lani had narrowed her eyes at Violet and squared her shoulders as if sizing up the competition. Suzy needed someone like herself, calm and kind.

Violet watched as Suzy began to dig through her purse, pulling out a plastic bag of oyster crackers. She opened the bag and began eating as quietly as possible.

"Do you have any packets of ketchup in there for me? Maybe some salt and pepper?" Violet joked.

"Give me a break," Suzy snapped through a mouthful of cracker. "This was all I had in the house."

Suzy was a chef. Even when she needed to go to the grocery store, there was always a block of expensive cheese or a bag of figs or almonds, a bar of fancy dark chocolate wrapped in gold paper. Violet looked again at her sister, the pieces suddenly falling into place.

"Are you hungover?" Violet asked. Suzy shook her head, holding her fingers against her lips, as if trying to keep from throwing up. "You're not pregnant, are you?" she joked.

"What? No," Suzy said quickly. Then she swallowed and let out a sigh. She dropped her head, bringing her palms to her face and pressing the skin of her cheeks and eyes. "You can't tell Cal."

"Holy shit, seriously?" She clutched the wheel in stunned silence. Suzy hadn't mentioned anyone of interest since she and Lani broke up. When Suzy announced she was a lesbian, Violet hadn't been shocked. The few men Suzy had dated had been quiet and gentle, their slender bodies as unthreatening as a teenage girl's. Lani had been tougher and more masculine than any of the men Suzy had ever brought home, and Violet witnessed the potent power she wielded over Suzy. Violet was relieved when they broke up, but it was hard to imagine how this unexpected pregnancy had come about. Suzy had never been one for one-night stands or quick flings, and she was the one who chastised Violet when her behavior flirted with danger. "But who?" she asked after a moment.

Suzy let out another sigh. "Ian."

"Ian?" Violet repeated in surprise. Suzy and Ian had broken up over a year ago.

"It shouldn't have happened. It was just once."

"Does he know?"

Suzy shook her head. "I'm not keeping it." She gestured to her phone. "I was supposed to have the appointment this morning."

"Oh." Violet pursed her lips, not sure which part of Suzy's news was most alarming.

They hadn't exactly been raised with religion. For much of their childhood, their father was a lapsed Catholic. When they were little, they'd gone to church on the biggies—Christmas, Easter, occasionally Thanksgiving. But when Violet was in middle school, their father began going again every Sunday. It hadn't occurred to her till now to wonder what made him start going again after all those years away. Each week he brought Suzy with him, the only one of the three of them willing to go. When he moved out, Suzy stopped going to church, and as far as Violet knew, she hadn't been since. But Violet doubted a three-year steady diet of Catholicism hadn't left its mark somehow.

"Seriously, you can't tell Cal. She won't understand. Especially now, with Dad." There was a note of pleading in Suzy's voice. Violet took her eyes off the road to look at her. Suzy's face was pale, her freckles nearly washed away. There were gray circles beneath her eyes.

"Okay, I won't. I promise." It occurred to her that of the three of them, Violet wasn't the only one who was falling apart. In fact, there was a good chance she might be in the best shape of them all.

Chapter Twelve

Suzy

Suzy wasn't used to needing to eat so often. She tended to go hours between meals, often forgetting to eat and then whipping up some elaborate meal with whatever was in her cupboard. Now it was as if her body were taunting her—she felt sick if she didn't eat anything, but the idea of food made her sick as well. By the time they arrived in Portland, it was late afternoon and Suzy was both nauseated and ravenous.

Violet took the exit off the highway, and they drove through the center of town. Portland was a pretty coastal town, the type of place that filled up in the summer and then quickly emptied out as the colder weather came, leaving behind locals and college kids from the nearby university. Quaint shops lined the wide street, and their windows were decked with knickknacks and souvenirs. Several of them were closed for the season, but the town was still busy.

Suzy was thirteen when their father moved to Maine, two years after he moved out of the Cambridge house. She'd only been to visit a handful of times, and she'd spent part of a disastrous summer here in high school. Though he didn't seem to have any ties to Boston anymore, other than Suzy and her sisters, on the rare occasions when she saw her father, it was because he came to them.

"Look." Violet pointed out Veg, halfway down the street. On the hand-painted sign outside, a bright-orange carrot and magenta beet flanked the *V* and *G*. The interior was dark, and the sign on the front door read "Closed."

The last time Suzy had been in Portland was three years ago, when she was just beginning culinary school. At her father's urging, she drove up for the afternoon, though she was jittery and anxious the whole ride. Her father led her proudly into the bright and airy restaurant, pausing every few feet to introduce her to a staff member or customer. Seated in one of the polished wooden booths at Veg, her father made her try several new dishes on his menu—an arugula pesto, a watermelon salad, a vegan dessert made with cashew paste. He was trying to connect with her, Suzy knew, trying to speak with her in their common language of food. It wasn't Suzy's type of cooking, but it was good; she'd been impressed, and she told him so. His face opened into an expression of such naked happiness that Suzy had to look away.

Her own eyes filled with tears at the memory and the recognition of how little effort it took to give her father love, yet how stingy she'd been with it, like pinching crumbs from a cookie and dropping them on the plate of a starving man.

"Do you know where we're going?" Violet asked.

Suzy pulled out her phone and scrolled to the page she'd loaded with directions to the property that Barry was letting them borrow. "Take this right up here and then your first left." Violet followed Suzy's instructions and turned down the street. "It should be up here on the right. Number twenty-two."

They pulled into the driveway, the oyster-shell gravel crunching beneath the tires. The house was a small, shingled Cape, and from the street Suzy saw the swirling gray ocean behind it. Cal's black Subaru wagon was already in the driveway. "Ready?" Violet asked, putting the car into park.

"No." Suzy opened the door and the icy ocean air hit her hard. "But let's go anyway."

"Let me get your bag," Violet offered at the open trunk. It was such an un-Violet-like gesture, and Suzy cut her with her eyes.

"Don't," she said, reaching for the small suitcase.

Violet raised her hands in surrender. "Fine. You can carry mine too, if you want."

Suzy rolled her eyes, leaving Violet's suitcase where it was. She wondered if Cal would be able to tell she was pregnant just by looking at her. It had taken Violet only a few minutes, and Violet wasn't particularly attuned to other people, though she'd always been able to read Suzy. But she worried Cal would pick up the scent of fear and regret as soon as Suzy walked into the house.

"Hello?" she called and dropped her suitcase by the front door. She'd expected to find the house full of Maisy's boisterous noise or the mindless prattle of cartoons, though she doubted Cal would let Maisy watch TV during the day, even now. They wandered through the downstairs rooms, but there was no sign of Cal.

"Wow, look at this place." Violet stood at the large picture window that faced the ocean. A few boats bobbed in the distance. A thin path led from the back door to a private strip of beach. The papery beach grass blew in the light breeze, though the sand was covered in a hard shell of snow.

"Cal?" Suzy called, but there was no answer. The kitchen was empty, of both Cal and food. The counters were bare, not even a bag of chips or box of muffins to nibble on.

"Where is she?" Violet asked.

"Maybe she went to the grocery store," Suzy said hopefully.

"Her car's in the driveway," Violet pointed out. "Maybe they brought two cars?"

"Let's check upstairs."

The house smelled clean, like new wood and lavender. Their feet were heavy on the uncarpeted pine stairs leading to the second floor. "Callie?" Violet called.

"In here." The hoarse voice of their older sister came from behind a closed door at the end of the hallway. They stood outside the room. Suzy knocked. "Come in."

When she opened the door, Suzy had to stifle a gasp at the sight of Cal. Though she'd seen her just two weeks prior, Cal was transformed. She wore yoga pants and an old Yale sweatshirt, which wouldn't have been remarkable on anyone other than Cal, who wore silk suits to work each day and relaxed on the weekends in button-down shirts and pressed khakis. Her shoulder-length dark hair was mussed, and there were creases on her cheek from lying in bed. There was a hollowness to her face, her eyes a little sunken, her skin a pale gray. Plus, she was *in bed*, actually lying down. Suzy couldn't remember when she last saw Cal sit still for more than five minutes, much less lie down in the middle of the day.

"You look like shit. Are you okay?"

"I'm fine," Cal snapped, pushing herself up in bed. "Just peachy."

Suzy bent down and hugged her big sister. Cal at least smelled clean despite her haggard appearance. Suzy blinked back tears as she rested her head on Cal's shoulder, but when she pulled away, Cal's eyes were flat and expressionless. Suzy felt a current of fear run through her.

"Where's Howard? And the kids?" Suzy asked.

"At home. They'll come up in a few days." Cal lay back down in bed, pulling the blanket over her.

"Oh. We just assumed they were coming," Violet said. "You could have driven up with us."

"I wanted to be alone." Cal closed her eyes for a moment. It seemed to take an enormous amount of energy to open them again.

"I just can't believe it," Suzy said. She realized now she'd expected Cal to comfort her, but taking in the fragile appearance of her oldest sister, it was apparent that wouldn't be happening. The foreignness of this was unnerving.

"Really, Cal. Are you okay?" Violet sat beside Suzy on the edge of the bed. Her voice was gentle. She was trying.

"Am I okay?" Cal repeated, staring out the window at the churning ocean. Cal hadn't made eye contact with either of them since they'd arrived. She seemed suddenly angry, though Suzy wasn't certain at whom her anger was directed. "Am I okay? No. I don't think I am." Suzy met Violet's eyes briefly. *What now?* Violet seemed to ask. Suzy wished Howard and the girls were here to diffuse the tension. She couldn't remember the last time it had been just the three of them. "Sorry," Cal said, rubbing her eyes. "I think I'm just tired."

"It's okay," Suzy said.

"So. What do we need to do?" Violet's words were directed mainly at Cal, though Cal didn't answer. "I guess we need to think about a service. Have you talked to anyone at the funeral home?"

Cal shook her head.

"Okay. We should probably head over there. Do we know what kind of service we want?" Suzy shrugged and Cal didn't answer. "Did Dad go to church up here? Should it be a Catholic service?" Again, nothing. "Hello? Anyone?"

"I need to lie down," Cal said abruptly.

"You *are* lying down," Violet pointed out.

"Alone."

"Didn't you just wake up?" Violet asked. Suzy waited for Cal's inevitable sarcastic quip, though none came.

"I need to lie down," Cal repeated and she did, rolling to face the wall and pulling the covers up over her shoulder.

Suzy and Violet stayed seated on the bed for a moment until it became clear Cal was not going to say anything else. Then they rose wordlessly, shutting the door behind them.

Chapter Thirteen

Cal

Cal lay in bed and thought about all of the things that didn't matter. This list was even longer than her usual to-do list. Maisy's upcoming parent-teacher conference. The new package of diapers Sadie needed at day care. The chicken she'd left out to defrost that Howard would forget to cook and then have to throw out. The stamped bills ready for the mail sitting on the counter. Maisy's hair in need of a trim.

The way Howard had been looking at her lately, like he was frustrated and sad and angry all at once.

Just yesterday these had all seemed so pressing, but today they were scraps of paper, light and worthless, floating through her consciousness. None of it mattered at all. She could summon the list back up, but none of the items held any significance.

The memorial service.

Her father's body, waiting for them, cold and inert by now. Just another thing on the list of things she wouldn't think about.

With her cheek pressed against the clean sheets, Cal's mind was quiet for the first time in ages. Attending to her father's memorial service was no more pressing than the patch of eczema on

Sadie's elbow. Her thoughts swam around like fish, slippery and ungraspable.

There was such freedom in not caring.

Out in the hall, Violet and Suzy were murmuring in soft, concerned tones. No doubt talking about her. Add another item to the list. Let someone else care about it all for once.

Chapter Fourteen

Violet

Violet stood in front of the open refrigerator, peering in at the absence of food. A half-drunk bottle of seltzer, some condiments, and a jar of pickles. She looked without looking, standing in the cool artificial air.

The last time Violet had spoken to her father was on Christmas, over a month ago. They'd spent the day at Cal's house. Usually they celebrated the holidays with their mother, but since she was in London, Cal had invited their father instead. It was one of the few holidays they'd shared with him in recent years.

He'd stayed the night in Cal's guest room, though Violet had seem him only for the hours of Christmas dinner. He'd invited them all for breakfast the next morning, but by the time morning rolled around, her father was already long gone from Violet's mind as she prepared to move out of the apartment she shared with Luka. Her father had brought an expensive bottle of red wine to dinner and presents for each of them, though Violet and her sisters didn't usually exchange gifts. Suzy had bought him a bottle of gourmet olive oil, and Cal had given him a wool sweater in a beautiful eggplant color. Violet had been embarrassed she didn't have a gift for him. He'd given her a soft moleskin journal with her initials embossed on the cover, the pages inside a heavy white stock. She knew he expected her to use it to write poetry, but the book was too beautiful to write in and Violet usually wrote her poems in a tatty spiral-bound notebook, which she then typed up on the computer later. The journal was now sitting in a storage unit with the rest of her books while she looked for an apartment. The thick white pages remained empty.

For the first part of Violet's life, her father had been a teacher at Beckett Day School, a private coed prep school in Cambridge. He taught history, was dean of the middle school, and coached the boy's high school swimming team. If you'd asked any student to name their top three teachers at Beckett, her father's name would have made the list. Until the winter of Violet's sophomore year, when he was accused of sexual misconduct.

Her parents never told her the story directly. They just said her father was taking the rest of the year off. But Violet was fifteen, and the halls were filled with the buzzing sounds of kids spreading rumors. Everyone was talking about it, but in a hushed, fractured way around Violet. Sarah Byron, a bossy girl in Violet's French class, had finally pieced the story together for her, though whether Sarah told her out of kindness or to watch Violet's shocked reaction, she wasn't sure.

The story went like this: There were three boys, young men really, since the youngest was sixteen. Thatcher Kennedy, a junior on the swim team, accused her father of watching him in the shower after swim practice. Victor Landley, another junior, echoed Thatcher's accusation. Jack Parr had been the nail in the coffin. He claimed their father propositioned him for oral sex in the locker room after practice one afternoon. They filed into the dean's office on a Wednesday afternoon in January, one after the other, to tell their sordid tales. By the end of the week, Violet's father had been put on administrative leave for the remainder of the semester. He didn't return to Beckett in September, and Violet attended the public high school for her junior year.

Violet now missed her father.

She didn't miss him just because he was dead. She missed the father who listened to her terrible middle school poetry and who helped her study for tests. She missed the father who waited up for her when she went out on dates and insisted the boys who called on the phone have a conversation with him first. She missed the father she'd had before he'd been accused of making advances on the boys, and before he only halfheartedly protested his innocence.

Already her memory of her father was growing distant, the picture of his face blurred around the edges, his voice a scrap of film she couldn't quite grab hold of. But the quiet reality was that this would have been true if Violet had tried to conjure up her father's face yesterday, before he was dead, before remembering him seemed so important. She'd lost her father a long time ago.

"I'm going to the grocery store." Suzy was beside Violet at the open fridge door. "Do you want to come?"

Violet startled and turned to Suzy. "No." She closed the door. "I'll stay here in case Cal needs anything."

"I'm taking your car, okay?" Suzy was already holding the keys.

"Sure." Violet opened the fridge again.

"It's definitely empty, Vi."

"I know. I was hoping for coffee." Violet sighed.

"Check the freezer," Suzy advised.

Violet opened it to find a yellow tin of French roast. "Don't forget cream and sugar."

"I'll be back soon."

Violet heard the wheeze of her old Honda out front and then the house was quiet. She settled on the couch and pulled out her phone, scrolling through her messages, hoping to find one from Luka. There was nothing.

She searched through her photos, wondering if she had one of her father. It suddenly seemed important to have his face in front of her, a tangible reminder of what she'd lost because she couldn't grasp hold of what was gone. And then there he suddenly was at Christmas dinner, his face the size of her thumbnail, his arms around the three of them in a shot taken by Luka. Violet enlarged the photo on her phone, focusing on her father. He was tall and thin, with close-cut white hair and clear blue eyes. A lean, muscled man who'd grown so clean and healthy over the past ten years that it seemed particularly cruel he'd died so suddenly. A restless grief clawed at her throat.

Violet closed the photos and went onto Facebook to distract herself from the complex brew of emotions the picture stirred up. She checked out Luka's profile page to see if there had been any recent activity, any love messages from Elena or telling posts. But Luka rarely posted on Facebook and there was nothing new. There was a new message in her in-box though, and she clicked on it, the name of the sender shooting through her body with ancient longing.

Michael Donahue.

Dear Violet, the message began. Violet narrowed her eyes so as to read the miniature print on her phone.

> I wanted to tell you how sorry I was to hear the news about your father. He was a wonderful teacher and a good man. We reconnected recently and I had hoped to make a visit up there. Please let me know when the funeral is, as I'd like to attend. Give my best to your sisters. —Michael

She wondered for a moment how he heard about her father's death—the obituary hadn't appeared in the paper yet. Then she realized that Michael was probably friends with her father on Facebook. Her father rarely posted or shared pictures, but he did have an account.

Violet suspected it was mostly to see the pictures that she and her sisters shared. Her father's timeline had quickly filled up with messages of condolence, though Violet didn't read through most of them. There was something creepy about sharing a death through social media.

Violet clicked on the image next to the message from Michael and then clicked again to enlarge the photo. He looked the same. Dark-haired and handsome, though his face had filled out, and he had the square look of a man now, as opposed to the angularity of a teenager. In his profile picture he was with a pretty blond woman, a boy, and a girl.

Michael Donahue was the first of a series of men Violet let treat her badly. None of them had been abusive. Their poor behavior was more inattention and a lack of interest beyond the first thrilling moments of newness. She suspected a psychiatrist would feel differently, but Violet didn't blame her father, though she wondered if she would have fallen into such a predictable pattern of disappointing men if he hadn't left just as she was becoming sexually active. Luka was the only man Violet was certain had loved her.

But Michael. He was her first. He certainly hadn't loved her, but Violet fell headfirst into an aching obsession that came only with being a teenager. And even though he had been a jerk to her (and he had, there was no doubt about that), the memory of her longing was burned into her skin, still alive and tingling below the surface.

He had been her math tutor. Violet had never been a good math student, and after she'd nearly failed her first few geometry tests her sophomore year, her father insisted she get a tutor. If her mother had been the one finding the tutor, she would have hired a girl. She knew Violet. Despite having three daughters, their father was blind enough to hire a handsome senior boy to tutor her and think it would help Violet's math skills improve. Michael was a straight-A student in AP calculus. He was the captain of the swim team, though the season didn't start till late November, far enough away that he could help Violet bring up her grade. For ten dollars an hour Michael came to the house three afternoons a week to tutor her.

Violet spent most of the first session admiring Michael's mouth. He had smooth pink lips and perfect teeth, so white she wondered if he had them professionally bleached. He smelled delicious, some piney, musky scent Violet had never smelled again on another man, though even now she could conjure up the yearning it had evoked in her.

He had received early admission to Harvard, and of course he had a girlfriend, a popular blond senior named Bettina, though everyone called her Bitty because she was so tiny. Even then, a girlfriend was never much deterrence for Violet.

Though she was only a sophomore, Violet was used to being noticed. She had red hair, which for some reason boys found irresistible, and she was the only one of her sisters to have large breasts. During their tutoring sessions, Violet flirted shamelessly with Michael, and it didn't take long before he stopped pretending he didn't notice.

At first they studied in the kitchen or the living room. Violet's textbook would be open, and Michael would work through the problems with her on a clean piece of graph paper, his numbers and letters small and square, the lines drawn precisely with the ruler he brought with him. While Violet was lucky if she could remember to bring pencils and paper to class each day, Michael had a separate notebook for each subject and another one dedicated to their tutoring sessions. He was the only boy she knew who carried a fully stocked leather pencil case in the pocket of his messenger bag, complete with a silver ruler, a protractor, and various other measuring devices and different-sized triangles. Tools that Violet couldn't remember ever having used since sophomore math class.

While Michael talked through the problems with her, Violet stared at his large, strong hands, the nails clean and square—the hands of a man, though he was just two years older than the boys in her class. Because he was on the swim team, Violet already knew what Michael looked like without most of his clothes on. She knew the smooth planes of his back, the broad terrain of muscle he carried in his shoulders and biceps. She'd already seen the swell of his quadriceps, the stretchy blue Speedo barely larger than an olive leaf.

Most days during their tutoring, Violet's father was still at work finalizing lesson plans or supervising the debate team. Cal was busy with Model UN or yearbook or some other extracurricular activity. Usually Violet's mother and Suzy would be home, but on Tuesdays, Suzy had gymnastics, so Violet and Michael had the house to themselves.

It was on a Tuesday that Violet suggested they work in her bedroom. It hadn't taken long before they were lying in her bed, and Michael's hands worked to unhook the lacy black bra she'd selected for him that morning. The following Tuesday, Violet didn't bother to take out her math book and they went straight upstairs. By the third Tuesday, she knew what lay beneath the olive leaf, had held it in her hands. By the fourth Tuesday, Violet was no longer a virgin.

In school, Michael barely talked to her. He was still with Bitty, and Violet was just the lowerclassman he tutored as a favor to his swim coach and for extra cash. But they had a few free periods that overlapped, and some days Michael would meet her beneath the bleachers of the stadium. The metal risers pressed against Violet's back, and she breathed in Michael Donahue's intoxicating scent, his mouth on her neck, and his hands in her hair. She'd arrive late to study hall, lips swollen and her heart still beating too fast. Her days became preoccupied by the snatched minutes under the bleachers and glimpses of Michael across the quad, waiting for Tuesday afternoon.

It was after school one December afternoon that Violet went looking for her father. She'd missed the bus because she'd been with Michael, her hips ground against the exterior brick wall of the gymnasium, his hand roaming under her winter coat and wool sweater. Though he had his own car, Michael couldn't drive Violet home because he needed to pick Bitty up from dance class. Violet had absorbed the snub and was trying not to be hurt by it. She didn't like to be the kind of girl who was hurt by this type of thing.

Because Violet's father was dean of the middle school, he had an office in addition to a classroom. It was on the third floor, a floor rarely visited by students because there weren't any classrooms up there. Violet had only been in his office a couple of times, though she knew there was a Dylan Thomas poster on the wall and a sagging couch usually covered in stacks of papers.

The school was eerily quiet. It was a slushy Friday afternoon and people had already gone home for the weekend, making plans over their shoulders for later that night as they hurried to the school parking lot where their secondhand Saabs and Audis waited for them. Most of the students at Beckett had money, and winter weekends were filled with ski trips and shopping expeditions. Violet attended Beckett for a small fee as a faculty perk, and she was always aware of the differences between her and the other students. Girls never liked Violet much anyway, equally threatened by and contemptuous of the way boys noticed her. Violet's weekends were spent pretending she didn't care that she was excluded from most social events, and the only invitations she ever got were from boys wanting to find out if she was a real redhead. Since she'd started seeing Michael, she hadn't given any of them the satisfaction of finding out. Usually Violet spent the weekend in her bedroom, hunched over a notebook, writing poetry or reading. Saturday and Sunday loomed emptily ahead of her.

That Friday afternoon, her father's classroom was empty, but his book bag and coat were still there. Before she climbed the stairs to the third floor, Violet paused to run her fingers through her hair and check that her clothes were not askew, or for some other telltale sign Michael left upon her. Her body felt tender and fragile. There would be a bruise in the middle of her back where her spine had pressed up against the brick wall of the school. For a guy so careful that he dated each page of notes and used reinforcement labels on his torn notebook pages, Michael was surprisingly forceful.

The third floor smelled musty, like furniture polish and floor cleaner. The hallway was dark, though a stream of light came from the closed door of her father's office. Violet's penny loafers were quiet on the linoleum floors, the soft swish of her tights the only sound in the empty corridor. She stood before her father's door but didn't go in.

There was little in the way of privacy in Violet's home. Someone was always coming into the bathroom while you were in the shower or borrowing a shirt without asking. But for some reason, Violet paused before the closed door, though her tendency would have normally been to throw it open and walk into her father's office as brazenly as if it were her own. There was no talking, but there were noises inside, the springs of the ancient couch and the scrape of feet on the floor. There was a sigh, not of frustration or exasperation—the kind Violet was used to—but the whisper of breath being released in pleasure.

She should have turned around, taken the train home or called her mother for a ride. But it was snowing and her father had a car. Michael had hurt her feelings, and Violet wanted her father's warm chatter on the drive home to take away the sting. She knocked. The noises stopped.

"Dad?" she called hesitantly.

"Just a minute." Her father's voice was odd, as if he were talking to a stranger, not his daughter. A moment later he opened the door. "You're still here." His face was flushed and he held a manila folder, though somehow Violet knew he'd just picked it up off the desk as a prop.

"I stayed late to work on math," she lied easily. "Are you going home soon?" He stood in the doorway, not inviting her in, but Violet peered under his arm to see who was with him. She didn't know whom she'd expected, but was surprised to see Mr. Louis, one of the lower school tech teachers. She'd taken typing class with him in middle school.

From his perch on the couch, Mr. Louis nodded to her. "Hello, Violet." He was a slight dark-haired man, one of the younger teachers in the school. When Violet was in his class, all of the girls had crushes on him.

"Hi," she answered back shyly.

"We were just going over the upcoming middle school dance," her father said, his voice a little too cheery. "I'm trying to convince Mr. Louis to chaperone."

Perhaps six months earlier, Violet would have believed him. But six months earlier, school had been a different place. It was a place of studying and learning, tedium and monotony. But since Michael Donahue's weekly appearance in her bedroom, school was now thick with lust and desire, and Violet was able to pick up the scent like an animal. She noticed Mr. Louis's rumpled shirt, her father's loosened tie, and the tension that crackled between them.

Something buzzed inside her body, a ringing in her ears—a vibration that made the length of her arms tingle and pricked her palms. Violet clenched her hands into fists to shake off the sharp shock that flooded her senses as her father's secret unfurled itself before them both.

"Can you give me a ride home?" She chewed on her lower lip, still raw from the stubble of Michael's chin. She focused on this rather than anything else, unwilling or unable to look either her father or Mr. Louis in the eye.

"Sure." Her father turned to Mr. Louis, who had risen from the couch. "We're all set here, right?"

"Yup, absolutely." Mr. Louis's cheeks smoldered a deep pink.

The three of them stood in the hallway while her father flicked off the lights and locked the door to the office. They trudged down the stairs silently, single file, Violet walking several feet in front. On the second-floor landing, Violet headed for the doors to her father's classroom.

"Have a good weekend," Mr. Louis called to Violet, raising his hand in a wave.

She pushed through the swinging glass doors, already questioning what had transpired upstairs, second-guessing what she'd sensed between them.

"You too," Violet murmured without turning around, not bothering to hold the door for her father.

Chapter Fifteen

Suzy

Suzy wasn't sure if she believed in God, but she knew her father had. Joseph Bloom had been raised by their strict Nana Dee and the church. Suzy had never met her grandfather, who'd left when her father was only a toddler. Instead, her father had turned to other fathers, the type that wore white collars and spoke to their children from behind a confessional screen.

Though their mother had grown up attending a Protestant church on a semiregular basis, she was a free spirit with her frizzy hair, peasant dresses, and a job as a social worker. She rubbed off on their father, for a while at least. After they bought their ramshackle house in Cambridge, one of the crunchiest enclaves of straitlaced Greater Boston, they stopped going to church, though their father eventually returned.

Even during the years when he didn't go to church, Suzy knew her father believed in God. He said prayers every night before bed and carried Nana Dee's quartz rosary in his pants pocket, fingering the beads throughout the day. He believed in right and wrong, and he spoke about this in his history classes; he also believed in sin and guilt. Though he never preached to his daughters, Suzy knew he would have thought the abortion was a sin. She also knew he would never have said so aloud.

This weighed upon her as she walked the aisles of the grocery store, absently filling the cart with milk, cold cuts, and fruit. She'd rarely discussed politics with her father, but Suzy suspected he wouldn't have dismissed all abortion as sin. There were the instances of rape, or teenagers becoming pregnant, or mothers who were in such dire financial straits that another child would put the whole family at risk. Suzy suspected he would have grudgingly assented to these. But Suzy was none of these exceptions. While she was single, she could support herself. She was educated; she was old enough. She was ashamed to admit it, but she'd scheduled the abortion hastily, as if such a mistake could be easily erased.

She'd been pro-choice her whole life, had long ago learned to use sterile terms like *fetus, embryo, bundle of cells*, but all she could think now was *baby*. A baby her father would never meet, though the irony was not lost on her that if her father hadn't abruptly died, he still would never have met this baby/bundle of cells.

Even though Suzy hadn't intended to tell either of her sisters about the pregnancy, she wished she could talk to Cal, but Cal was falling apart. The terrifying fact of this reality was apparent, made clear to Suzy by her own simple presence alone in the grocery store and by the foodless house she'd left. At the very least, the normal Cal would have sent her with a carefully numerated list, with even the most obvious basics like bread and milk, as well as more easily overlooked items, like dishwashing detergent and trash bags, written in her curling script.

But this was not the normal Cal. This was Cal after her father died. Cal was the only one who remained close with him after the divorce, the only one to come up to Portland to visit, the only one to call—not every month but every week—and not out of guilt or obligation, but because she wanted to. The loss had obviously undone her.

Suzy couldn't remember ever seeing Cal undone, even as a child. She was the glue, the rock, the boss—the one you could count on. It drove her and Violet nuts at times, but what else would they have done without her? Because she and Violet were both children, really. They were children and Cal was an adult, and as long as Cal stayed the adult, they could remain children.

Suzy didn't know what needed to be done when a person died. She didn't know where to even begin. She suspected the funeral home had brochures on this sort of thing, though the fact that no one had been to the funeral home yet further confirmed that Cal had fallen apart.

Her stomach growled and a wave of nausea rolled over her. She needed food.

Suzy looked into her cart. It was still nearly empty, though she'd somehow added a jar of pickled beets and a tub of rice pudding. She gripped the plastic handle and blinked back the tears that sprang to her eyes. She needed to figure out dinner for tonight and lunch tomorrow and enough food to get through at least a few more days. She didn't even know how to do this. The simple task was beyond her.

Pull it together, Suzy. Her father's voice was suddenly clear in her mind. *One step at a time.*

In a house of four women, their father's voice was often the rational one, the calm in the center of the storm. Suzy could picture his thin face and easy smile, the way he tilted his head to the side when he was being serious. If her father were here, he would tell her to slow down and think about each task individually.

Suzy took a deep breath. In the cart was a bag of pretzels, which she opened and began to eat. She took another breath, ate another pretzel. The nausea subsided, and after a moment she felt a little calmer.

Suzy maneuvered her cart back to the beginning of the store. Produce. They would have sandwiches for lunch, and she could make a salad for dinner. She placed vegetables in the cart and then moved on to the next aisle. Instrumental music hummed over the speakers. She said the items aloud in her mind as she plucked them off the shelves, the list Cal would have sent her with if she'd been able to. Bread, milk, eggs. Carrots, hummus, crackers. Coffee, cream, turkey, cheese.

In the health aisle, Suzy stood before a row of prenatal vitamins. She pulled a bottle off the shelf and dropped it in the cart, then put it back on the shelf, then dropped the bottle in again before pushing the cart down the aisle toward the toilet paper.

She could do this.

One step at a time.

Chapter Sixteen

Cal

Cal's cell phone buzzed on the nightstand. The pale winter light in the room was blinding when she forced her eyes open and looked at the screen. Howard. She was tempted to ignore it, but it was the third time he'd called today.

"Hi." She heard the flatness in her voice, but didn't have the energy to disguise it.

"Hi. How are you doing?" Howard's voice was cautious, as if she might start sobbing again at any moment.

"Fine. Terrible." It was early evening and Cal imagined him sitting on the couch in the living room, Sadie tucked into the crook of his arm, drinking a bottle. Maisy would be in the den watching *Curious George*, her mouth parted open in that dull, transfixed expression she got when in front of the television. The expression that made Cal want to throw the box out the window, if she didn't desperately need the thirty minutes' peace that *Curious George* could provide.

They'd been married for almost ten years. They'd met at her office holiday party soon after she'd started working at the firm. Howard had shown up with one of her coworkers, and he offered to buy Cal a glass of champagne. When she informed him the drinks were free, he said he'd buy her two. Age, marriage, and two children had changed him, but back then Howard was always willing to follow an open bar.

They were both single and in their twenties, and he wasn't her usual type. Cal tended to go for serious academics, the type to ignore her for two weeks during finals. Howard was more fun than any man she'd been with. He wasn't irresponsible—he'd gone to Princeton and gotten a position at a top firm—but he didn't take any of it too seriously. For their first date, he brought Cal to the aquarium because he loved to watch the penguins. Then they had dessert and cocktails at the Top of the Hub, a restaurant that overlooked all of Boston. It surprised her how quickly and completely she fell in love with him.

Cal knew the love was still there. It was just buried under years' worth of petty worry, haggling over chores, and an endless fatigue. She was only half sitting up in bed, her back propped against the bed frame with a pillow, but she lay back down now, pulling the blanket over her body.

"Have you made any plans?" Howard asked.

"Plans?"

"For the service."

"Oh. No. I don't know, actually." She closed her eyes and yawned. She was so, so tired.

"You don't know?"

"I'm resting. I'm going to let Violet and Suzy take care of it." Howard would have started dinner for Maisy by now, probably something frozen involving french fries. There would be ice cream for dessert because Mommy wasn't home, and Howard wouldn't know how to explain why. She heard Maisy's voice in the background, and for a moment Cal's heart ached.

"Do your sisters have any idea what they're doing?" Howard asked.

"They'll figure it out."

"But Callie," Howard continued, "don't you want to be part of it? You were the closest to your dad. Don't you think you know best what the service should be like?"

Cal felt a sudden flare of anger, though it wasn't directed only at Howard. It was at all of them. "Why should I have to be the one to do it all? Why can't someone else ever take care of it?"

"I'm sure they can," he said carefully. "I just think you'll regret not being part of the decisions."

"I won't."

"Okay." He paused, searching for a topic. In the background Maisy whined again. "In a minute, Maisy," Howard said, then turning back to Cal, "Sadie's fever's gone. I think you were right: it was probably just teething."

"Good." Cal focused on the painting beside the bed, a red buoy in a blue-and-gray ocean. Her breasts throbbed at the mention of Sadie, milk tingling in their ducts, waiting for an open mouth. She still hadn't pumped, though she'd squeezed milk down the bathroom sink a few hours earlier, the pale liquid shooting from her body as if from a sprinkler. No point in saving it.

On the other end of the line Howard shushed Maisy again. "Someone really wants to talk to you."

"Not now." Cal could not care about it all as long as she held everything at a distance. But Maisy was her heart. Her voice alone pierced to the soft and tender center of Cal's soul.

"Cal, she misses you. She doesn't understand what's going on. Just for a minute?" In the background Maisy was asking for the phone, the stream of *Mommy, Mommy, Mommy* bringing up the tears Cal couldn't bear to start. If she started again, she might never stop.

"Tomorrow. I need to rest," she said.

"Cal." Howard was always patient, but she could hear his frustration rising.

"Tomorrow," she repeated, pressing the "End Call" button—the first time she'd ever hung up on him, leaving Howard to explain to their daughter.

Chapter Seventeen

Violet

Violet wrote back to Michael quickly.

> Thank you for your message. We haven't figured out the
> funeral arrangements yet, but I'll let you know. —V

She pressed "Send" before she lost her nerve or added anything else, like how she still remembered the feel of his muscled forearm under her hand, the soft and fine hairs smooth against her palm. She dropped the phone on the couch beside her as if it were a magic bottle and Michael a genie who might suddenly appear in the living room.

Outside it had started to snow, fat wet flakes dropping into the bay. Violet's stomach growled. Where was Suzy with their food?

Michael had been one of her dad's favorites, a young man he'd taught in middle school and went on to coach for four years in high school. Her father had been raised by a single mom and then surrounded by girls his whole adult life, but at school there were his boys. Boys he'd written recommendations for, boys he'd counseled through problems at home, boys he'd been kind to. Though all of the students revered him, it was the boys whom he most impacted. They were the ones who came back to visit after graduation, the ones who nominated him for graduation speaker three times. They were the ones who remembered his compassion. That was the part about the accusations that was so cutting. All of that kindness suddenly seemed suspicious and duplicitous. Self-serving.

She picked the phone up and clicked back on Facebook, some invisible current pulling her to whatever lay on the other end. Only a few minutes had passed, but he must have been online. There was a notification that she had a new message. Heart pounding, Violet clicked on the message from Michael.

Thank you, Violet. I hope to make it.

Violet placed the phone back on the couch.

As a teenager, she spent a lot of time alone. She had acquaintances to eat lunch with at school and a few girls who sometimes invited her to the mall on weekends, but she didn't have anyone she could confide in. There was Cal, but unburdening herself to Cal was never simple and usually resulted in Violet feeling worse than she had before. Cal had already been accepted to Yale and was so busy with extracurriculars that Violet barely saw her. Suzy was four years younger, and in high school four years felt like a lot. So when she needed to tell someone what she'd seen in her father's office, she confided in Michael.

The Tuesday after Violet saw her father with Mr. Louis, she and Michael lay in her bed. They'd already had sex, but sometimes Michael liked to do it twice. The swim season had started, and he wasn't able to tutor her as often, though he still managed to make their Tuesday afternoons. Violet was still only getting low Cs in geometry, and she knew Michael's days as a tutor were numbered. They didn't give tests in school for the type of things Michael was teaching her.

He closed his mouth around her breast, and his hand roamed down the length of her body, tall and curvy, so unlike compact Bitty. More and more Violet thought about what he did with Bitty. Not just in bed, but out of bed. Dinner and movies, taking her to parties with their mutual friends, driving her home in his car. At school, Violet would see them walking through the hallways together, his arm wrapped protectively around Bitty's shoulders, or his hand resting gently at the small of her back. His meetings with Violet behind the gymnasium or under the bleachers were getting rarer and rarer.

He must have felt her preoccupation because he pushed himself up on an elbow. "Do you want to go again?" he asked.

"If you want," Violet answered. She wanted him just to lie there with her, but she knew he wouldn't want to hear this. It was Bitty he held. With Violet . . . there was a word for what he did with her.

"I've got to get to practice by four, so if you don't . . ." He trailed off, his black hair falling into his eyes.

Violet had gone to his first swim meet just a few weeks earlier. She'd sat in the stands of the swampy pool and watched Michael waiting for his heat, swinging his arms and rolling his shoulders, his familiar body in constant motion.

Her father had been at the meet too, of course, in a pair of blue swim trunks and a T-shirt, a whistle around his neck as he paced the length of the tiled pool, calling out encouragement to his swimmers. He was affectionate with the boys, a hands-on type of coach: slapping one of them on his wet back after a good performance, speaking softly to another, so close their faces bowed together, his arm around the young man's dripping shoulders.

At the time she'd been preoccupied with Michael, and with Bitty cheering in the stands just a few rows below, her blond ponytail bouncing with each shout. But now her father's behavior seemed odd in light of what she'd seen with Mr. Louis, his manner a little too chummy. Had it really, or was Violet just looking for a reason to keep Michael in her bed for a few extra minutes, a reason she knew would make him stay?

"I saw my father with Mr. Louis last week," Violet began. Michael had already sat up in bed and was looking for his shirt. Violet reached out a hand to still him, placing her palm on his warm, flat stomach. "The tech teacher?"

"Yeah?" Already he was miles away, practicing the butterfly, his signature stroke, those beautiful, muscular arms arcing through the air like a flying fish.

"It was weird," Violet continued, waiting for his eyes. She already knew how she'd feel after he left, lonely and unsatisfied, the four walls of her untidy bedroom pressing in on her. Michael always seemed to leave a void behind. She just wanted to postpone that feeling for as long as possible. "They were in his office."

"What's weird about that?" Michael pulled on his "Beckett Swim" T-shirt.

"They were . . ." Violet paused.

It wasn't just to get Michael to stay, though there was that, of course. But she was confused. She didn't understand what she'd seen. She needed someone to assure her she'd misunderstood, and there was no one else to tell. Michael knew her father. Michael *loved* her father. How many times had he told her what a great coach her dad was, how smart he was, what a cool guy? Michael could find a way to explain away what she'd felt. "They were . . . I don't know." She bit her lip. "Disheveled. Like I'd interrupted something."

"What do you mean?" Finally Michael looked at her, but his face was twisted into a grimace.

"I don't know. They just seemed . . . intimate." She let the rest remain unsaid, though from Michael's expression he understood.

"Your dad's a fag?" Violet winced. It wasn't a word that had ever been used in her home as far as she could recall. "Sorry," Michael added, seeing her distaste. "I mean, your dad's gay?" His eyes scanned her face for some sort of explanation that would make sense.

"What? No," Violet protested. She watched Michael's face, his features rearranging themselves as some realization dawned on him.

"It makes sense," he said softly, standing to pull on his boxer shorts and jeans.

"What?" Violet pulled the sheet up to cover herself. "No, it doesn't."

He shook his head. "Something one of the other guys said. About the way he acts. Always touching us. Like he's looking for an excuse."

"No." She shook her head wildly. This had been a mistake. She didn't know what she'd hoped to get from Michael, but this wasn't it. "You can't say anything. Please."

Michael turned to look at Violet, and for the first time all afternoon she knew he really saw her. His face softened. He sat back down on the bed beside her. "Look," he began. Violet swallowed the lump that had already formed in her throat. She knew where this was going. She'd been waiting for it for weeks. "I'm not going to be able to keep tutoring you. The season has started, and I've just got too much going on."

"That's okay," Violet said. She dropped the sheet and leaned against him so her breasts pressed against the bare skin of his arm. "We can still see each other."

He inhaled quickly, his fingers fluttering along her nipples before dropping his hand. "I don't think so."

"Why not?" Violet hated her own voice, thick with unspent tears. She would not cry. She wasn't the girl who cried.

"I feel bad about Bitty. And you too," he added, though she knew this was an afterthought.

"What's different now?" Violet asked bitterly. "What's changed?"

"Nothing." He scratched his head. "I just, I feel bad about it."

"Well, *don't*," Violet said.

Michael let out a harsh laugh. "I just can't anymore, okay? I'm sorry."

"It's fine," Violet lied. He scooted a little closer to her on the bed, his hand once again reaching for her breast.

"I'm sorry, okay?" he asked, his mouth coming closer to hers. His hair smelled of chlorine, but underneath that was the smell that made her miss him even when he was right there. She let him pull her in, breathing in his nameless scent one last time.

Chapter Eighteen

Suzy

Suzy spread out the fixings for sandwiches and soup and brewed a fresh pot of coffee. There was something comforting about the hiss and gurgle of the coffeepot, something so everyday and normal. The heat in the little house had finally kicked in and the kitchen was warm and cozy, though Cal still hadn't emerged from the bedroom upstairs.

Suzy poured a carton of tomato soup into a pot and then began to make ham-and-cheese sandwiches while Violet went upstairs to try to coax Cal down for some lunch. When the doorbell rang, Suzy lowered the flame on the soup, crossing the kitchen to answer the front door. A tall, thin man stood on the stoop, carrying a basket covered with a checkered dish towel. Cold air and the steely scent of snow poured into the cottage.

"Hello, Suzy," the man said, and when Suzy stared back at him blankly, he added, "I'm Barry. Your father and I own Veg together?"

"Oh, of course. Sorry." It was Barry who had found her father, Barry who had broken the news to her. Suzy had met him before, but only a few times, so rare were her visits up here. She hadn't even realized he was co-owner of Veg. She thought he was an employee.

"I'm so sorry for your loss," he said, folding his body to embrace her. He was younger than her father, she realized when he pulled away, though his white hair was cut close to his scalp much like her father's had been. His pale blue eyes were rimmed pink and watery, though Suzy wasn't sure if this was from emotion or if they always looked this way.

"Please come in." Suzy stepped back to allow him to follow her inside.

"I brought muffins." He held up the basket. "Carrot-walnut. They were your dad's favorite."

"Thank you." She took the basket, ushering him into the kitchen. "I was just making some lunch. Would you like a sandwich?"

"Oh, no thank you. I just came to pay my respects. I don't want to put you out." He didn't sit or even take off his coat, but stood with his arms clasped in front of him.

"You're not, really. How about a cup of coffee?" Suzy offered.

He smiled and nodded. "Coffee would be nice."

"Please, sit." Suzy gestured to one of the stools at the counter. She pulled out mugs and poured a cup for each of them. He unzipped his coat, but still didn't remove it.

"I hope you don't mind if I eat." Suzy gestured to her bowl of soup and sandwich. "We just arrived."

"Please, go ahead." Suzy lowered her face toward the soup, burning the tip of her tongue with the first bite. Barry looked around the house. "The place is working out okay for you, then?" Suzy stared at him blankly before remembering it was Barry who had arranged for them to stay in the house.

"Oh, yes. Thank you so much for setting it up for us." She lowered the spoon back into the bowl, embarrassed by the slurping noises in the quiet kitchen. She took a bite of sandwich instead.

"Are your sisters here with you?" Barry glanced around the quiet downstairs.

Suzy nodded, chewing and swallowing. "Violet should be down in a minute. And Cal." She faltered. "Cal's not handling things very well right now."

Barry nodded. "They were close." It wasn't a question.

"They were," Suzy agreed.

Suzy ate her sandwich and soup as Barry sipped his coffee. There was something companionable about the silence, as if there were no need for small talk.

Violet burst into the kitchen, shattering the quiet with the loud clack of her shoes and the louder presence of her existence. "She's still not getting out of bed, though I think I've persuaded her to have a cup of coffee. Oh, sorry," she added, seeing Barry seated at the counter.

"Vi, this is Barry. He owns Veg with Dad." She turned to Barry. "You've met Violet before?" Suzy couldn't remember the last time Violet had come up to Maine either. Their father had always visited them.

"I'm afraid I haven't had the pleasure." Barry rose to standing and reached to embrace Violet. She held him awkwardly. "I'm so sorry for your loss."

"Thank you." Violet straightened, blinking quickly.

"I made some sandwiches," Suzy said, pushing the plate toward Violet. She turned back to Barry. "Were you close to him?"

Barry swallowed hard and then nodded. "Yes." His voice cracked, and he cleared his throat. "Yes, we were close. We'd known each other for nearly ten years."

"You found him?" Violet sat down with them at the counter. She held her sandwich but didn't take a bite.

Barry nodded. "He didn't come in to work, and he wasn't answering his phone. It was unlike him. I went by his house." He lowered his eyes and then stood up from his stool. "He was on the floor beside the treadmill. I called 911, but he was already gone. I checked his pulse. And I could tell." Barry looked away.

They were silent, digesting this news. The image was sharp in Suzy's mind of her handsome father in his running gear, lying on the floor beside the spinning rubber, dying alone.

"Does it hurt?" Violet's voice was quiet. "A brain aneurysm?"

Barry's face was full of such kindness when he spoke. "I think only for a minute. It's usually a very quick death." Violet nodded and put the uneaten sandwich back down on her plate.

"I really didn't mean to intrude. I just wanted to come by to see you all and to offer my condolences." He brought his mug to the sink and rinsed it out.

"You don't have to do that," Suzy protested.

"Occupational hazard," he joked. He zipped up his heavy winter coat. "I also wanted to offer my help with the service. I don't mean to overstep," he said quickly. "But I'm happy to do that if it would be helpful."

Violet and Suzy exchanged a glance of gratitude and relief. "Please," Suzy said. "That would be wonderful. We haven't done anything yet. We don't even know where to begin."

Barry nodded. "It's a small town. I know the funeral director. I'll stop by on my way home, get things started. I'll be in touch later today to let you know how things go. If that's okay?"

"Yes," they both said quickly.

"Okay, then." He walked to the door, and Suzy and Violet rose to follow him.

"Did he still go to church? I never asked him," Suzy said.

Barry's face tightened for a moment, and he nodded. "He did. Every Sunday. St. Mary's Star of the Sea on the bluff."

"I think a Catholic service might be best, then." Suzy glanced at Violet, who shrugged. "I think he would have liked that."

Barry nodded. "Of course. St. Mary's will do a lovely job. And a wake too?"

Suzy nodded. "I think so."

Barry nodded again. "I'll see what I can do." He ran a hand over the stubble on his chin and gave them a small smile. "I'm so glad to finally meet you both," he said, opening the front door and letting a blast of cold into the warm house. His eyes filled with tears. "I just wish it weren't this way." Violet stood and watched him walk down the path toward his car, his broad shoulders stooped as he trudged slowly into the cold.

Chapter Nineteen
Cal

Cal's sisters were talking downstairs. There was a lower voice as well, the voice of a man, though Cal wasn't sure whose. The funeral director, maybe. A friend of her father's. Howard? But no, Howard would have come upstairs by now, his kind face creased with worry.

Then it was Barry, most likely. At the thought of Barry, her chest tightened and another spasm of grief shot through her.

Every time Cal came to Portland, her father invited his "good friend" Barry over. He'd come for dinner or join them for lunch at Veg or some other restaurant in town. Barry and her father never touched, but the intimacy between them was clear in the easy way they spoke, like two people who shared the mundane details of daily life. At first she wondered if maybe he really was only a friend, but her father's odd manner when she tried to bring up the topic had confirmed that he was more.

"You and Barry seem like such good friends," she said on one visit before Sadie was born. Howard was getting Maisy ready for her nap, and she and her father were sitting on the deck that overlooked the backyard. Unlike the yard of her childhood home, this one was absent of flowers, only a bright green sheet of artificial grass and a few neat bushes. "I'm glad you have someone here that you're so close to."

Her father shrugged, sipped his iced tea. The day was hot and bright, and he readjusted his baseball cap. Cal couldn't see his eyes behind the dark sunglasses he wore. "Friends are good. Everyone needs friends," he said.

"Right," Cal agreed, not sure if she should leave it at that or keep pushing. "But some friends are more important than others."

Her father didn't answer. The empty glass sweated in his hand, and he kept his eyes trained on the lawn. Inside Maisy was fussing, and Cal could tell from the tone of Howard's voice that he was losing patience. Cal stayed in the chair, waiting to see if her father would say anything more. She wanted to ask why he couldn't tell her, why he wouldn't admit it out loud. But there was something about the quiet control her father was working so hard to keep intact that prevented her from pushing him. His mouth was a steady line, and his Adam's apple bobbed along his neck as he swallowed down whatever he might have said.

"Mommy!" Maisy's voice cut through the sliding glass door and echoed outside.

Her father turned to her with a wry grin. "Never a moment's peace."

"I'd better check on them," Cal said and stood slowly, taking her time in case he wanted to add anything more. He didn't. The moment was lost, swallowed up in the chaos of a toddler and pushed away for now. Cal picked up their empty glasses. "I'll get some more iced tea," she added, when what she really wanted to say was *I'm right here when you're ready.*

Since then, she'd brought the subject up two other times, always in the same vague terms, checking to see if he wanted to say more. He never did. She hadn't said anything to either Violet or Suzy. Though many times she wanted to, out of respect for her father, she didn't. If he wanted to tell them the truth about his relationship with Barry, he would, and for her to gossip about it, even with her sisters, felt tawdry and disrespectful. She wondered if her mother knew, but since their divorce, talking with her about their father was off-limits. For so long, their mother's pain was palpable any time his name came up, and to share this revelation would have been like rubbing salt in a just-healing wound.

So Barry had come to pay his respects, and Violet and Suzy likely thought he was just the business partner that their father worked with for many years. Or maybe not. Maybe they both knew all along. She wondered if it would all come out now, but at this point it didn't even matter. Cal's throat swelled with emotion. She lay back down in bed.

From the kitchen she heard the sound of dishes, cups scraping against the countertop, the clink of silverware. She smelled coffee, and her stomach growled, finally admitting to hunger, though there was no way she would venture downstairs to fix herself something. If she left this bed, they would expect her to be in charge again. Without a word, the responsibility of everything would be foisted back upon her, the burden of the everyday. So she would remain tucked in this tiny bedroom, the white walls and glimpse of the bay cocooning her from the darkness that waited outside. Eventually someone would make her a plate and leave it on the bedside table.

Chapter Twenty

Violet

Since moving to Maine, Violet's father hadn't mentioned any significant other, either male or female. Violet hadn't asked if there was anyone special in his life, partly because she didn't want to remind either of them of what she'd seen so long ago at Beckett and partly because they rarely spoke about anything personal. Their infrequent conversations focused on vague pleasantries, like movies they'd seen or book recommendations. Her father would squeeze in a few questions about work and Luka (or whoever her romantic interest was at the moment), and before she hung up, he'd extend an invitation to Maine that they both knew she'd ignore. The phone calls occurred every few weeks and usually lasted less than ten minutes.

Unlike her conversations with her mother, which happened nearly every day, sometimes even more. Violet could talk to her mother for two minutes or an hour. Her mother knew the nooks and crannies of Violet's life, every boyfriend she'd ever had, every colleague she gossiped about. Violet's mother understood her in a way her father could not.

Violet put one of Suzy's sandwiches on a plate, poured a cup of coffee, and brought them upstairs to Cal's room. She stood outside the bedroom door, listening for the sound of crying or Cal talking on the phone to Howard. The room was quiet.

"Cal?" There was no answer. Violet bent to put the coffee cup on the floor in order to knock softly on the door. "Cal? I made you a sandwich."

There was another moment of silence before she heard Cal's muffled voice. "Come in."

Violet opened the door and picked up the coffee from the floor, making her way into the small bedroom. Cal was lying in bed, a pillow propped behind her and a tattered paperback resting on her knees.

"I made you some lunch." Technically Suzy had made it, but Violet was the one who'd thought to bring it upstairs. "Are you hungry?"

"A little," Cal admitted, pushing herself up to sit. She placed the book on the bed, spine facing up to hold the page, and reached for the dishes. If possible, Cal looked even worse than when they'd first seen her a few hours earlier. The circles under her eyes seemed to have deepened despite the hours in bed, and her hair was coming out of her ponytail in greasy strings. Violet watched as Cal reached for the sandwich and ate an entire half, one quick bite after another. She wondered if Cal had eaten anything since learning of their father's death the previous day. She ate the second half the same way, then reached for the cup of coffee. She let out a long, slow sigh, like air being released from a tire.

"Callie," Violet said gently, using her childhood nickname and lowering herself to the edge of the bed. "What can I do?"

Cal shook her head. She blew on her coffee and then took a careful sip.

"I'm so sorry," Violet offered. She knew right away it was the wrong thing to say.

"You're *sorry*?" Cal said. She gripped the mug so tightly Violet worried it might crack in her hands. "What are you *sorry* for?"

Violet searched for the right words. "For your loss. I mean, I know it's all of our loss, but for you it's different. You were the closest to him."

"Yes, I was," Cal agreed, and there was an accusation in her words. "What about your loss? He was your father too."

"I know." Violet ran her fingers through her hair. Just looking at Cal made her want to take a shower. "But I don't know what that means yet. I'm still trying to wrap my head around it." She was trying to be honest. She didn't know what the magnitude of her loss was yet. In some ways she envied Cal's unadulterated grief. Violet's was wrapped up in anger, guilt, and regret. Pure sadness was simple in comparison.

She and her father had not been close. This was largely Violet's choice, but it was a choice made when she was a teenager, born out of anger and confusion, a choice she hadn't been able to change, even as she grew into adulthood. The rift that began when she was fifteen grew larger each year. He moved, and she didn't visit, and the fury and betrayal she'd felt as a teenager for his actions had morphed into an impassable distance between them. Somehow the father of her childhood—a patient and kind teacher, a brilliant and quick-witted man, an affectionate and loving dad—had been lost to Violet over the years. In his place was just a sounding board for her own frustration.

"You hurt him." Cal's voice cracked. Tears began to stream down her cheeks, but she didn't bother to wipe them away. "You and Suzy, the way you just cut him out of your life."

"I didn't cut him out," Violet said weakly, but she knew Cal was right. While she had spoken with her father on the phone occasionally and saw him a couple of times a year, he was largely unaware of the shape of her life. When he asked her questions about her life, she responded with pat, single-sentence answers. He'd only met Luka once, had never been to their apartment, never been to a poetry reading, never eaten with her at her favorite restaurant—not because he wouldn't have, but because Violet had never bothered to invite him.

"Don't bullshit me, Violet. I know what it was like. I called him every week. I came up here to visit. We stayed with him. He brought Maisy to church and took her bowling and got up early in the morning with her so Howard and I could sleep in. He was a wonderful father and grandfather, and you never even gave him a chance." The tears continued to pour freely, and Cal continued to ignore them. Violet couldn't remember the last time she'd seen Cal cry, but it was almost as if she wasn't crying. Her body was taking over and acting independently.

"Are you sad or angry?" Violet asked.

"I'm both!" Cal exploded. "I'm sad he's gone, and I'm angry with you for being such a shitty daughter. Even if he never said it, you hurt him. *You hurt him,*" she said again.

"Did he tell you that?" Somehow Violet had convinced herself that her father didn't care about their fractured relationship. It was easier to assume he was content to leave it the way it was—distant yet civil—than to face the difficult task of mending it.

"He didn't have to." Cal shook her head in disgust. "Every time I talked to him, every time I saw him, he asked about you. He wanted to know about Luka or whoever the hell you happened to be sleeping with at the moment. He asked about your job. He asked about your friends and your roommates. He asked if you were *happy.*" Cal hurled the words at her as if they were glass ornaments. The shards lay shattered at Violet's feet.

Their father's departure from Beckett was not something anyone in the family discussed. Ever. Not then, and not later. Violet had heard the whispers at school, and she knew Cal must have too. But even in high school her relationship with Cal was tenuous, and having a heart-to-heart about their father's fall from grace and the state of their parents' relationship would have meant putting aside all of the petty day-to-day arguments—borrowed shirts and missing tubes of lipstick and torn stockings—that seemed to get in the way of true intimacy. By the beginning of the next school year, Cal was already safely cloistered at Yale while Violet had to face her junior year in a new school. A line had been drawn in the sand, with Cal on one side and Violet on the other.

When Violet first heard about the accusations by the boys at Beckett, she hadn't believed it. What she thought she'd seen with Mr. Louis was different than the line they claimed he crossed with his students. Her father would never do such a thing. She tried to bring it up with him during the final weeks of the semester. By then she already knew that neither of them would be coming back to Beckett. Her father had already been asked to leave, and a long-term sub was hired to cover his classes for the rest of the year. Cal graduated at the beginning of June. Violet was allowed to finish the school year, but the days were painful to get through. Her few friendly acquaintances distanced themselves from her, and Violet spent each day trying to blend into the scenery at school, to become as invisible as the desks and chairs. Each day she left physically depleted, marking down the final days of school in her date book with a red Sharpie.

Her father still came to pick her up each day, though he asked Violet to walk several blocks to the parking lot of a small shopping center nearby. Violet wasn't sure if he didn't want to see anyone or if he was forbidden from being on campus.

One June afternoon, Violet waited in the blazing heat of the parking lot for her father. Her last class had let out early, and her father wasn't due for another ten minutes. She was sitting on the wall that lined the perimeter of the parking lot, watching her pale skin flush with sunburn, when she spotted several boys emerging from the convenience store across the street, holding paper soda cups. Violet watched the cluster of young men, Victor Landley, Thatcher Kennedy, and Jack Parr at the center of the group.

They were joking in the easy way of boys, slapping and elbowing each other as they walked. Violet's whole body tensed with an overpowering desire to disappear, but there was nowhere to go. As they neared, their roughhousing grew more subdued and they shot each other looks of warning. Violet braced herself for whatever was to come, insults or catcalls or slurs, but they shuffled past her quietly, a few of them nodding briefly in acknowledgment without meeting her eyes. All except the last boy in the group, Jason Brickman, a sophomore like Violet. Freshman year, Jason was a scrawny boy with a face full of acne, but he'd proved himself to be an excellent swimmer and had somehow shot to popularity this past year. As he neared Violet, she watched his newly clear face contort in a sneer.

"You know your dad's a perv, right?" Jason asked. "He got what he deserved."

"Fuck off," Violet spat out, though her voice came out high-pitched and whiny, like someone who didn't swear often enough for it to come naturally.

"Shut up, Brickman," Thatcher tossed over his shoulder, his eyes briefly catching Violet's.

Jason's ugly face wrinkled in confusion. "Whatever." He threw his empty cup at her feet. They kept walking, and Violet tried to breathe. She clung to the rough concrete wall, gripping it so tightly that the pads of her fingers stung.

When her father arrived several minutes later, the boys long gone, Violet collapsed against the seat and tried not to cry.

"How was school?" he asked, which always seemed like such an absurd question under the recent circumstances, but it was still the first thing her father asked each day.

Violet ignored the question. "What they're saying about you—it isn't true, is it?" she said instead.

Surprise flickered across his face, but he kept his eyes trained on the road. "Of course not." He was quick to answer, his voice mechanical.

"Are you . . ." Violet faltered. She didn't know how to talk about this with him. She *hated* talking about this with him, but even more she hated not talking about it. Nights at home were spent with the five of them in separate rooms of the house, passing in the kitchen as they foraged for food in the sparse fridge. The quiet was eerie in a house typically full of noise and life. She and her sisters weren't even bickering in an unspoken agreement of maintaining peace.

Violet looked out the window, trying to distance herself as much as possible from her words. "Are you attracted to them?" The silence stretched between them for so long that Violet turned to look at him. His face was flushed an unfamiliar purplish shade. "Dad?"

"How dare you ask that?" His rage was only barely contained.

Violet recoiled against the stiff plastic of her seat, frightened by her father's response but unwilling to drop the conversation, not now, when she'd finally mustered the nerve.

"But I saw you. With Mr. Louis."

Her father blinked several times. He clenched the steering wheel so tightly that the knuckles on his hands bulged. "You saw nothing," he hissed.

"I saw—"

"You saw nothing," he repeated. A long silence stretched between them. Finally her father broke it. "There are some things we don't need to talk about. Ever. Is that clear?"

Violet shivered in the air-conditioned car. She stared at the pink sunburn that had blossomed on her bare arms. "Yes, sir," she whispered.

What was it in that moment that caused her to suspect the accusations were true? Even now, Violet wasn't sure. The closest she could come to understanding her own judgments was in the automatic way her father answered her question and the scent of guilt that seemed to fill the car, something sharp yet subtle, like a bag of garbage left in the kitchen a day too long. It all got tangled up in Violet's mind somehow, what she thought she'd seen on the third floor of Beckett, her father's swift denial, Jason Brickman's nasty words. She didn't actively believe the story, but she didn't disbelieve it either. It was like going outside on a bright day. You never stared directly at the sun, but you were always aware that it was there. Her doubt had taken root.

Violet looked at Cal pressed against the oversized pillows of the bed. Her face was pinched with hurt.

"I'm angry you went on believing a lie for almost twenty years, and you let it keep you from having a relationship with him. And now it's too late," Cal said, then collapsed back against the pillow, the rage leaving her physically exhausted. Violet's cheeks burned as if Cal had reached across the bed and slapped her. Her own emotions were a twisted knot of shame and anger, frustration, guilt, and confusion all coiled together so tightly she didn't even know how to begin to untangle it. And just like Cal needed to be angry at Violet, Violet needed to be angry with Cal.

"It wasn't a lie!" she burst out. "You want to think it never happened, but it did. I know you loved him and he was your hero, but he was a . . . a pervert." Violet hated the word, the one Jason Brickman had thrown at her so casually that day, but it was the only one that made sense. What other word was there for a man who did that with his students? Had there been other students before the ones that came forward? Younger ones? What about the twelve- and thirteen-year-olds he taught? She trembled with emotion. "Those guys were his students, and I know they weren't little boys, but they weren't adults either. They trusted him and he took advantage of that. I know you can't stand to think about Dad as being anyone except this perfect pillar of morality, but he wasn't, Cal. He just wasn't." Violet's heart beat quickly in her chest and her head felt heavy, like her ears were stuffed with cotton.

"What are you talking about?" Somehow while Cal and Violet were arguing, Suzy had stepped into the bedroom. She wrinkled her nose at the fetid scent of the closed-in room.

"Nothing," they both said at the same time. Violet smoothed her skirt, trying to recompose herself.

"What boys?" Suzy asked. She hovered in the doorway, her hands stuffed deep in the pockets of her oversized hoodie.

Violet looked at Cal, their anger from just a moment before gone in Suzy's presence. Suzy had been just eleven at the time, not even a student at Beckett, far from the fray of whispers and accusations. Suzy hadn't been close with their father either, and a part of Violet assumed some of this had to do with Beckett, that somehow she'd caught traces of the story. Violet had never told her, out of some twisted allegiance to Cal, who wanted to believe their father was better than he was. It dawned on her now that it was possible Suzy knew little about what happened at Beckett and that her strained relationship with him was born out of something else.

"Nothing, Suzy. It's nothing," Cal insisted.

"Who did he take advantage of?" Suzy's delicate features were furrowed in a frown, and Violet and Cal remained silent. Suzy took a step into the room, though there was no place to sit other than the crowded twin bed. She lowered herself beside Violet. "What are you talking about?"

Violet shifted on the bed. She felt Cal's warmth through the blankets. She searched Cal's face. The angles and planes of Cal's face were sharp, and her expression was rigid and blank.

"What are you talking about?" Suzy asked again. Her freckled face was tense with worry, her curls sticking out of the patterned headscarf she wore. Though she was twenty-eight years old, Suzy still looked like a little girl to Violet, and she was sure Cal was thinking the same thing. Despite their own tumultuous relationship, Cal and Violet had always been united in protecting Suzy. Violet looked back at Cal, a question on her face.

"Go ahead," Cal said flatly.

Violet took a breath before she began. Suzy only had one chance to hear this story for the first time, and Violet wanted to make sure it would leave as little damage as possible. Which was ridiculous, because no matter what Suzy believed, all that this story left behind was wreckage. "Do you remember when Dad left Beckett, right before he and Mom got divorced?" Suzy nodded. "Did you ever know why he was let go?"

Suzy frowned and then shook her head. "Not really. I thought he quit."

"To what? Sit around in his pajamas all day in his new crappy apartment?" The sarcasm flared inside Violet, frustrated and edgy.

"Shut up, Violet," Cal snapped.

"Sorry." She cracked the knuckles on both thumbs, a nervous habit that both her sisters hated, and then held her restless fingers in her lap to avoid cracking the rest. "He was let go because there were some accusations made." Violet paused, waiting for Suzy's inevitable question.

"Accusations of what?"

She looked to Cal before answering. There would be no going back. Once Suzy had that knowledge of their father, she could never unknow it, whether she believed it or not. There had been many times over the years when Violet wished she could erase what she'd heard from Michael and seen that wet afternoon in her father's office.

"*Ridiculous* accusations," Cal jumped in, and Violet didn't disagree. Let Suzy get Cal's version. At this point, there was no reason for her to believe otherwise.

"What do you mean?" Suzy pressed.

Cal went on. "Some boys claimed Dad had been inappropriate with them. They said he'd looked at them in the locker room while they were showering. One of them claimed he propositioned him."

"For sex?" Suzy asked incredulously. Her eyes were wide.

"It was all made up. None of it was true." Cal's voice was hot with indignation. Suzy looked to Violet for confirmation. Violet remained silent.

"None of it was true?" Suzy asked.

"No, of course not," Cal said, but Suzy was still looking at Violet.

"I don't know," she finally answered.

"God, Violet, how can you even say that?" Cal screamed, and the blankness on her face was taken over by a dark storm of fury. Yet she stayed in bed, unmoving. "What the hell do you even know about it?

How could you have believed any of it?" Her dark eyes were pinholes in the pale flatness of her face. "You are still such a self-centered, helpless little brat. How would you know anything?"

"Shut up," Violet yelled, closing her eyes against Cal's words. "I saw him, okay? I saw him with Mr. Louis, okay? They were in his office, and they were . . ." Violet trailed off, her rage at Cal diminished as she recalled that cold winter afternoon when the ground started slipping beneath her feet. "Weird. They were weird together."

"Weird," Cal repeated, throwing the word back at her like a Nerf ball, fluffy and insubstantial. "*Weird?* What the hell does that even mean?"

She knew it sounded weak. Even to her, it sounded meaningless. Violet tried to remember what she'd seen that afternoon. Her father and Mr. Louis in the office. The sounds of movement inside. Her father's flushed face. Was that all? Was it possible she'd been wrong all along? At fifteen, what she'd seen had seemed like the smoking gun. All these years later, the memory felt flimsy for so much to have depended on it.

"I don't know," Violet said. "I don't know. They were in his office alone. They were . . . disheveled, and he was acting, just weird. Like he'd been caught doing something." Suzy looked from Violet to Cal and then back to Violet as if watching a tennis match, waiting for the winning point, unsure whom she was rooting for. "I think they were having a relationship." Violet pressed a hand to her lips, the words finally having tumbled out after all these years. Maybe she didn't know the full story, but she'd seen something. She was tired of Cal's self-righteousness in the absence of any real knowledge.

"He was *gay*, Violet. That doesn't mean he did anything with those boys." Violet blinked quickly, taken off guard by Cal's flippant response. The way Cal spoke made it sound so obvious. Violet had assumed that Cal was oblivious to what she'd known since high school. Suzy looked from Violet to Cal, her face slack and expressionless.

Violet pushed on. "It wasn't just that. Michael Donahue." She turned to Suzy. "Michael, a boy I knew from the swim team, he said Dad was always looking at them, touching them, like in an overly friendly way."

"Michael fucking Donahue?" Cal spat the name out. "That asshole you were sleeping with even though he treated you like shit, like you didn't exist, even though he had a girlfriend? You believed *him*?" It was so rare to hear Cal swear that Violet nearly flinched.

"You knew?" Violet asked, genuinely surprised. In her memory, the thing with Michael had been so quiet, so covert. It was part of what had added to the allure. Until it didn't.

"*Everyone* knew, Violet," Cal said. "You're so blind. You believed him over Dad?"

"He hardly denied it!" Violet stood from the bed, no longer able to sit in such close proximity to Cal. She worried she might actually hit her. "He just resigned. He didn't talk about it with us; he didn't say it wasn't true. He just left."

"Why should he have had to defend himself to us?" Cal's face was blotchy and red, and she wiped her nose with the sleeve of her sweater. "Of all the people he should have been able to count on."

They were quiet, Cal's words hanging in the air between them.

Violet's body seemed to hum, the palms of her hands tingling. "It was a long time ago. It doesn't really matter either way," she finally said.

"Of course it does," Cal snapped.

"How old were they?" Suzy asked. She looked small on the bed, her legs pulled into her body, and her back pressed against the wall.

"High school," Cal answered. Apparently Violet's turn to tell the story had ended, and Cal would answer questions from now on. "Two juniors and a sophomore. But nothing ever happened." Cal turned to Violet, her eyes narrowing. "He was gay, Violet. That's all."

Suzy brought her hand to her mouth. "I'm going to be sick." She scooted off the bed and bolted from the room. A moment later they heard her in the bathroom down the hall retching.

Cal narrowed her eyes at Violet. "Nice," she said.

"Oh, give me a break. She's pregnant," Violet said, then immediately regretted it as she watched Cal's eyes widen. "She's not keeping it, so don't get all moony," she added, the icing on the cake. This was not her news to share, but Suzy should have known by now that Violet wasn't good with secrets. Yet somehow she'd managed to keep the one about their father for seventeen years. Violet knew that the truth was she *could* keep a secret. She just wanted to hurt Cal and knew Suzy's planned abortion would sting Cal like a slap to the face. And right now Violet wanted someone else to feel as bad as she did.

Chapter Twenty-One

Suzy

How long did Suzy stay in the bathroom? Ten minutes? Twenty? She lay down on the floor, her cheek pressed against the cool gray tiles. She hadn't cried all day, but the tears came fast, as if they'd just been waiting for the opportunity.

Who had her father been? A pedophile? A homosexual? Either was completely unfathomable to her. But then again, how often had Suzy asked her father about his life? Had she asked him if he was seeing someone? Had she ever asked him *anything* about himself? Their conversations, rare and impersonal as they tended to be, focused on food—his work or hers. Like a child, it hadn't occurred to her to ask him about his needs, his dreams, his desires. Suzy had taken it for granted that the conversation would revolve around what mattered to her.

She was filled with a dark rage—at herself but also at her father. She'd asked if it was true, and Violet wasn't sure. Of course Cal was sure—she had always stood beside their father, even when it meant standing against Suzy and Violet and even their mother. Cal was Daddy's little girl, and he could do no wrong. But that didn't actually mean he had done no wrong.

There came a quiet knock at the door, followed by Violet's voice. "Suze?"

Suzy didn't answer.

"Suzy? Can I come in?"

Suzy forced herself to sit up, but she still didn't answer. Instead, she crawled across the bathroom floor and sat with her back pressed against the wall. The door opened slowly and Violet peered down at her in concern.

"Are you okay?" Violet wrinkled her nose in displeasure. The air still held the acrid tang of vomit. Suzy closed her eyes, burying her face in the tent of her knees.

"I was so mad at him." Her words were muffled against the fabric of her jeans. "I thought you were mad because he left us."

At eleven, Suzy never thought much about her parents' jobs. His employment at Beckett had little to do with her—she hadn't even been in middle school yet. And when she'd attended the public middle school with the rest of her friends, she hadn't mourned her opportunity to go to Beckett.

When she looked back on her parents' divorce, it hadn't been obvious. They rarely fought, even at the end. If anything, there was tension between them, a heavy atmosphere of something unspoken in the air, though maybe that was only in retrospect. She only knew that when her parents did announce their father was moving out, Suzy had been stunned. Had they apologized? She didn't remember.

Suzy could only recall one vague conversation she and Violet ever had about what happened at Beckett. At the time, Suzy was aware of Violet's sudden pulling away from their father, even before they announced the divorce. She stiffened when he came into the room. She directed conversation to their mother whenever possible. She answered him in clipped, one-word responses. And then, later, after he moved out, Suzy remembered the excuses Violet came up with to avoid having to spend the day with him. But Violet was a teenager; she was always moody and easily annoyed. It hadn't occurred to Suzy that her behavior toward their father was actually related to anything. After the divorce,

Suzy found herself emulating Violet's brusque coolness toward him, easily fueled by her own hurt and confusion.

One evening, Suzy and Violet returned home after a painfully uncomfortable Saturday afternoon spent at the ice-skating rink with their father. He had plied them with hot chocolate and barbecue potato chips, but Violet had left hers practically untouched. Suzy felt guilty for finishing her own chips, but didn't quite have Violet's willpower to throw the uneaten food in the trash. Violet rolled her eyes at nearly every comment their father made and spent most of the afternoon sitting in the stands, reading a book. Their father didn't skate, so Suzy had skated alone, making endless circles around the rink to some nonexistent destination. Cheerful music of her father's generation blasted over the speakers, catchy songs by the Beach Boys and the Supremes, and Suzy kept skating, though her nose was running and her ungloved fingers tingled in the iced air. Her father waved each time she went by, an awkward smile pasted to his face. Each time she passed him, Suzy's anger and pity had grown in equal measures, to the point where she couldn't get off the ice to face him, despite her aching ankles.

Later that evening, Suzy and Violet sat on opposite beds in their shared bedroom, doing homework. Violet was reading *Wuthering Heights*, and Suzy was doing math problems. "I hate Daddy," Suzy said. The words felt dangerous and she knew they weren't true, but she wanted Violet's reaction. "Don't you?"

"No," Violet said unconvincingly. She didn't look up from her book.

Suzy frowned. "Then why are you being so mean to him?"

Violet looked up for a quick moment and then stared down at her book. "You wouldn't understand. It doesn't matter."

"I would too understand." Suzy was sick of always being treated like the baby. "I'm almost twelve."

Violet rolled her eyes. "It's a grown-up thing. It's complicated. He broke a rule at school."

"What did he do?" Suzy asked, frowning. Their father wasn't the type to break a rule without a reason.

Violet sighed. "He . . ." She looked up at the ceiling, searching for a way to explain. "He was friends with some of his students in a way he shouldn't have been. Teachers aren't supposed to be friends with their students. It's against the rules."

"Oh." Suzy nodded, not wanting to let Violet know she didn't understand as predicted. "So why are *you* mad at him?" she asked after a moment.

"Because I don't like that he did that." Violet returned to her novel, not looking up again.

"Oh." Suzy stared down at her rows of math equations, more confused than before the conversation began.

On the bathroom floor, Suzy rested her head in Violet's warm lap, recalling the conversation from long ago. She hadn't understood it then and as she got older, no one had stepped in to fill in the holes of her father's departure, and she hadn't thought to ask for more information. "I wish I'd known," she whispered, closing her eyes. She felt Violet's fingers gently combing her hair.

"I'm sorry," Violet breathed.

They sat on the floor for a long time.

Chapter Twenty-Two

Cal

Before Cal got pregnant with Maisy, she had three miscarriages. She'd spent two and a half years trying to get pregnant, and Maisy was finally conceived after several rounds of in vitro. Somehow, like other women she'd heard about, her body's chemistry had changed after Maisy's birth and Sadie was conceived naturally and unexpectedly, a trick of biology and a surprising blessing even though they'd planned on only having one child. Cal's sisters knew how Maisy was conceived and about some of the difficulty she'd had getting pregnant, but only Howard and her father knew about the miscarriages. She hadn't even told her mother. For some reason, it had always been easier for Cal to confide in her father.

Cal was a private person. She wasn't outspoken and social like Violet, and she wasn't warm and kind like Suzy. She didn't do well with expressions of emotion or sharing her feelings. She knew some might think of her as aloof or standoffish, but her guarded demeanor was born out of anxiety, not indifference. Cal was an action person.

She had learned this from her father. Her father was calm and patient, and he was the smartest person she'd ever known. His nose was constantly stuck in a book, a giant tome of the history of World War I, an anthology of British poetry, or a slim volume of modern philosophy.

He'd stay up late at night reading, learning, consuming knowledge. He'd gone to Harvard on a scholarship and then disappointed Nana Dee by becoming a teacher. Such a waste of that valuable education when he could have made some real money going into business or medicine: this was Nana Dee's judgment of her father's chosen profession. But her father didn't care about money or status. He cared about ideas.

Cal shifted in the tiny bed, closing her eyes and seeing Nana Dee's formidable presence. The chunky pumps and netted hats she wore, her steel-gray hair set in curls, and her occasional smile always sticky with pink lipstick as she criticized something or someone.

But what Nana Dee didn't understand was that Cal's father was an amazing teacher. Both Violet and Cal had him in eighth grade, and he'd always come up with the most creative assignments—music journals when they were studying the civil rights movement, photography montages of the Great Depression. He was a fluent and entertaining lecturer, the rare kind of teacher able to carry the class with only his words. He held the students to high expectations and didn't give in easily, but he was very kind to them.

It was her father who encouraged Cal to go to law school. He told her a law degree could open doors even if she decided not to practice. When she first started law school, she imagined she'd end up working for an organization like the ACLU or the Southern Poverty Law Center. She was still naive enough to believe lawyers did work that mattered and that she could help change people's lives through the law. But she took an internship at Fitch, Lowe, and Dunn and was offered a position at the end of it. It was a corporate law firm and the last kind of job she imagined she'd take, but she told herself it was just for a year or two, just long enough to pay off her student loans and put away a little money.

Howard worked at the same type of firm, though he'd never really harbored fantasies about saving the world or doing more meaningful work. Not that he was selfish or uncharitable, but he tended to think of work as work and separate from who he was as a person. Cal had always had a hard time identifying herself as something separate from her job, even when her job was being a student. She'd always been consumed by her work, whether it was a sugar-cube replica of the pyramids in second grade or a lawsuit against a soda company. Her father had never said so, but she knew he was disappointed by her decision to stay at the firm. They both thought she'd become someone else.

Cal's mother was a social worker. Until her retirement two years ago, she worked for DCF, the Department of Children and Families. Part of her job was monitoring families that were in the system, checking in with them to see how the court-appointed therapy, rehab, or AA meetings were going; looking in the cupboards of the pantry to make sure there was enough food to scrape together a few decent meals; making sure the house wasn't filthy or unsafe. Many of her days were filled with these check-ins followed by writing up detailed notes that documented what she saw and did. Were there diapers in the house for the baby? Asthma medication for the teenager? Enough beds for family members? Cal knew that on a day-to-day basis her mother saw the squalor and desperation of poverty and neglect, families stretched to the breaking point and just barely surviving. Those were the good days.

The bad days were when she'd arrive to discover the family had stretched beyond the breaking point. Visible bruises on a child's skin. Ketchup and mustard in the refrigerator, and nothing else. Too many missed appointments at the methadone clinic. On these days, Cal's mother had to pick the better of two awful and traumatic choices. On these days, Cal's mother removed children from their homes and took them away from their parents.

Cal could always tell when it had been a bad day. From the moment her mother walked in the door, they could all see it on her face. The sadness and regret covered everything. She'd try to smile and be present for her own children, but Cal knew that even while their mother was doling out dinner, she was thinking about today's children sitting at an unfamiliar table, eating unfamiliar food. The plus side was at least they were eating dinner. The downside was that they were probably with strangers. The distraction would be with her for the rest of the evening.

One night, on her way to the bathroom, Cal overhead her parents talking about a particularly bad day—syringes on the kitchen counter, an unattended baby crying in a crib for hours, feces on the living-room floor. Cal had listened to the details with a fascinated revulsion. Cal thought she understood her mother's job, but it never occurred to her that people could live like that. She couldn't believe her mother had to see such horror on a daily basis. Through the closed door of their bedroom, Cal heard her mother crying softly.

"Christian, the older boy, was crying, and he kept calling me a bitch, over and over again. 'You stupid bitch,' he kept saying. Six years old and that's the way he talks. And I just kept thinking, all I'm trying to do is help this child. Ten years from now, will he understand that I was trying to keep him safe? No. I'll just be the bitch who took him away from his mother. Oh, Joey, what am I doing?" Cal's mother began weeping all over again. Her mother was always so upbeat and optimistic. Cal had never heard such despair in her voice. Her father murmured soothingly, and Cal stood silently outside the door, clutching the glass of water she'd risen to fill.

The next morning, her mother greeted Cal cheerfully when she came down to breakfast. All signs of the night before were erased, and she hummed to herself while she stood at the stove making eggs. Cal wondered if her mother was naturally optimistic or just good at hiding her feelings.

Since she'd retired two years ago, her mother had blossomed. Even after overhearing her mother's private grief that night, Cal hadn't realized what an emotional toll the job had taken on her. Her skin brightened. She got a new haircut. She started shopping in different stores and wearing different kinds of clothes. Though Cal had always thought her mother was content, now she seemed lighter, free of the invisible burden she'd been carrying.

Recently, Cal asked her mother if she regretted the job she'd had all those years. She seemed so much happier now that Cal wondered if maybe she wished she'd done something else for so much of her life. Her mother's reaction had surprised her.

"Not at all," she said without a moment's hesitation. "There are jobs in this world that are hard and at times feel futile. But never forget, Callie, those are the jobs that need to be done. What the world needs are more good people willing to do those hard jobs."

Cal knew her mother wasn't trying to indict Cal for her own career choice, but she still felt guilty for the rest of the day.

While lying in this bed, intentionally not thinking of all the things she should be thinking about, Cal had come to a few truths. The first was that she hated her job. Or if not actually hating it, certainly she didn't enjoy much about it. She didn't like many of her colleagues: mostly arrogant, red-faced men who spent too much money on expensive bottles of whiskey and Italian shoes and who didn't see enough of their children, leaving the business of everyday parenting to their wives and then swooping in at the last minute with an expensive toy or trip to Disney World. She didn't like the work she did every day, the hours of tedious paperwork to meticulously comb through, the client meetings with CEOs and CFOs. She didn't like the office where she spent most of her days, all sharp angles and glass and chrome. She didn't like how she felt at home, as if her body had been fractured into pieces: the largest piece for work, somehow disproportionately followed by a chunk for the girls, a swatch for Howard and her sisters, then finally a sliver left for herself.

Maisy and Sadie were her lifeblood, her heart walking around and beating outside of her body. Yet Cal had come to view her interactions with them as another job on the endless list of things to get done. Cook breakfast. Check. Drop off at day care. Check. Pack a healthy lunch with a paper-heart note tucked in the zippered pocket. Check. Stare at Sadie's incredibly long lashes while she slept in Cal's arms but don't hold her too long because then she wouldn't transfer well to her crib. Check and check.

Even her interactions with Howard were part of the list. Saturday dinner date because it was important they have time together alone as a couple. Check. Sex so she didn't have to question the strength of her marriage. Check.

The other truth she'd come to was that if she wasn't able to change how miserable she was, she would lose Howard. Maybe he wouldn't divorce her, but she'd seen the way he looked at her lately. Like he didn't know how he'd ended up in this life with her. She'd felt his disappointment and sadness, but she knew that resentment and anger simmered just below the surface, and one day soon, all those emotions would rise up and consume them both.

At some point, Cal had stopped having fun. Or, when she really looked at her life closely, somehow Cal had never learned how to have fun. She knew Violet would be the first one to point this out, though an argument could be made that Violet had too much fun. Once, Howard had been able to help Cal have fun, but no one in their house was having much fun these days.

Her father hadn't been "fun" either, but he knew how to access something in Cal that few others did. He had seen through the external shell she offered up to the world. He'd seen the fear and insecurity that lay beneath it. With her father, she could doubt herself, because she knew he would build her back up. Most of Cal's life was about being in control, taking care of others—taking care of *everything*. But with her father she could be needy and soft, because he would be strong and in control for her. With her father she could be herself, though it now struck her as terribly sad that the only person in the world who knew her true self was dead. Did that mean that the best part of her was now dead too? She felt the tears prickling again, but she closed her eyes against them, swallowing the lump in her throat.

Cal wondered if everyone walked around the world feeling as if the face they presented was just a mask, or if not a mask, only one small dimension of who they really were. Cal suspected her sisters didn't feel this way. Violet was Violet to her core—brash, opinionated, entitled. But also funny and smart and charming. Suzy might have felt a little like Cal, but Suzy was so good. She was kind and gentle and with only the slightest edge, though Cal knew she wished it were sharper. Suzy had always wanted to please the people around her, and Cal wondered if part of her recent declaration that she was gay had been because she'd gotten caught up in Lani and the idea of what Lani wanted.

And now Suzy was pregnant and about to have an abortion. Not that anyone would use the word *abortion*. No one ever used the word *abortion*. People talked about "choosing not to keep it" or "terminating the pregnancy." They never said they were getting an abortion. Those words were just too blunt.

Cal wasn't pro-life, though she was less pro-choice than she'd once been. It was impossible to go through multiple miscarriages and fertility struggles and then imagine not keeping a baby. To imagine the sex of your baby and paint his bedroom in your mind, to fight the urge to buy miniature socks and yellow ducky onesies only to watch the dream of that unborn child drip out of your body in tablespoonfuls of blood. It made the idea of willfully having an abortion abhorrent.

Cal sighed and rolled over in bed, propping a pillow behind her and reaching for the tattered mystery she was nearly halfway through. She didn't know why she never told Suzy and Violet about the miscarriages. Part of her wished she had. They were close, but their closeness wasn't about sharing secrets and unburdening feelings, at least not on Cal's part. Cal's role had always been to listen and offer solutions. No one ever thought to listen to Cal's problems, or maybe she just never thought to show her sisters the vulnerable side only her father and Howard ever saw. Her closeness with Violet and Suzy was about their shared history, their continued close proximity, the understanding of the day-to-day. It was about the balance they'd struck when they were children and the roles they'd all come to fulfill. Cal in charge, Violet rebelling against everything, Suzy trying to make peace. They were the classic stereotype of birth order.

Down the hall, she heard Violet's and Suzy's soft voices in soothing tones coming from the bathroom. Cal knew she should be shocked about this news of Suzy's, and she was, but she found she also didn't care. Didn't care how it had happened, didn't care that Suzy planned on getting rid of it (the ugly yet still vague euphemism), didn't care that this baby (there, she'd said it) would have been Sadie and Maisy's cousin. It was this deep indifference that was most frightening to her. But if she examined this further, she would have to face the truth of the day, the reason she was in this bed in the first place.

Cal opened the book back up and began to read about what had led the killer to arson.

Chapter Twenty-Three

Violet

The winter morning sun was merciless as Violet stood on the door-step of her father's house. She jiggled the key Cal had given her in the gold lock until it turned. She swung open the front door and stepped inside, Suzy on her heels. Cal had refused to come, and neither of them had bothered to press very hard. After yesterday's argument, Cal hadn't emerged from the bedroom for the rest of the day or night, other than a few surreptitious trips to the bathroom.

The night before, Violet had counted on getting stinking drunk with both of her sisters, but Cal was semi-comatose in bed and Suzy was pregnant. If Suzy wasn't even planning on having the baby, Violet didn't see why she couldn't have a couple of drinks, yet Suzy refused. That left Violet on her own. She'd finished off nearly an entire bottle of cheap red wine on the couch while Suzy chastely drank seltzer water, and this morning Violet had a splitting headache and felt fuzzy around the edges. Suzy was bright-eyed, if a little pale. Violet had heard her retching in the bathroom again before breakfast.

Violet had only been to her father's house in Portland once, the sum-mer Suzy stayed there and she and Cal picked her up to bring her back home. It hadn't occurred to Violet to return, to make the two-hour drive this far north, despite her father's multiple invitations. Violet was a city girl and had never understood the fascination with nature. The idea of living in a place where it was possible to have a house not near anyone else's sounded awful to her. The quiet, the open space, the emptiness, the solitude—all of the things people enjoyed about the country were unappealing to Violet.

But Portland turned out not to be the incarnation of *Deliverance* she'd imagined. There was a small but vibrant downtown center where she and Suzy had breakfast. The whole foodie scene was clearly big here as evidenced by the eggs, kale, and goat cheese all from local farms. There were funky shops and a surprising hipster population, probably students who'd graduated from the nearby university and then settled in town. Veg was still closed today, but when Violet peered through the windows, she saw burnished-wood tables and a chalkboard menu with a basket for communal newspapers. It looked like the type of place she and Luka would have gone for brunch, lingering over their coffee and reading the paper long after they'd finished eating. Yet she'd never been to see this place while her father was alive. She hadn't tasted his cooking as a professional chef. She hadn't thought any of it mattered, that *he* mattered, enough to make the effort.

By the time they arrived at his house, Violet was feeling fragile and teary all over again. Inhaling the scent of her father, which she hadn't known would be so strikingly identifiable, Violet realized the memory she would have of him would be of the sour distance between them these many years. She felt a dull ache behind her breastbone and in the back of her throat.

"You okay?" Suzy stood beside her. Violet nodded, swallowing hard.

"I just didn't expect it to smell like him." Violet wiped her palm across her cheek. They stood in the front hallway, arms hanging uselessly by their sides. "So . . ." Violet glanced at Suzy. "Where do we begin?"

Suzy sighed. "Look for photos, I guess." Barry had called the night before to tell them he'd arranged to have a wake at the funeral home the following evening, and a funeral at St. Mary's on Tuesday. Suzy and Violet were charged with finding pictures to display in the funeral home. They headed deeper into the house.

The hall opened into a modern kitchen and great room. The cabinets were light wood, with cream carpeting in the living area. The room was tastefully decorated with a few pieces of quality furniture and several paintings hanging on the wall. Violet examined a landscape of the coast, trying to figure out if it was an original or a print.

"Vi. Look at this." Suzy stood by the mantel over the fireplace holding a glass-framed photo. Violet peered over her shoulder at a picture of their father as a young man surrounded by his three daughters at the beach. "Do you remember that day?" Violet looked closer at the picture, nodding. She must have been ten or so in a striped bikini, Cal twelve in her simple red Speedo, and Suzy just six in a pink-skirted suit and sun hat. They'd rented a house on the Cape for a week, one of the infrequent family vacations they'd taken together.

In her memory, the week was perfect, filled with all of the culinary delights of a Cape Cod summer—lobster with drawn butter, fried quahogs, clam chowder, and ice cream every night. The photo was taken in the late afternoon as the sky fell to evening, the time of day when the light was honey gold. They'd spent a long afternoon at the beach and then their father had ordered lobster rolls from the takeout window up the road from the beach. They'd just taken a final dip in the ocean before their mother snapped the photo and their father stood with a towel draped along his back, cloaking his three girls in its flimsy terrycloth warmth. Violet remembered feeling full and sleepy and happy.

"God, look at this one." Suzy was peering at another picture, this one of Suzy as a toddler sitting on their father's knee. Her light-brown hair was in ringlets around her face, and their father was staring down at her with a look of enchantment.

They wandered down the length of the mantel, marveling at each photograph, all of them of Suzy, Violet, and Cal, most of them taken during the time when their parents were still married, a shrine to their family's previous life. There was Violet sitting on the back steps of the Cambridge house, her head bent over a book, long hair brushing the pages. There was Suzy grinning on the soccer field, a plastic medal around her neck. There were Cal and Violet tucked into the booth of their local ice cream parlor, lips sticky with chocolate syrup.

There were more recent ones too, one of Cal on the day she graduated from law school, looking proud and young in her cap and gown. There was another shot of a weekend a few years earlier when their father had come for a visit and they'd all gone to dinner at a restaurant in the South End. They were squeezed into a booth, but their smiles were strained, revealing how uncomfortable the evening had been for everyone. Most recently, Violet noticed a photo of the four of them at Christmas just a few months earlier. Luka had been the photographer. They were huddled on Cal's couch, all of them dressed up, and strewn in the background were crumpled wrapping paper and ribbons. Violet's cheeks were red from the wine she'd been drinking all night, and after the evening came to a close, she and Luka would go home and have a big fight, which would lead to their breakup. Looking at the photo, Violet was sad for all she'd had in the moment the photo was taken, all she'd had and not appreciated, not realizing how quickly it would be gone.

The mantel seemed to stretch on forever, pictures Violet had never seen, moments she'd forgotten, carefully preserved behind glass. Choosing the pictures to take with them wasn't easy, but they managed to select a small stack.

"Let's see if there's a bag or something we can put them in," Suzy said. They headed into the kitchen.

Violet had forgotten how neat their father was. The Cambridge house was always untidy, the kitchen counters littered with crumbs, and piles of papers and books everywhere along with the detritus of female life—makeup and bottles of lotion, hair products, and jewelry somehow left on every surface. Their father was the one who insisted the house get cleaned every Saturday morning.

"It's time for a blitz!" he would say, clapping his hands like a schoolteacher and then doling out chores for each of them to do. Cal usually did the vacuuming, Suzy mopped the floors, and that left Violet to clean the bathrooms, a chore she detested to this day. Their father would sweep through the house with a laundry basket and throw every stray item inside for the girls to sort through. Often the basket would stay full until the following week, when he'd dump out its contents onto the floor of one of their bedrooms and then refill it with their junk.

Looking at his spotless kitchen now, Violet wondered how difficult it had been to live with four rather messy women for so many years. The kitchen countertops were clean, the floor swept, not a dish in the sink, only a single mug left to dry in the dish rack. Violet imagined it was the cup he used to drink his last sip of coffee that morning. Or maybe tea. She thought she recalled her father switched to tea in recent years, though she couldn't be certain.

"Here we go." Suzy was digging around in one of the drawers under the sink, and she held up a canvas bag, returning to the living room to put the photos inside. Violet lingered in the kitchen, looking at the collection of items stuck on the fridge with magnets. A flyer for church services at St. Mary's, a list of phone numbers for the staff at Veg, a schedule for a yoga studio in town, a magazine clipping of a restaurant review of Veg. A few more pictures, but these weren't of Violet or her sisters. These were shots of her father's life in Maine. There was a picture of him with the staff at Veg, Barry and her dad flanking the cheerful-looking crew. Another one of her dad and Barry hiking in the woods, wearing heavy backpacks, the red-and-orange foliage bright behind them. A photo from a Halloween party, her dad dressed as Charlie Chaplin, a neat little bowler hat on his head and an ink mustache drawn on.

Two lives. Their father's life had been split neatly down the middle: his family life in Cambridge on one side, and his solitary life in Maine on the other. One life on display on the mantel in the living room; the other one, his real life now, in the kitchen, plastered to the door of the fridge. If you paused in just one room, you'd never know the other existed.

Chapter Twenty-Four

Suzy

They left the house quickly, not ready to sift through the remnants of their father's life, not ready to turn up anything more. The photos were enough for today. Suzy locked the door behind them and followed Violet to the car.

Next stop was the funeral home. It took a few minutes for the heat to kick on, and Suzy rubbed her hands together in her lap, trying to keep warm in the frigid air. It had to be at least ten degrees colder up here than in Boston. They were both quiet on the drive. Suzy was shaken by the strangeness of walking around their father's house, seeing Friday's newspaper sitting on the kitchen table. His morning routine interrupted forever. But more than that, the surprising familiarity of the house had done something to her, unearthed feelings from the brief summer she'd spent in Portland during high school. Feelings Suzy did her best to never recall.

"Who's going to say something?" Violet asked. For once she wasn't fiddling with the radio or trying to apply lipstick as she drove.

"What do you mean?"

"At the funeral. Someone needs to say something. That's the way it works, right? A eulogy?"

"Cal?" Suzy suggested. Of course it would be Cal. Who else could it be?

Violet's eyes were hidden behind enormous sunglasses. "She doesn't seem like she's in any shape to do it."

"I can't," Suzy said quickly. "I hate public speaking. What about you?"

"Me?" Violet raised her eyebrows. "I don't think that's appropriate. Dad and I weren't exactly close."

"Well, neither were we," Suzy said quietly. The car had turned stuffy, the heater filling the small space with musty-smelling air. She wished they'd taken Cal's car. She rolled down the window, breathing in the cold, watery smell of the sea. Violet turned the heat up a notch.

"What about a friend of Dad's? What about Barry?"

"That's kind of weird when he's got three daughters, don't you think?" Suzy unzipped her coat. Her wool scarf suddenly felt tight and scratchy around her neck, and she unwound it in a rush, feeling a wave of nausea coming on. She took a deep breath, digging through her bag for her water bottle and crackers.

"Are you okay?"

Suzy nodded, sipping slowly from the bottle and crunching a cracker.

Violet pulled into the driveway of the funeral home, a simple white colonial that looked more like someone's personal home than a place where people went to say good-bye to loved ones. She parked the car, and Suzy unbuckled her seat belt, ready to go inside.

"Hang on." Violet's fingers were warm against Suzy's wrist. "I need to tell you something."

"What?"

"Don't be mad." Violet bit her lip and spun a silver ring around and around on her finger. Violet always wore lots of rings, and when she was nervous, which was rare, she'd fidget with them.

"What?" Suzy repeated flatly.

"You have to promise not to be mad," Violet pleaded.

"Oh, come on," Suzy said. "We're not ten. I can't promise not to be mad when I don't even know what you did."

Violet looked down at her hands and then met Suzy's eyes. "I told Cal."

Suzy leaned closer to Violet, hoping she'd misheard. "You what?"

"I told Cal. That you're pregnant." Violet pressed her lips together, as if she wanted to squeeze the words back inside.

"Violet!"

"I'm sorry," Violet cried. "I was mad and she was being such a bitch. It just came out."

"I specifically told you not to tell her," Suzy said, surprised she wasn't angrier at Violet. She'd been dreading telling Cal, really. Maybe she'd secretly told Violet in the hopes she'd do it for her.

"I know, and I'm really sorry. You were throwing up, and she was giving me the evil eye, like it was my fault you were sick. So I told her. Are you mad?"

That was the thing about Violet. Even when she did stuff like this, Suzy could never stay mad at her for long. Suzy was able to forgive Violet for her endless stream of selfish, careless mistakes while Cal was forever counting them up to hold against her.

Suzy sighed, sinking back into the seat. "What did she say?"

Violet frowned. "Not much, actually. I told her you weren't keeping it, and I kind of figured she'd freak out. But she didn't really say anything. Just said she wanted to rest."

It was so unlike Cal not to have an opinion on something. "That's weird."

"I know. It was." A gray Volvo pulled into the spot beside them. Barry waved as he put the car into park. He got out and stood by their car, waiting for them. "To be continued," Violet said, opening the door. Suzy followed her.

"Morning," Barry said.

"Morning," Violet and Suzy echoed.

"No Cal this morning?" Barry asked, looking down on them. He was more than a full head taller than Suzy, probably six three to her five four. Suzy felt the urge to lean into his weight, to press her face into his blue parka and let him comfort her. Instead, she shoved her hands deep into the pockets of her own coat.

"She hasn't really gotten out of bed since we saw you yesterday," Violet told him. They trudged up the walkway toward the house. Small potted evergreens lined the path.

"When is her family coming up?" Barry asked. "Shouldn't they be here?"

"I don't know. She says she doesn't want them here. But I'm sure they'll come for the funeral, if not before," Suzy said.

Barry frowned. "She needs her family to get through this."

"Cal doesn't need anyone," Violet said, a note of bitterness in her voice. "She never has."

Suzy looked up. It couldn't be true, of course, but there was an element of truth in it. Even now, as she came undone, Cal couldn't show them her sadness, only her anger and indifference. She wouldn't ask Suzy or Violet for help. Then again, what could they actually offer?

"People have different ways of grieving," Barry said gently. "I'm sure having Howard and the girls here could only help."

"You've met them?" Suzy asked, surprised.

"Sure. Cal comes up to visit a few times a year. They always come in for a meal."

"Oh." Suzy felt another pang of guilt. Over the years she'd forced herself to drive up for a couple of day trips, but she'd never spent another night in Portland. Last night was the first since she was a teenager.

It had taken her father some time to get on his feet after the divorce. For reasons Suzy hadn't thought to wonder about before now, he hadn't looked for another teaching job. Instead, he'd found freelance work writing curricula, but it wasn't a reliable income and certainly not enough for the child-support payments he owed each month. Even married, money had been tight on the salaries of a social worker and private-school teacher. But after he moved out, it got even harder. Suzy's mother didn't bad-mouth their father, but Suzy overheard the tense phone calls, and she watched her mother pore over the bills after dinner, sipping a glass of red wine as she added up numbers on a calculator. She'd sigh heavily and scratch something out with a pencil, trying again to make the money stretch. Suzy hated her father in these moments.

He'd moved to Maine when one of the publishing companies he freelanced for offered him a full-time position. The cost of living was cheaper up here, and a stable salary would allow him to meet his child-support responsibilities, though by then Suzy was the only one left at home. Violet would be a sophomore at UMass Amherst, and Cal would finish her final year at Yale.

The summer after her father moved up here, it was agreed Suzy would spend part of it with him in Maine. She was the only one still living at home, and she would come on her own for the month of July.

Suzy was fifteen, an age when summer vacation meant hanging out with friends, not being isolated in Maine with just her father for companionship. She wasn't angry with him in the way she'd been when her parents first split up. Their interactions were cordial yet distant, despite his efforts to win her over. Even though she wanted to be won over, she didn't know how to be with him anymore.

Suzy had always been an athlete—the only one of the three of them to share their father's passion for sports. As an eleven-year-old, Suzy had tried everything—soccer, softball, swimming, tennis—and her father had coached many of those teams, from the time she was in kindergarten all the way up through middle school. On hot summer days he'd take her swimming at the Beckett pool, and they'd race each other in parallel lanes and then go home and throw a baseball in the backyard after dinner. Back then, she still sat on his lap occasionally in the easy way of children and kissed him good night on the mouth.

When they'd last lived together, she'd been an eleven-year-old child. She was skinny and flat-chested. But now she was fifteen, an almost-woman with breasts and hips she didn't know what to do with. Her body required more equipment than it did back then—an underwire bra, tampons, a special cream for the breakouts on her chin, a mousse for her unruly curls, Advil when she got her period. The paraphernalia of her sudden womanhood filled their shared bathroom in Maine. She felt her father's unease, and her own embarrassment at the clutter being a woman seemed to require.

When Suzy first arrived in Maine, she hadn't seen her father in almost six months. He looked healthy, lean and strong from the yoga he'd started doing and his new vegetarian diet. Despite all his years as a swimmer and coach, he didn't swim much anymore. Instead, he exercised on land, on a small blue mat, his stiff body pretzeled into unnatural poses. He tried to convince Suzy to come to yoga class with him, but it was the days before yoga was trendy and she'd balked at the idea, opting for swimming at the local pool instead.

It was at the pool where she met Zach. She learned later he was a sophomore at the University of Southern Maine, and he was on the swim team. They had the same schedule, both of them arriving at the pool a little after nine and then swimming for half an hour. They often ended up in adjacent lanes, and more than once Suzy had seen him looking at her between breaths as she turned her head to inhale.

Suzy had never had a boyfriend before. At home she was friends with a cluster of girls who managed to straddle the divide of the social hierarchy of high school. They were not part of the cliquey popular group, but they were not social outcasts either. Suzy had never been on a date, but she couldn't imagine going out with any of the boys in her school. The boys had a harder time balancing between elite and exile. They either walked around in the cocky, indifferent manner of the popular, or they had some obvious flaw—the doughy hips of a girl, a full-blown case of acne, a paralyzing stutter. So far, the choices for a boyfriend seemed slim.

Suzy had been in Maine for a little over a week when Zach first talked to her. When she finished her laps that day, she made her way to the edge of the pool to float and catch her breath. She looked up, and he was standing above her on the edge of the tiles. He wore baggy blue swim trunks, though he swam like an athlete. He had a square jaw and sharply angled face, a slender build, and dark hair. Until she saw him out of the water, she hadn't realized just how good-looking he was.

"Hey." He tilted his chin toward her. Suzy was still breathing heavily from her workout, and she knew her face was flushed.

"Hi," she said between breaths.

"You're good. Do you swim for USM?" Suzy would be a high school junior in September. She was petite, with the small features of a young girl and a halo of pale brown curls that ranged from frizzy to corkscrew, depending on the weather. She knew she didn't look like a college student. But she didn't try to dissuade him and didn't tell him she was only in high school.

She shook her head. "I'm on the team at my school in Cambridge," she said instead.

"Cambridge?" He raised his eyebrows.

"Massachusetts. I'm visiting my dad for the summer."

"Nice." The boy lowered himself to the edge of the pool and sat down, his legs dangling in the water. He extended a hand. "I'm Zach."

Suzy reached for it. It was cold and pruny, like her own. "Sue." She'd always gone by Suzy, a nickname created for her before she had a chance to decide whether she liked it. Suzy was quiet and shy, ready to please everyone. Suzy didn't date, and she wasn't acknowledged by boys as good-looking as Zach. She felt like being someone else for a while.

"Do you want to go for a cup of coffee or something?" Zach asked. She didn't drink coffee, but she knew better than to tell him that. She'd learn to drink it today.

"Sure."

He grinned at her, and she saw that his nose was slightly crooked, as if it had been broken and not properly healed. The nose made him a little less perfect-looking, more regular, and Suzy relaxed a little. It was the nose that made her trust him, a decision she would soon come to regret.

In the locker room, she hurried in the shower and then toweled herself off quickly, as if he might not wait for her. She pulled on a pair of gym shorts and a T-shirt, kicking herself that she hadn't brought anything nicer. She finger-combed her curls, patting them into submission. She stared into the mirror at her freckles, her hair, the white T-shirt with the neck cut out of it. She didn't usually wear makeup, but she wished she at least had lip gloss. She sighed. This was it. Take it or leave it.

Zach was waiting for her in the lobby of the pool, his short hair already dry. When he saw her, he smiled and she no longer cared about her ratty clothes or unruly hair. She smiled back.

Chapter Twenty-Five

Cal

Cal's back hurt. She'd slept poorly the night before, probably because she'd been dozing off and on all day yesterday. She'd been in this bed for over twenty-four hours, though she was still tired and groggy. She wondered if she was coming down with something, some flu or disease. Terminal exhaustion, maybe. She felt like she was recovering from years of exhaustion, not just recently but as far back as her school days, when she spent nights poring over legal briefs in law school, cramming for exams and writing papers in college, and even staying late to meet deadlines as the editor of her high school paper, then rising early to start at dawn, a cup of coffee her only company.

"Just relax," her mother was always telling her when she was growing up. "You don't have to do everything. Take some time to relax."

But Cal couldn't relax. It wasn't in her nature. These days relaxing meant checking Facebook or saving projects to Pinterest she'd never get around to doing. Otherwise, there was work to be done, and if she didn't do it, who would?

As if on cue, her phone rang, Howard's grinning face lighting up the screen.

"Hey," she said, answering his call for the first time all day. It was close to noon.

"Hi," he said. "You're there."

"Where else would I be?" she asked, then immediately felt guilty for snapping at him.

"I tried calling a few times earlier this morning, but you didn't pick up."

"I was helping my sisters figure some stuff out," she lied.

"Good. Do you know when the service will be?" His voice was patient and soothing, the way one might talk to a child.

"There's a wake tomorrow night. The funeral will be Tuesday morning." Suzy had left a message earlier with the times, though Cal still didn't know any of the details.

"Okay. So we'll come up tonight," he said.

"You don't need to come," she told him. "There's no reason for the girls to go."

"Cal, of course we're going to come," Howard said, exasperation creeping into his voice.

"No, really. I don't want them here. I don't want to explain this to Maisy. And what's Sadie going to do? She'll be tired and cranky. There's no reason they have to come." She lay back down against the pillow, closing her eyes.

"Cal, I want to come. I knew your father. I'd like to come to his funeral." The word stuck in her throat. A *funeral*. Her father would have a funeral. "Have you talked to your mother?" he asked, changing the subject. "When is she coming?"

"I'm not sure." Cal had been dodging her mother's calls as well. The last message had said she was trying to catch a flight out today, though there were some delays because of weather. "Are the girls okay? How's Sadie sleeping?" At the mention of Sadie, her breasts ached, her nipples tingling as the unspent milk rushed to the surface. She still hadn't used the pump. Soon the milk would begin to dry up.

"She's doing all right," Howard said. "She's been okay with the bottle. She woke up once last night but went right back after I fed her."

"And Maisy?" Cal's changeable older daughter always left her feeling depleted and insufficient. Her wants were so great it seemed Cal could never fill them. "How is she?"

"She's doing okay. She misses you." Cal nodded, though Howard couldn't see her. She brushed a tear from her eyelash. "She's right here. I promised her she could say hello to you." His voice was firm this time. There was no way around it.

"Okay," Cal said softly. There was a muffled sound as the phone was passed.

"Hi, Mommy." Maisy's voice was soft and bright, and Cal's eyes filled with tears.

"Hi, baby. How are you doing?" She pulled herself to sitting, her knees drawn to her chest.

"I miss you. When are you coming home?"

"Soon, sweetheart. A few more days." She could imagine Maisy so clearly, still in her pajamas, her hair an unbrushed mess.

"Papa died," Maisy informed her.

"I know," Cal said.

"Why did he die?" Maisy asked, and Cal put her hand to her eyes, grateful at least that Maisy couldn't see her. She swallowed hard so the tears wouldn't be audible in her voice.

"I don't know, baby."

"I don't want him to be dead," she said firmly.

"Me neither."

"Daddy said there's a party for him."

"A party?" Cal asked in confusion.

"To say good-bye," Maisy explained.

"Oh." She imagined Howard trying to describe the purpose of a funeral, something he shouldn't have had to do on his own. "I guess it's a kind of party."

"Will there be cake?" Maisy asked.

"I don't think so. There might be. I'm not really sure."

"I want to come," Maisy said, a note of excitement in her voice.

"We'll see."

"Can you make sure the cake doesn't have any nuts?" The conversation was tiring, the way Maisy tugged on a string and pulled to see where it would go, and Cal had no choice but to follow.

"Sure, honey," Cal said. One more thing to think about.

"But we're visiting the fire station this week. I don't want to miss the fire trucks," Maisy added.

"Okay. You can talk to Daddy about it." Cal sighed, overcome again by exhaustion. She couldn't negotiate the funeral, cake, and the fire trucks. "Put Daddy back on the phone, okay, honey? Give Sadie a kiss for me."

"Okay, Mommy. Bye." There was another shuffle against the phone and then Howard was back.

"Hi," he said.

"A party, huh?" Cal said, a wry smile finding its way to her face.

"Sorry. I didn't know how else to explain it. I didn't do a very good job."

"It's fine."

"I miss you too, Callie," Howard said softly.

Cal swallowed a lump in her throat, the tears infuriatingly back yet again. How many tears was her body actually capable of producing? Acknowledging his tenderness would only make it worse. "I just remembered, Maisy has a birthday party today. Chloe, from school. The invitation is on the fridge. The present is in a bag on the bookcase in the hall." She could picture it clearly, a Polly Pocket snowboarding set, the tiny figures dressed in pink plastic goggles and snow pants.

Howard sighed. "Can't we skip it?" he asked.

Normally, the answer would have been no. It was on the calendar, she'd RSVP'd, the gift had been purchased. But Cal didn't care.

"If you want. I just thought you might want an activity for the afternoon."

"Okay. We'll see how the day goes."

"Just watch for nuts if you do go," Cal couldn't help but add. "Birthday parties get crazy. It's hard to keep track. And probably everything there is processed in a nut facility."

"Okay. I know," Howard said. He knew she couldn't help but remind him. It was like a nervous tic—it accomplished nothing but made her feel a tiny bit more at ease.

When Maisy was first diagnosed with a severe nut allergy, she was fourteen months. It hadn't occurred to Cal that nuts were something to worry about. There were no food allergies in either of their families; she had just been following the recommendations of her pediatrician by holding off till Maisy was at least one.

Cal had made herself a slice of peanut-butter toast that morning, and when Maisy toddled over to her and reached for a bite, she'd hardly thought twice about breaking off a piece for her to eat. Maisy had smacked her lips and reached for more. Cal twisted off another bite of bread, slathered with what she'd ultimately come to consider poison. It was after the third or fourth bite that Maisy started to have a reaction. First, Cal noticed her lips looked puffy. Cal felt her heart pounding in her chest as she called to Howard to come downstairs. By the time Howard arrived, a prickly flush had formed around Maisy's mouth, and her breath was coming in shallow gasps. Cal scooped Maisy up from the floor and clutched her.

"What's wrong?" Howard asked, his eyes wide. "What happened?"

"I don't know!" Cal shrieked.

"Is she choking?" Howard reached for Maisy, but Cal clung to her.

She shook her head. "It's the peanut butter. She's having a reaction to it. She needs to get to the hospital."

"Okay, let's go." Howard patted his pocket for his keys, still not grasping the magnitude of the situation.

"Call 911," Cal ordered. "Now!"

Later, after the EMTs had jammed the EpiPen into Maisy's fat little thigh and strapped an oxygen mask to her face, Cal replayed the moment over and over in her mind. It was a moment that came back to haunt her at night when she was having trouble falling asleep. It was the knowledge, terrifying and certain, that her child was dying before her eyes. She thought of all those peanut-butter sandwiches she and her sisters had eaten carelessly as children, their lips and fingers sticky with the substance, never realizing its unleashed force.

The allergy was inconvenient and socially awkward, but Cal had long since stopped caring what others thought of her vigilance. Once she'd seen her child's lips turn blue from lack of oxygen, she no longer cared about social pleasantries. Since that pivotal afternoon, the allergy had become a crucial part of their lives. The pack with the EpiPen that needed to be carried everywhere, the extra ones needed for her pre-school classroom, the special snacks kept on hand for occasions when Maisy wasn't allowed to eat the food, the extra minutes and hours in the grocery store reading labels, her insistence on having all play dates at their house where she could feed the children, and the constant nagging fear anytime Maisy went anywhere without her.

Cal knew it would only get worse next year when Maisy moved from the small, safe world of her preschool to the larger, more unknown public elementary school. Eventually, Cal would have to trust the other adults and systems that cared for Maisy, and not so long from now she would have to trust Maisy herself. Maisy was old enough now to know not to eat nuts, but the toxic legume was everywhere. In cereals, in granola bars, in cookies and crackers and desserts. No food was safe, unless Cal had prepared and packed it herself after scouring the label for any trace.

So she knew Howard understood her need to remind him to check for nuts at the party. It had become a touchstone, as much a safeguard against tragedy as "be careful" or "I love you" on the way out the door. But tragedy could strike anywhere. Death and disaster were always lurking, only a handful of nuts or a brain aneurysm away.

Chapter Twenty-Six

Violet

The funeral had been arranged. Through some miracle, Barry and several other close friends Violet and Suzy had never met took care of nearly all the details that needed to be managed. Phone calls were made, an obituary with the information about the wake and funeral was in the paper, flowers had been ordered, and Barry would take care of arranging the photos they'd brought. Violet and Suzy's earlier conversation about who would give the eulogy turned out to be a moot point anyway, as they'd learned there was typically no eulogy at a Catholic service. They could choose a reading or blessing if they wanted to; otherwise, the priest would say the service. There would be a reception back at Veg, and Barry and the staff would take care of organizing and preparing the food.

When Violet and Suzy arrived back at the cottage, Cal was still locked in the bedroom, and Suzy went straight upstairs to lie down. Violet wandered into the kitchen, restless and depressed. She was grateful for all of Barry's help, and it was becoming clear that he was more than just her father's business partner, but it saddened her how little she or Suzy knew about what their father would have wanted.

Violet sat down at the counter with a bag of pretzels and her phone. She scanned through e-mails, replying to a few colleagues about how long she'd be away and which classes she needed covered. There was another message from Michael asking about the details of the wake and funeral, and Violet responded quickly before she could think too much of it. She thought about e-mailing Luka or calling him, but the way they'd left things the other morning didn't allow any room for such a gesture.

Their breakup had both come out of nowhere and been building for a long time. Christmas was the first time Luka had met her father, and it was strange for Violet to see them together. Luka was so tall he made even tall men appear short, but her father had always been such a large presence in Violet's mind that it was odd to see him so diminished by Luka.

They'd gotten along immediately, Violet's father asking Luka questions about where he was from, his family, and the bar where he worked. Violet watched their conversation with detachment. At one point, her father would have wanted more for her than Luka. He would have wanted her to be with a professional, someone who had regular hours and an annual paid vacation and a 401(k). But sometime in the past fifteen years her father had given up his investment in Violet's future spouse and was now just grateful to be spending Christmas with her. For some reason, his ready approval of Luka made her angry, though she knew this was ridiculous. Yet part of her wanted him to grill Luka, to press him about his intentions, his ambitions, to question his worthiness as a mate. She couldn't articulate any of this to Luka, because it was absurd and hurtful. So she picked a fight instead.

They arrived home after Christmas dinner a little after nine. Violet was sluggish and full from the roast beef and pies Cal had made and the multiple glasses of red wine she'd drunk before and during dinner. The day had made her tired. Between the excessive food and the emotional drain of spending the day with her sisters and father, all Violet wanted to do was get into bed and read for a few minutes before falling asleep.

But Luka was in the mood to talk. He stripped to his boxer shorts and slid up against her, not picking up on her sleepy, sullen mood.

"Tonight was nice," he said, nuzzling against her shoulder. His stubbled chin was rough against her skin.

Violet nodded, focusing on her book. "Mmm-hmm," she murmured.

"Your dad is great," Luka continued. "He's a chef?"

"Supposedly," Violet said, unable to keep the sarcasm from her voice. She still had a hard time believing her father made his living from cooking. Violet hardly remembered him ever cooking for them while growing up. Occasionally, he'd make a big breakfast or spend a weekend afternoon baking pies or making popovers or some other novelty food, but Violet didn't remember him ever doing the boring day-to-day cooking. Making sure the pantry closets were full and there was dinner on the table every night when they all got home—that had fallen to Violet's mother.

"What kind of a restaurant is it?"

"A vegetarian place, I guess. I've never been." Violet's head hurt, and she knew she'd have a hangover in the morning.

"You've never been?" Luka asked in surprise. His face was only inches away, his breath stale from the wine, and Violet found herself examining his teeth. They were crooked and slightly stained, the uncorrected teeth of someone who had not grown up in the world of American orthodontics. She'd never paid Luka's teeth much attention before, but she suddenly found them off-putting.

"No. I haven't been up there in years."

"We should go up sometime to visit. Check out his restaurant. Go eat lobsters." Luka grinned.

Violet rolled her eyes. "Maybe." She reread the same sentence for the fourth time, having lost the thread of the chapter.

"Your dad seems really nice," Luka said earnestly. He brushed Violet's hair out of her face, trying to catch her eye. "You don't talk about him much."

"There's not much to say." She kept her eyes on the page. "He and my mom split up when I was in high school. He moved to Maine a few years later."

"You didn't visit?"

"Not really. By the time he moved up there I was already in college. When I came home on break, I wanted to be in Cambridge, to see my friends." She closed the book, ready to turn off the light.

"You seem mad at him." Luka's eyes held her in place. This was one of those times when he was trying to draw her out, to get inside her, but Violet didn't like his probing gaze. During these times, her automatic reaction was always to deflect him. Especially when it came to her father.

"I'm not mad at him," Violet snapped. "We're just not that close. We never have been."

Luka stretched out, his ankles and feet nearly hanging off the end of the bed. "Do you think he liked me?"

"Sure," she said without enthusiasm. "I'm tired. Can we go to bed?"

"Don't you want him to like me?" Luka asked, frowning. "Because you don't seem like you really care."

"It's fine if he likes you; it doesn't really matter if he doesn't." Violet sat up and adjusted the pillow behind her. "We're not that close. I told you."

"Why haven't I ever met him before?"

Violet sighed in frustration. "Because I hardly ever see him. We talk every few months."

"So?" Luka said. "You don't see him often, but you've seen him since we've been together. Why haven't you invited me to meet him until now?"

"Because he has high standards!" The words burst forth. She hadn't meant for it to come out so tactlessly. She watched Luka process the words, finding the barb among them. "I don't mean it like that," she backtracked. Was this even true? Did her father actually have high standards? Or was it Violet herself who had the high standards, and it was easier to blame her father?

"Really?" Luka's voice was cold. "How do you mean it?"

Violet rubbed her eyes. Her head was pounding, the hangover already upon her. "I just meant I didn't want to introduce you to him until I knew if it was serious."

"And is it?" Luka was propped up on one arm. "Have you decided yet?" She couldn't gauge his mood, if he was upset or playful.

"Of course," she said unconvincingly.

Luka picked up her hand and squeezed it. His fingers were like the rest of him, long and thin. And strong. "So let's get married."

"Luka." She rolled to face him.

"Why not?"

They'd had this conversation before, but he'd never asked so directly. The other times had been discussions, abstract conversations about marriage. This was the first time it felt like a proposal.

"Luka," she said again, not knowing what more to add.

"Violet." He smiled, showing his imperfect teeth.

"We've talked about this. I'm not ready." She didn't know why she was putting him off. She loved him. She did. She'd never been with a man she felt so utterly herself with, a man who saw her and was willing to take her the way she was. While most of the women she knew were waiting to find the right man to marry, marriage had always felt like the end of something to Violet. Once she got married, so many of the uncertainties in her life would line up. All those open doors would close, one after the other.

"Why not? What are we waiting for?" He placed his hand on her hip. Its warmth felt solid.

"We want different things," Violet told him.

"What different things? I want what you want." He clasped the curve of her body, trying to pull her closer.

Violet shook her head. "No you don't."

"Violet." He kissed her fingertips one at a time. "You don't know what you want. You want everything, and you want nothing."

Violet rolled her eyes, frustrated by the intangible way he spoke. "And what do you want?"

He held his open hand in front of her. "I want you. I want to bring you home to meet my family, to show you where I come from. I want my mother to come and visit her grandbabies in America. I want us to have a life together."

It sounded so simple when he said it like that. So simple Violet wondered why she always pulled away when part of her just wanted to lie down in the life he'd mapped out for them. She didn't answer.

"What do you think you want?" Luka asked, finally growing frustrated.

"What do I *think* I want? God, do you have to be so patronizing?" Violet sat up and pulled away from him on the bed. "I'm not a child, Luka. I'm capable of knowing what I want and don't want." Just moments earlier he had proposed. Now they were fighting. Yet somehow Violet knew she was the one driving this fight. Luka would go back to the proposal if she let him. He would go back to the easy intimacy of his warm hand holding her in place, if only she would let him.

"So tell me. Tell me what you want." He sat back in bed, crossing his arms.

Pressed so directly to articulate, Violet found she didn't know what she wanted, but she couldn't admit this to Luka. "I want to be a poet," she said instead.

"You *are* a poet," Luka pointed out. "You're a wonderful poet, and you get paid to teach poetry to others."

"That's not what I want. I don't want to spend my day praising awful poems written by superficial college kids and illiterate high schoolers." She didn't really feel that way, at least not about the students she worked with in the schools. But the work barely supported her. Adjunct professors and public school writers-in-residence hardly made enough to pay the phone and electric bills, much less rent in Somerville. Before she and Luka moved in together, Violet had shared a crowded apartment with three other people, and she'd waitressed at night in addition to the day jobs in order to pay her share of the rent. Even two years ago she was getting too old for this lifestyle. Luka's bartending job made it possible to survive on the work Violet did without the waitressing, though Luka was dependent on the good graces of the owner who could have fired him at any time because he wasn't legally supposed to be working. She was trying to make a point, though already she seemed to have forgotten what the point was.

"So what do you want to do?" Luka asked. "Spend the whole day alone writing poetry?" Luka shook his head. "You're an adult. You need to support yourself." She looked away from him. He sounded so much like the version of Violet's father in her head. Though Violet had rarely had a real conversation with her father about her career. Only imaginary ones. "I know a lot of people who do a lot worse than teach poetry all day to support themselves," he added.

"What's that supposed to mean?" She knew what it meant, and she knew he was right. When Luka arrived in the country, he'd immediately been absorbed into Boston's Czech community but also into the extended world of immigrants in the city. He had friends who drove cabs, tended bar, worked construction, and cleaned hotels. They supported themselves, and they often sent money back home. The world Luka inhabited outside of their cozy apartment was foreign to Violet.

No matter how much he invited her in, she felt like an interloper around this extended family of friends and acquaintances. Luka could fit in anywhere, comfortable chatting with the eclectic collection of yuppies, college students, and businessmen who came into the bar where he worked. He could stay up late drinking vodka and playing poker with his Slovakian friend Leo one night, and the next night socialize with Violet's friends and colleagues at a poetry reading. Everyone loved Luka. Violet, on the other hand, worried his friends thought she was entitled and stuck-up, a rich American with the cushion of family and country behind her.

"It means you're lucky to have a job doing something you enjoy," Luka said now. "What else do you want?" His eyes were brown with flecks of amber, and they watched her closely.

They had been together for nearly two years, living together for one. For much of that time, Violet had tried not to think about the future, though she knew this was unusual for a woman in her thirties. She wasn't certain she saw herself with Luka twenty years from now, but she loved being with him. She loved the weight of his body, the way he carried himself, confident and graceful. She loved going to see him at Luxe, the bar where he worked, to watch his quick movements behind the bar, to see girls younger and prettier than her eyeing him but to know he would come home to her at the end of the night. She loved the way he seemed to know her, to understand her sharp edges, even the twang of meanness masking insecurity that tended to drive people away eventually. He got her, though she wondered if she always got him.

"I don't know." Her voice was barely above a whisper.

"Do you want me?" Luka sat rigid in the bed, his narrow chest bare but for the curly dark hair that felt soft when she ran her hand along his skin. She wished she'd clicked the light off when she first got into bed or turned into his body when he'd rubbed his face against her shoulder. She wished she'd accepted the invitation she'd ignored.

"I don't know," she whispered again, tears burning behind her eyes.

He watched her for a moment and she could see something inside of him shifting, settling, accepting whatever he'd managed to look past for all this time. He stood slowly, unfolding himself from the bed. He reached for his pillow and crossed to the closet where they kept the spare blankets.

"What are you doing?" Violet asked.

"I'm sleeping on the couch."

"Luka, don't," she protested. When he turned back to her, he looked older. He *was* older than her, thirty-nine to her thirty-two, but there were dark circles under his eyes though it wasn't even ten o'clock.

"I can't do this anymore, Violet." His voice was somber.

They'd found themselves here a few times in the last two years, but Violet had always been able to bring him back. She rose from the bed and moved toward him, but this time he held her at bay with a hand. She tried to put her arms around his waist, but he caught her, his fingers surprisingly tight around the fragile bones of her wrists.

"Luka," she said helplessly.

"I'm done with this," he said.

"I'm sorry. Please, come back to bed," she pleaded.

"No, Violet. *No.* I'm tired of you fucking me around." Violet's breath caught in her chest. There was a new and unfamiliar bitterness in Luka's voice. He'd never spoken to her so cruelly.

"I'm not," she said, though she wondered if there was some truth to this. She'd never meant to; it just seemed to happen.

He dropped her hands and crossed to the door.

"What are you doing?" she asked. "What's happening?"

"We can figure out the details tomorrow," he said. "You can have the apartment if you want it. I don't care."

"What?" Violet was stunned. Just minutes earlier he had proposed and now they were talking about who would keep the apartment. "No, I don't want this," she said.

"It's too late." He shook his head. "Merry fucking Christmas." He let the door slam behind him.

Violet stood in the center of the bedroom, her arms still raised from where Luka had released them. She thought about following him down-stairs but knew they would just end up fighting more. He wouldn't want her to go to him now. With nothing left to do, she climbed back into bed and turned off the light. Maybe he would feel differently in the morning.

But he hadn't, of course, and even now, two months later, Violet still couldn't believe the swiftness with which her life had unraveled. He'd offered her the apartment, but she couldn't afford it nor could she afford anything halfway decent on her own, which was why she'd been at Annie's for so long. She'd need to either pick up a waitressing job or move into a roommate situation. Probably both.

Her father had wanted her to be a teacher. In one of the only career-related conversations they'd ever had in real life, he'd tried to convince her she could both teach and write poetry and that she didn't need to be tenured at a university to be a poet. Violet had dismissed him with little more than a roll of her eyes. Being a teacher seemed like such a boring and uptight profession, a lifetime of petty rule enforcement and haggling over hall passes.

So she was surprised by how much she enjoyed the high schoolers she worked with in the Poets in the Schools program. Though the writing wasn't usually very good, she found the emotion behind it to be more honest than the college-age students she taught. The teenagers were at a crossroads—the crucial moments between childhood and adulthood. Violet remembered the magnitude every moment seemed to hold during that time.

The coordinator for the Poets program mentioned quietly to Violet that one of the teachers would be retiring at the end of the school year and Violet might think about applying. Though Violet wasn't certified to teach, she had an English degree and could get a temporary license if she passed the educator tests. Violet had nodded and smiled politely, but since their conversation the idea had risen to the surface of her consciousness more times than she would have expected.

From a young age, she'd declared herself a poet. As a child, it meant she was constantly scribbling in a journal, terrible self-absorbed rants she was embarrassed to return to weeks later. As an adult, it meant poetry workshops, an MFA she would be paying off for the rest of her life, a chapbook followed by a small run on a slim collection of her work that did modestly well, though that didn't really say much considering how few people bought poetry these days. Few people made their living as a writer. No one made his or her living as a poet.

She was far from getting a tenured position at BU, and the only alternative was to consider applying to far-flung colleges across the country, to leave everything for a tenured job at a tiny college in Kansas or Wisconsin. Yet to apply for the high school job felt like denouncing the person she believed herself to be. It also felt like admitting her father was right, that she could teach and be a poet.

She was growing tired of the artist's struggle. She was too old not to be able to pay her rent, too old to be living with roommates, far too old to be sleeping on someone's couch. Maybe a little stability wasn't such a terrible thing. And maybe it was time to let go of an identity she'd created for herself when she was too young to know any of those things would matter. Maybe her father really had known what was best, but Violet had shrugged away his words, too stubborn and angry to bother listening.

Chapter Twenty-Seven

Suzy

Suzy lay in bed with her hands clasped atop her belly. The website she'd looked at this morning said the fetus was the size of a kidney bean. She knew it was not yet fully formed, but she imagined a perfect baby a little bigger than her thumbnail swimming inside her.

Suzy hadn't called the clinic to reschedule her appointment. She wasn't sure what had changed. She never would have told her father anyway, but now she worried he was looking down on her, silently judging, quietly disappointed.

There was a knock on the door, and Suzy opened her eyes. "Come in."

Violet threw open the door, hands on her hips. "I'm staging an intervention," she announced.

"What?" Suzy pulled her hands away from her stomach, though she was certain Violet had already taken note of the position.

"You and Cal. Enough of this wallowing in bed."

"Give me a break. I just lay down for a little while," Suzy said.

"You've been up here for over two hours," Violet corrected. "And Cal hasn't gotten out of bed since we got here. Enough." Violet yanked the covers off Suzy and pointed to the door. "Let's go get Cal." Suzy sighed and hauled herself out of bed. There was no point arguing with Violet when she got like this.

Violet and Cal had squabbled since they were children. They were like oil and vinegar; they were always fighting over something. At this point, Suzy suspected it was an automated response on both their parts. But despite the constant bickering, despite the intense rivalry, there was also a fierce bond between them. Though Cal and Violet weren't close the way Suzy was with each of them, there was a grudging and unwavering loyalty. They might not have been friends, but they were sisters, and that bond was deeper than the surface irritation.

They stood outside of Cal's door and Violet knocked twice, then opened the door before Cal had a chance to answer. Cal lay on her side reading a fat paperback. She looked up, startled at their entrance.

"What?" Her hair was pulled back into a slick ponytail, and the bones in her neck protruded. The air held a fuggy smell. An empty mug with the dregs of coffee sat upon a crumbed plate on the night-stand. Suzy breathed in through her mouth, teetering on the edge of nausea.

"It's time to get up," Violet told her. Suzy stood quietly in the door-way, letting Violet take charge.

"Vi," Cal sighed. She closed the book and rolled over, her back closing them out. But Violet wouldn't be shut out.

"I said it's time to get up," Violet repeated, slightly louder this time.

"I don't want to fight with you, Violet. Okay? Can't you just leave me alone?"

"I'm not here to fight. I'm here to get you out of this bed." She yanked the blanket off Cal much like she'd done to Suzy just moments earlier. Without the blanket covering her, Cal looked even sadder, her slender body curled into the fetal position, her T-shirt and sweats hanging from her like rags, bare feet tucked into each other.

"God, Violet, just leave me alone," Cal said, but her voice lacked the authority it usually carried. "I just want to sleep." Cal buried her face in the pillow, but not before Suzy saw the tears. She couldn't remember ever seeing Cal cry as an adult, and now she seemed unable to stop.

"I know you do," Violet said gently. She lowered herself to the bed and put her hand on Cal's legs. "I know how close you were to Dad. And I'm sorry this is so hard. But you need to get up now."

"Why?" Cal demanded. "Why do I need to get up?"

"Because this isn't healthy. You've locked yourself up in this room, and you've pushed us all away. You're shutting down."

"So?" Cal asked. "My dad just died, for God's sake. Can't I shut down? Can't I ever take a break?" Her voice bordered on hysterical. "Why do I have to be in charge of *everything*?" Her red face contorted in a look of raw grief. Suzy shuddered inwardly. She wanted to turn from this, to look away. It was too intimate to stay here, too intrusive to force Cal's hand if she wasn't ready. But Violet bent closer. She reached out and cradled Cal's face in her hands.

"Everything's under control. You don't have to be in charge of anything. I promise." She ran her thumbs lightly along Cal's cheekbones. "You just need to get out of bed."

They were quiet for a moment, just looking at each other, and Suzy could see Violet had finally cracked through Cal's wall of grief. "I just can't believe he's dead," she whimpered finally.

"I know," Violet whispered. "Neither can I." She smoothed Cal's hair out of her face. "But it's time to get up now."

Cal took a deep breath as if steeling herself for what lay ahead. "I don't have to do anything?" she asked.

"Nothing. Suzy and I will take care of it all," Violet promised.

"Okay." Cal nodded. "Okay," she repeated softly, sitting up.

"One thing actually," Violet said, her nose wrinkling in displeasure. "You do need to do one thing."

"What?" Cal looked ready to retreat back to the dank refuge of pillows and blankets.

"You need to take a shower."

Violet unpacked toiletries from Cal's suitcase and found a towel for her in the linen closet, then ushered her into the bathroom and turned the water on. Her gentle caretaking reminded Suzy of the time her sisters had intervened on Suzy's behalf, the summer she stayed with her father in Maine.

Suzy often wondered if her father had wished for a boy, if maybe her birth had been a final and unsuccessful attempt. He'd never made her feel like a disappointment, but she knew there were times he felt outnumbered and out of his depth with the problems and drama of raising three daughters. As children they were as close to him as to their mother, but as they entered adolescence, each of them had slowly distanced themselves from him. It was hard to know how much of this had to do with the divorce or if it would have happened eventually, but the three of them came to rely on their mother instead of him, or more often, on each other.

The summer Suzy stayed with him in Portland was a perfect example. After she met Zach that afternoon at the pool, she didn't tell her father about him. Over coffee that afternoon, she learned that Zach would be a junior in the fall, he was from Portland, was majoring in biology, was a snowboarder, and planned on moving to Colorado upon graduation, where he could live the life of a ski bum for a few years. She let Zach believe she was in college too, and she told him about her sisters.

"We're each named after flowers," she said.

"Oh yeah?" He smelled like chlorine and soap. His arms were propped on the small wooden table, and his forearms were strong and muscled from hours in the water.

She nodded. "My dad's last name is Bloom. My mom was a big hippie, and when they got married, she had a huge garden in the backyard of their house. It was filled with flowers." Suzy took a sip of the iced coffee she'd ordered. She'd loaded it with cream and sugar, so it was more like a milkshake than coffee. "She convinced my dad to name my oldest sister Calla Lily. You don't see them on the East Coast very much, but my mom planted calla lilies in her garden. They were the flowers in her bouquet when they got married." Her mother's garden was incredible, though in the past few years she favored fruits and vegetables over flowers.

"That's cool," he said with a smile.

"My next sister was named Violet," Suzy continued. "When she was born, my mom planted a whole patch of violets next to the calla lilies."

"And what about you?" Zach asked, leaning closer.

"Black-eyed Susan." She rolled her eyes. "By the time I was born, even my mom was over the whole flower thing. But they could hardly leave me out."

"It's cool your name means something." He added more sugar to his coffee. "That it has a history."

Suzy murmured noncommittally. She hadn't told him the full story. The part she left out was what happened a few weeks after their father moved out of the house. Suzy came home from school to find her mother on her hands and knees in the backyard. This wasn't unusual for a day like this. Autumn came late that year, and October still held the warmth of summer. Suzy hadn't thought anything of it till she looked closer at what her mother was doing. She was deep in the bed of violets, and Suzy watched in shock as she pulled out handfuls of the fragile purple flower by the roots. Beside her was a pile of calla lilies, their slender green stalks arranged in a haphazard group.

Suzy ran outside and caught her mother by the shoulders. "Mom, what are you doing? Stop. Stop!" She hadn't yet gotten to the black-eyed Susans, and the cheerful yellow flowers waited unknowingly for their death. Her mother looked at Suzy as if she'd been in a trance. Her face was stained with dirt, her eyes wide and glassy. Soil dripped from her hands, and her jeans were stained with mud and grass. "That bastard," she said softly. And then again, louder. "That *bastard.*" Her mother leaned forward on her knees and took several deep breaths. When she looked back at Suzy, her eyes had lost their wildness and she looked more like herself. "Time to start fresh," she said. "I was thinking tomatoes and peas." She pushed herself to standing and went to fill the compost bucket. Suzy looked at the mound of dead flowers on the ground and then back at her mother, as if she'd murdered each of them with her bare hands.

It was the only time Suzy saw her mother visibly break down over the divorce. True to her word, her mother planted peas and tomatoes in the spring, along with squash and lettuce. The plot of black-eyed Susans remained where they were, along with the last few violets. The calla lilies were all gone though.

Suzy changed the topic by asking Zach about snowboarding. She listened and nodded, sipping the cold, sweet drink he'd bought her. By the time their cups were empty, he'd invited her to a party at his house the following night.

Suzy didn't know what her father would say if she asked to go. Her mother would have unequivocally said no. But the rules with her father were all mixed up. He often acquiesced out of guilt or an attempt to apologize for all he couldn't give her.

Yet his guilt only superseded his common sense by so much, so Suzy told him she was walking into town to go to a movie with a girl she'd met at the pool. Luckily, the party was within walking distance from her father's house; otherwise, she would have had to figure out a way to get a ride. In her bedroom before the party, Suzy stood in front of her sparse summer wardrobe, trying to figure out what to wear. She finally settled on a pair of cutoff jean shorts and a black T-shirt. She added some beaded jewelry and tried to tame her hair with a headband. She added a stroke of mascara and a smear of lip gloss, hoping her father didn't notice or comment.

Back home, Suzy didn't go to parties. She didn't drink, except for the one night she and her friend Liane had snuck glasses of peach schnapps and apple juice when Liane's parents were out. The one drink left them giggling and fast asleep before the adults made it home. The idea of going to a party alone where she didn't know anyone was terrifying to Suzy, but she couldn't bear the thought of her father as her only companion for the rest of the summer, and she didn't think Zach would invite her for coffee again if she didn't show up tonight. So far the whole summer felt as if she were living someone else's life—an only child for the first time, living in an unfamiliar house in a town where she knew no one, even her father little more than a distant acquaintance these days. This wasn't a life she was comfortable living, so why not try some things she wouldn't ordinarily do? The goal of the summer had become to be someone other than herself.

Suzy walked the mile and a half to the address Zach had given her, the thwack of her flip-flops mixing with the sound of crickets and the swish of leaves rubbing against each other in the light breeze. She passed several people on the main road—families out for ice cream, a few couples strolling arm in arm—but on the quiet side streets Suzy walked faster. Suzy wasn't used to walking alone at night, and though it was barely nine, she found herself glancing over her shoulder every few feet and wondering how she would feel walking home later that night.

Within a half hour she turned down Spruce Lane. As soon as she rounded the corner, she heard the telltale signs of a party—the deep thrum of music, the loud voices of young men followed by the cackle of girls. The noises were coming from a dilapidated gray-shingled house with a fenced-in backyard where the party was spilling over. Suzy let herself in the gate, the rusted hinges creaking loudly as she shut it behind her. The front door was ajar and with a knot of anxiety in her chest, she made her way inside. The living room was crowded with people and what she later realized was the makeshift furniture of college kids. Instead of a couch, a row of striped beach chairs was lined up against the wall, and a neon Budweiser sign and a free drugstore calendar were the only décor. A Beastie Boys song was playing loudly from a stereo system in the corner of the room.

She was relieved to spot Zach in the alcove of the kitchen, drinking from a red plastic cup and talking with a blond girl in a strappy white tank top. When he spotted Suzy he smiled, raising his glass to her, but he didn't make his way over. Suzy stood in the living room, unsure where to go, and she considered turning around and hurrying down the steps and home. Her father would be lying on the couch, drinking his one nightly cocktail, a tall gin and tonic, flipping channels on the TV. When Suzy arrived, they would have an awkward conversation and try to find something to watch together, though each would be waiting for the other to go to bed. At one point Suzy used to watch football with her father on Sundays, but it was baseball season, and Suzy could never muster much enthusiasm for the game. Last week, they'd watched a romantic comedy on TV. Suzy cringed inwardly during the sex scenes, and they both stared stone-faced at the television. Despite all this, turning and going home was something Suzy was tempted to do.

But Zach had met Sue, not Suzy, so she swallowed down her pounding heart and scanned the room, looking for someone to talk to. She spotted a slight young man with thin brown hair standing alone by the music system, scanning CDs. She could tell he wasn't really interested in the discs but, like her, lacked anything better to do with his hands or eyes. She crossed the room till she was just a foot or so away from him.

"Hi," she said, forcing him to look up from the Nirvana CD he was examining intently.

He looked up and scanned her face. "Hey," he said after a moment. "How's it going?"

"Okay." Suzy nodded at the CD he held. "Are you the DJ?" Over here by the speakers the music was even louder, and she had to shout to be heard.

He looked down at his hands and seemed surprised to find the disc there. "Not really." He reached out his hand, an oddly formal gesture in the loud room. "I'm Oliver." His hand was warm and slightly damp.

"Suzy." He tilted his head toward a smaller sitting room off the living room, motioning for her to follow. It was quieter in here. Oliver had the delicate features of a girl, a slender pointed nose and high cheekbones.

"How'd you end up here?" he asked.

"Zach? Who lives here? He invited me?" She hated how her sentences all came out as questions. "How about you?"

"I live here too," Oliver said. "I hate these stupid parties, though." He took a sip of the near-empty beer he was drinking. "Do you want a drink?" he asked, noticing her empty hands.

She hesitated. "Sure." Of course she'd known everyone would be drinking at the party, but she hadn't formulated a plan for herself whether she would drink. She hoped her father would be asleep by the time she got home, though she suspected he'd be on the couch reading, waiting up for her.

"Be right back," he said and then made his way through the living room and toward the kitchen. Suzy leaned against the wall and examined a photo of a dog wearing sunglasses and was relieved when Oliver returned after a moment carrying two full plastic cups.

"Cheers." He handed her the cup.

"Cheers." They both sipped the watery beer. Suzy had tried beer before, usually the foam off the top of her father's drinks, but never a whole one herself. It tasted like pennies, metallic and bitter.

"What year are you?" Oliver asked, just as Zach appeared beside them.

"You made it." He leaned forward and kissed her on the cheek, his mouth grazing the curve of her jaw and landing just below her earlobe.

Suzy felt a quiver of excitement in the pit of her stomach. "What's up," he said to Oliver.

"Hey." Oliver stayed where he was for a moment and then he nodded at Suzy. "See you around," he said and turned toward the living room. Suzy watched the narrow shape of his T-shirt as he was swallowed into the crowded room. She was pleased to see Zach, but a little disappointed to see Oliver go.

"I'm glad you came." Zach let his hand rest on her hip. His eyes had a slightly faraway look, the lids more hooded than usual.

Suzy smiled into her cup. "Me too." They stood for a moment without talking, both of them scanning the room. "Did you swim today?" Suzy asked.

"Nah. I'll be hurting tomorrow though." The music in the room was louder than a few minutes ago, and Zach leaned forward, directing the words into her ear. His breath was warm against her neck. A girl bumped into him as she walked past, and he stumbled slightly, spilling beer on Suzy's foot. "Sorry, I'm kind of wasted. We started early," he explained.

"So you live here?" She scrunched her wet toes in her flip-flops.

"Yup. I've got a room upstairs. Want to see it?" He grinned at her, and Suzy couldn't help but smile shyly back.

Later she wondered what would have happened if they hadn't gone upstairs. What if she'd spent the night talking to Oliver instead? Would it have unfolded the same way somewhere else, that night or another night? Or was it just the beer and the weed he'd obviously smoked earlier dulling his judgment? She'd never know because she followed him up the green-carpeted stairs, into a small bedroom with a tie-dyed tapestry hanging on the wall and a rumpled twin mattress on the floor. Despite the open window, the air was close and stuffy. Zach flopped onto the bed and reached for Suzy's free hand, pulling her down beside him.

"There, that's much better," he said. "It was too loud down there." Up here, the thin wood-paneled walls buffered the music. He placed his hand on her bare knee, tracking the freckles with his forefinger. In the coffee shop he'd been talkative and expansive. In the relative privacy of his room, he grew quiet, the air between them anticipatory of what would happen next. When he leaned in to kiss her, Suzy was waiting for it, his open mouth gentle against hers. She'd only kissed one other boy before, behind a pine tree at sleepaway camp the summer she was thirteen. This was different. Even as she kissed him back, she imagined telling Violet, her guide on all things boy- and sex-related.

Zach's palms roamed the planes of her face, and she couldn't help but imagine what they looked like together, the heat and tenderness like something from a movie. He lay her down upon the mussed bedclothes.

"Black-eyed Susan," he said softly. She gave an embarrassed smile. "God, it's hot in here." He pulled his T-shirt off in a fluid movement. "You want to cool down?" He tugged at the hem of her shirt, sliding it up to reveal her stomach.

Like Suzy hadn't thought about drinking, she hadn't thought about this either. In the back of her mind, surely she must have known they'd end up here. Hoped even. But she hadn't figured out how far she was willing to go or how she would get out of doing more than she wanted. Even while she was contemplating the question, Zach was already sliding the shirt over her head and bringing his face down to the warm crevice where the cups of her bra met. She inhaled quickly as his mouth roamed her skin, his fingers finding the way to the back of her bra and expertly unhooking the clasp.

His hands traveled the length of her torso, and Suzy closed her eyes. She felt warmth in the places his fingers grazed and in other places as well, shooting stars of pleasure firing through her body. She let out a surprised gasp as his mouth came to her breast, but there was another part of her trying to figure out when to stop and how. What words did one use in a situation like this? Suzy certainly didn't know, though she suspected Violet had learned the etiquette long ago. Then again, Suzy doubted Violet tried to stop things like this very often.

Before she'd gotten much further in her mind, Zach's fingers were pulling at the button on her jeans, and she heard the zip of her shorts coming undone. If she didn't slow things down soon, they wouldn't stop. He wouldn't stop.

"Wait," Suzy breathed into the slightly sweaty smell of his hair. By now Zach was unzipping his own jeans and sliding them down to reveal just a pair of plaid boxers and socks. "Hold on," she whispered. Her shorts were in a heap at the foot of the bed.

"It's okay," he murmured, pulling her cotton underwear off with surprising force. For the first time she felt a flurry of fear, a recognition of how quickly things had gotten away from her. "Just relax."

"Zach, wait," Suzy said again, though her words were quieted by the weight of his body pressing against her, both of them now naked. Suzy felt him against her leg, hot and hard, and she twisted out of his grasp, believing he would finally understand what she was trying to say, though she still lacked the words. But he held her fast, his legs pinning hers, his chest pressing her into the overly soft bed.

And then suddenly he was inside her. The pain was excruciating, a hot ripping violence tearing through her. She hadn't given much thought to the pain of sex, but she'd never expected this. She let out a cry, as the hurt collided with her panic at what was actually happening. "You're hurting me," she whimpered, tears appearing in her eyes. "Please." Had she said stop? Later she tried to remember and wasn't sure, though the word was blinking in her mind like a traffic light. *Stop, stop, stop.*

"Shh, it's okay," he murmured, though his eyes were closed and he wasn't even looking at her. Suzy struggled again in his grasp but he held her close, burying his face in the curve of her neck. He smelled of beer and sweat, a choking combination she hadn't minded just minutes earlier but that now made her stomach turn. Downstairs the music was playing, and the deep thrum of bass vibrated the flimsy walls of the bedroom. Suzy closed her eyes tightly and waited for it to be over.

His jerking motions sped up, and his breathing grew heavier. Suzy's insides burned with fire, and for a moment she wondered if something had split irrevocably inside her, if maybe he'd broken some tender part that could never be healed. He bucked against her, his body suddenly gone limp. When he rolled off and lay on the bed, his face was damp with perspiration and his eyes were still closed. Suzy lay motionless beside him, her body rigid.

"Fuck." He exhaled the word, a breathless curse of satisfaction. He let out a long sigh and then finally opened his eyes, rolling to face her, a lazy smile on his face. "Sorry that was so fast," he said. "When I get going like that, it's hard to stop."

Suzy nodded, though no words came out. She stayed where she was on the bed, though Zach was sitting up and feeling around on the floor for his clothes. He pulled on his T-shirt and boxers and turned to look at her, as if surprised to find her still in bed.

"You okay?" he asked. "I didn't hurt you, did I?"

She blinked at him, her mouth parted dully, speech seemingly gone. She shook her head slightly, though she wasn't sure which of his questions she was answering.

Zach tugged up his jeans. "Let's go down and get a drink." He found Suzy's underwear and shorts bundled on the floor and tossed them to her. Suzy forced herself to sit up, though her limbs felt weighted with cement. She found her bra on the bed, though her fingers struggled to work the hook. Tears pricked at the corners of her eyes as she fumbled with it for several minutes, terrified he would try to help. Eventually she managed to fasten it and pulled on her shirt, sliding her feet into the still-damp flip-flops. When she stood, her legs ached as if she'd been running for miles. They felt like jelly, and she was surprised when they worked enough to follow him downstairs. Her whole body was tender and sore, a sticky burning between her legs, and her breath came in shallow pants, though Zach didn't seem to notice.

In the living room, when he stopped to talk with several people, Suzy's eyes and ears didn't seem to be working properly. The conversations were happening underwater in low, warbled tones, and his friends were faceless to her, melting wax sculptures with blurred features.

"You're quiet," Zach said, turning to her with a smile, his crooked nose practically winking in betrayal. "I'll get us some beers." He disappeared finally into the back of the house. Suzy stood alone in the living room. Not more than half an hour could have passed since she'd last been here, but her life had changed. *She* had changed. There would be no going back from this.

Chapter Twenty-Eight

Cal

Cal had to admit she felt better after Violet forced her out of bed and into the shower, handing Cal a clean pair of jeans and a wool turtleneck from the still-packed suitcase. Suzy pulled out a package of fancy cookies, and Violet made them all tea. They sat on the living room couch overlooking the ocean. Cal's hands were hot from the heavy ceramic mug, and she stared out at the grayness of the sky and sea.

"So do you want us to tell you what's planned?" Violet asked cautiously. "If you don't care, that's fine too."

"No, tell me," Cal said. She listened while Violet went over the details of the funeral and wake, all of which Barry had helped organize.

"You can do a reading if you want," Suzy offered. "The funeral home gave us a few recommendations."

Cal shrugged, feeling tired and overwhelmed again. "I don't know. Someone else can do it."

Violet and Suzy exchanged a glance. "We don't need to decide now," Suzy said.

"Though we will need to decide by tomorrow," Violet added. "They'll be making up the program."

Cal stared out the window. In the distance, a freight boat chugged slowly and determinedly across the steely sea. "What about Mom?"

"She's trying to get out of England, but the weather's terrible and most of the flights have been canceled. Don't worry; she'll get here," Suzy said. Cal shrugged. She wasn't sure her mother's presence would make things easier for any of them.

"I brought back a few photo albums I found on Dad's bookshelf," Violet said. "We could look through them if you want. Isn't that what people do?"

"What do you mean?" Cal sipped her tea and then placed the mug back on the table. It was some fruity herbal blend.

"I don't know. I just remember when Nana Dee died, we all sat around in the living room looking at photo albums."

She remembered sitting in the living room of the Cambridge house, flipping through the cracked and musty pages of Nana Dee's albums. Behind each yellowed sheet were pictures of Nana Dee and her husband, the grandfather they never knew. He was a handsome dark-haired man, tall and thin like their father, with a smile that sparkled wickedly even through the faded black-and-white images. Nana Dee looked happy in the pictures, her rare smile flashing easily in every shot. According to their father, it was their grandfather's sudden abandon-ment that turned Nana Dee into the chilly, unforgiving woman they knew, though their father was only three when he left, and Cal couldn't believe he'd stored many other memories of his mother before that time. But their father believed that if his father had stayed, Nana Dee would have been different.

Cal shook her head. "I don't want to look at pictures."

"Okay," Suzy and Violet said in unison, their voices infuriatingly tender.

There was a long pause during which Cal considered going back up to bed. But Violet was right; it was time to get up.

"I hear you're pregnant," she said to Suzy instead. Suzy's freckled cheeks flushed instantly, as if a switch had been flipped on, and she glanced at Violet with a look of annoyance. "Don't be mad at her; you would have told me eventually." Cal took another sip of tea, surprised that the taste was growing on her. "She says you're not planning on keeping it."

"I don't know," Suzy said. "I haven't decided." Suzy looked down at her mug of tea, then back up at Cal. "I didn't want to tell you because I knew you'd be upset."

"I'm not upset," Cal said.

Suzy continued, as if Cal hadn't spoken. "I love Sadie and Maisy, and I know you think having children is important and all, but you have Howard, and you planned on having them. It's just different." Suzy tugged on the string of her tea bag, making it bob up and down in the cup until a few drops spilled over the side.

"I don't think having children is important. Not for everyone. Not if you don't want them," Cal said with a frown.

"What are you talking about?" Violet asked. "You're, like, mother of the year. You're the spokesperson for motherhood." Violet fished the tea bag out of her mug and squeezed the liquid into the cup, leaving the curled-up bag on the wooden table.

"What are *you* talking about?" Cal said, feeling a familiar flare of irritation. "Don't get me wrong: I love my kids, but parenthood is hard. I don't always love it. I don't even like it a lot of the time."

"You really shouldn't try to talk her into keeping it," Violet said sarcastically. "It's her decision after all."

"I'm just telling the truth. She'll do what she wants," Cal said. She pulled her legs up under her on the couch. "Who's the father?"

"Ian," Suzy said sheepishly. "It was a mistake; we're not back together or anything." She sighed. "The thing is, I've been thinking about keeping it lately. It sort of seems like fate." She gave Cal an embarrassed look, avoiding Violet's gaze. "I mean, here I am all ready to get an abortion and then Dad's death interferes and I have to cancel it. Maybe I'm meant to keep it after all." She looked at Cal hopefully, as if for confirmation.

Violet let out a sharp laugh. "Oh, come on, Suzy. Have the baby if you want, but don't bring fate and Dad's *spirit* into it."

"It's okay to want it," Cal told Suzy gently, ignoring Violet.

"It just feels wrong to go through with it now. I can't explain it." Suzy sank back into the plush cushions of the couch.

"Why don't we just get through the next couple of days? You don't have to decide anything yet." Cal reached over and held onto Suzy's hand for a moment, squeezing it. "It's a big decision either way." Suzy nodded.

"Let's go out for dinner," Violet said. "We need to get out of the house for a bit. And I'd really hoped to get good and drunk with the two of you last night, but both of you left me on my own." She looked from Suzy to Cal. "Suzy seems to be out, but you can join me, Callie." A smile played at her mouth. When Cal didn't answer, Violet continued. "Come on. Why not? Look at photo albums and get drunk. Isn't that what people do when someone dies? You don't want to look at pictures, fine. But you're going to have a few drinks with me tonight. I'm going to get dressed." Violet pushed herself up from the couch and headed upstairs, leaving her empty mug and tea bag on the table. Cal looked at Suzy and rolled her eyes. She went to find a rag to clean up the table before Violet's tea bag left a water mark on the wood.

They ended up at a Mexican restaurant in town. The room was brightly decorated and crowded for a Sunday night, but they were seated at a plush red booth after a few minutes. Violet ordered them all margaritas, a virgin one for Suzy, and the waitress brought chips and salsa.

Violet raised her glass. "To Dad."

Cal's eyes instantly filled as she raised her glass and clinked it against Suzy's and Violet's. The drink was sweet and strong. She was thirsty and took another long sip. "I'm so tired of crying. It's like I've lost control of my own reflexes." She wiped at a stray tear rolling down her cheek.

"It's natural," Suzy said. "It's a shock to all of us."

"I know. I still just can't believe it." Cal drank from the rim of the glass, the sharp tang of salt stinging her lips.

"Slow down," Violet ordered. "We've got all night."

Cal peered into her drink, surprised to see the tops of the ice cubes peering out of the glass. Mexican music played over the speakers, easing the need for conversation. The waitress came and took their order, and Violet and Cal got another round of drinks.

"Why didn't anyone tell me about what happened with Dad at Beckett?" Suzy asked when their new drinks arrived.

Cal opened her mouth to speak, but Violet answered in just the way Cal would have. "You were too young, Suzy. You didn't need to know any of the details. But let's not talk about all that tonight. Another time we can. Tonight, if we're going to talk about Dad, let's not go there." Cal gave her a grateful look, and Violet gave a little nod of acknowledgment, then reached for a chip. "I never realized how many friends Dad has here," Violet said with her mouth full. "Did you know?" she asked Cal.

Cal tipped her head to the side, thinking about it. Usually when she came up to visit, her father devoted the weekend to her family—playing with Maisy, cooking dinner, bringing them to Veg to show them off to the staff. They didn't socialize with anyone else. "Not really. I knew he had friends up here, but he didn't talk about any of them in particular. Except for Barry."

"You've always known he was gay?" Violet asked.

Cal shrugged. "Kind of. He never talked about it, but I knew."

Suzy shook her head. "I didn't. It didn't even occur to me. How ridiculous is that? I just figured he hadn't met the right woman."

"It's like he had this whole other life, and I knew nothing about it. I never tried." Violet was now wiping her own face discreetly. "I know I never made much of an effort, but I guess I wish he'd made more of one too. It's so silly, but I wanted him to fight for me. You know?" She directed the question to Suzy, who nodded.

Cal frowned. "What do you mean?" she asked, looking back and forth between her sisters.

Violet sighed. "You and Dad were always close. What happened during the divorce . . ." Violet waved her hand to indicate she wasn't going to elaborate on that topic. "It didn't change your relationship. You were able to stay as close to him as always." Violet took a long sip from her drink. "I wasn't close to him like you to begin with, and we got further away after that." She met Cal's eyes, trying to explain. "And I know I did that. It wasn't him; it was me." She paused, trying to gather her thoughts together to put them into words that would be understood. "But he was the parent. He should have tried harder." She shook her head in frustration. "He didn't try hard enough, and I didn't try at all. And then he stopped trying and just became resigned to the way things were between us. And I wish he'd fought harder for me." Violet looked down at the table to avoid the eyes of the other diners. "I just wish he'd fought harder."

"Me too," Suzy said softly. Cal looked at her in surprise and Suzy nodded. "I felt the same way."

The waitress came with their food. Noticing the heavy mood at the table, she placed the dishes before them and hurried away as quickly as possible.

Cal looked down at her dinner, the steam from her fajitas rising up to leave her face warm and damp. She didn't want to look at the hurt on her sisters' faces. So long had she blamed them for the pain they'd caused their father. So long had she been angry about the distance they'd created, between themselves and him, but also between the three of them. It never occurred to Cal they might have felt hurt by him or that he might be culpable in any way.

The distance between her sisters and father had grown over the years. She had seen the way it chafed at him, the way he peppered her with eager questions about Suzy's cooking career and Violet's writing.

Cal had been stingy, her anger with her sisters giving way to vague responses, single words that left so much unsaid.

Her father was never one to deal with conflict, and while she had taken this to be evidence of his kind and easy nature, she worried now it was borne out of fear. He'd chosen the quieter route through all of the difficult things in his life, the dismantling of his career, the dissolution of his marriage, the distance between him and his children. How hard had he tried? A few phone calls here and there. A visit once or twice a year, most of which he spent with Cal anyway. It was easier to be with Cal, and he hadn't pushed through the hard stuff to be with his other daughters. Suzy and Violet weren't the only ones responsible.

"I didn't know," she finally said. "I didn't realize."

"I know," Violet said. Her face was blotchy, but she'd stopped crying. She waved her hand to push the conversation aside. "All right, enough already. They're going to kick us out of here if we don't pull it together." Violet blew her nose on a napkin and then picked up her burrito, taking a big bite. She chewed silently for a moment, took another bite, and then put the burrito back down on her plate and turned to Cal. "Should we order another round?"

"Yes," Cal answered, though she knew she'd probably regret it in the morning. "Definitely, yes."

Chapter Twenty-Nine

Violet

Violet awoke the next morning with an empty sense of dread and an aching head. When she looked at the clock on the nightstand, it was after eleven and Suzy's bed was empty. When she finally made her way downstairs, Suzy and Cal were already dressed, sitting at the kitchen table and sipping coffee without talking. There was a feeling of foreboding in the air between them, a nameless anxiety of what the day would bring. A newspaper was spread on the table, but neither Suzy nor Cal was reading it. Violet pulled a large mug from the cupboard and poured herself a cup, joining her sisters at the table.

"Tired?" Cal asked, raising her eyebrows. Once Violet had pried Cal from the bed, she'd emerged stronger and clearer, nearly herself, and once again ready to be the leader. Violet was happy enough to move aside and let Cal resume her role, though it hadn't taken long for her to start grinding on Violet's nerves.

"I didn't sleep well." Violet had slept heavily the night before, but not restfully. She'd woken off and on all night, the events of the day looming before her. Though the wake wasn't for another few hours, Cal was already dressed, somber and elegant in a black suit. Suzy wore gray slacks and a black turtleneck sweater. Only Violet still wore pajamas.

She ran her hand across her face, rubbing the sleep from her eyes. "God, I don't know what was in those drinks last night. My head is pounding."

"It's called tequila," Cal said, rising from the table and pouring herself another cup of coffee. Oh, yes, Cal was back.

"I made a frittata. There's some left on the stove," Suzy offered.

"Coffee first."

"Well, you should probably get moving pretty soon," Cal said. "I want to be out of here by one."

"The wake doesn't start till two," Violet said.

"I need to stop for gas. And we need to be there early." She had already applied her makeup and done her hair.

"Fine." Violet stood up and refilled her mug, then sat back down at the table.

"Aren't you going to eat?" Cal asked.

"God, Cal, give me a minute. I just got up." Violet felt her irritation flash. Maybe they should have left Cal in bed. She was certainly more amenable.

"It's nearly noon, Vi."

"It's eleven *fifteen*, Cal." Violet sighed and took another sip of coffee before putting the nearly full mug in the sink. Standing by the stove, she cut off a sliver of frittata and shoved the whole bite into her mouth. Bacon with cheddar cheese and spinach. Suzy really was a great cook. She licked her fingers and cut off another chunk.

"Don't you want a plate?" Cal asked.

"Someone's feeling better," Violet muttered without bothering to get a plate. She ate a few more bites, then wiped her fingers on a paper towel. "Satisfied? I'll take a shower now."

Upstairs Violet took her time, partly to annoy Cal but largely because she wasn't ready for the rest of the day to start. She let the hot water run for ages, waiting for Cal to come banging on the door or for the water to turn cold, surprised when neither happened. Finally, she emerged from the bathroom, light-headed from the steam, her skin red from the heat.

In her suitcase Violet found a black skirt and an emerald-green blouse. She put on the outfit, fully expecting Cal would reprimand her for wearing too festive a shirt. She brushed out her hair and afterward spent a long time blow-drying it, then tying it into a loose braid that fell over her shoulder. She dotted on lip gloss and slid silver hoops through her ears. By the time she finished, it was nearly one. Violet turned to examine herself in the mirror. She was as ready as she was ever going to be.

Downstairs, Cal was sitting on the couch looking at her phone and Suzy was back at the table, this time reading the paper.

"You look nice," Cal said, and Violet was grateful she sounded sincere and didn't comment on the color of her shirt. She didn't think she was up for changing.

"Thanks." Violet sank into the couch beside Cal. "So what exactly do we do today?"

"We just have to stand by the casket and accept people's condolences when they come up to pay their respects to Dad." Cal pulled a compact from her purse and gently wiped her lower lid with a tissue where her mascara was slightly smudged.

"So we just stand there the whole time?" Violet asked.

"Pretty much. You might want to wear different shoes." Cal gestured at Violet's two-inch heels.

"I'll be fine. Fashion first," she trilled, looking pointedly at Cal's simple black flats. Cal ignored her. Violet's feet were already starting to ache, but she hadn't brought another pair of shoes. "God, I can't even remember the last wake I went to."

"Nana Dee's," Suzy called from the kitchen. "At least that's the last one I can remember."

Violet shivered inwardly. She remembered seeing the old woman laid out in the coffin, and she was like a caricature of herself, her gray hair fluffed into stiff curls, her makeup expertly applied by the mortician just as it had been in life. Even her unsmiling red-painted lips were only a more severe version of her everyday expression.

Nana Dee had not been the cuddly grandmother who came bearing chocolates and presents. No, that was Grandma Beth, their mother's mother. Nana Dee was an old-school grandmother. Children should be quiet and well behaved, and if they weren't, well, then you could expect a quick swat to your bottom and a sharp word that could cut you raw. If Violet dared to speak above a whisper, Nana Dee would shoot her a pointed glance that would make Violet bite her tongue and forget what she wanted to say in the first place. The amount of time they spent alone with her was minimal, but Violet was pretty sure each of her sisters had at least one memory of Nana Dee's wooden palm striking her rear end. Violet couldn't imagine growing up with a mother like Nana Dee.

Her father must have had an incredibly lonely upbringing. He was raised singly by Nana Dee after his father walked out on them, leaving him alone with no siblings. Despite their grandmother's severity, Violet and her sisters were raised to have a grudging respect for her and all she had done on her own. Her father had been devoted to her until she died when Violet was ten.

Nana Dee hosted every bleak and sparse holiday in the cramped home where she'd raised her only son. Her house was a tiny fortress of dark and quiet. The curtains were always pulled, even on a sunny afternoon, and she started using the heat in early October, so the living room was a hot, musty cave. Her house had been like a Catholic memorial, with crucifixes, embroidered psalms, and china statues of the Virgin Mary crowding every surface. Violet felt guilty every time she was in that house, for every forgotten and nameless sin she'd ever committed.

Despite her abrasive manner, their father clung to his mother into adulthood in a way he was unable to do with his own children. Every Sunday morning he brought Nana Dee to church and then back to their house for brunch. Unlike Saturday morning breakfast, Sunday morning was a stilted and disappointing meal of grapefruit juice and raisin scones from Nana Dee's favorite bakery. She was the only one who liked the scones, eating them with a thick layer of butter and jam, her weekly indulgence. Violet and her sisters picked out the raisins and left them in a sad pile on their plates.

Nana Dee, in her stiff lavender blouse, frowned imperiously at everyone, her lips pursed in distaste when Suzy spilled crumbs on her shorts. When Cal asked for more juice, Nana Dee commented on the ill effects of sugar in growing children. Their mother remained quiet for most of the meal, and by the time it was over, she was wrung out, her curly hair drooping as she feverishly washed the dishes, grateful to have survived another week.

Nana Dee's death was a slow and drawn-out affair. Like the rest of her life, she was both silent and willful in her dying, clinging to life for her final days—as pointless as they had become—as if desperate to live only to spite death.

Violet always assumed her father's loyalty to his mother was one of obligation rather than affection. When Nana Dee died, Violet was certain the rest of the family breathed the same sigh of relief that she did. Yet the sadness enveloped her father completely. At the funeral he wept openly, and Violet sat stiffly beside her sisters, both confused and embarrassed to see her father moved to tears by such an unpleasant and unknowable force.

Violet knew little of her actual grandfather, but it was Father O'Connor who helped Nana Dee during the hard years of being a single mother. As a child, Violet's father had been an altar boy in his parish, and Father O'Connor had been a regular fixture in Nana Dee's house over the years, coming over weekly for her stale macaroons and cups of watery tea. He had a full head of silver hair that glittered when it caught the light. He was a gentle man, always taking an interest in Violet and her sisters, asking what they were studying in school, which books they were reading. Even Nana Dee softened in his presence, the unfamiliar sound of her trilling laughter filling the small, dark house. When Nana Dee was dying, it was Father O'Connor who came to the hospital each day. While Violet and her sisters would skirt in and out of the room as quickly as possible, Father O'Connor sat patiently in a chair by the bed, hands clasped in his lap, as if there were nowhere else in the world he needed to be.

When the sex-abuse scandal in the Catholic Church first broke, Violet had just finished college. She was living in Boston, and the local papers were filled with the news of the scandal. Violet read the articles carefully, waiting to see Father O'Connor's name mentioned. It would make sense, wouldn't it, her father's misdeeds a result of abuse he'd suffered as a child? But she never stumbled across his name, and the list of offending priests was long. It seemed Father O'Connor was one of the good ones, a man who cared for his flock and took care of the children with the steady patience of a father.

"Let's go." Violet looked up as Cal snapped the compact shut and stood. Violet took a deep breath and followed her sisters out the door to Cal's car.

It wasn't until they pulled up to the funeral home that Violet began to grow afraid. She was the last one out of the car because she'd noticed her hands were trembling, and she couldn't seem to stop them. When she pulled down the mirror on the back of the visor, her face was ghostly white, all the blood drained from it.

"Vi?" Suzy called from the sidewalk. Cal was already halfway up the steps of the funeral home yet Violet was still sitting in the car, the door open, and one high-heeled leg on the road. "Are you okay?"

Violet shook her head, suddenly unable to speak. In minutes, she would be forced to face her father's dead body. In her mind, she knew he was dead, had known it for several days now. But this was the first time the realization had physically hit her. Seeing him painted with makeup, his hair sprayed into place, was terrifying.

Cal turned to Suzy. "Can you deal with her?" she asked, not unkindly. "I'm going to tell them we're here." Suzy nodded and Cal hurried inside. Suzy approached Violet.

"Come on," Suzy said, extending her hand to Violet.

Violet shook her head. "I can't. Not yet. I'm not ready."

"Violet, it's one thirty. People are going to be arriving soon." Suzy had dark circles under her eyes, as they all did, and Violet felt suddenly sorry to be adding one more thing to Suzy's burdens. She had enough on her plate at the moment. But Violet couldn't seem to get out of the car. It was as if her body had shut down and her legs wouldn't work.

"Go on. I'll be in soon," Violet reassured her. Suzy glanced back into the funeral home. The lights were on, and through the glass panels beside the heavy wooden door Violet saw Cal talking to a man in a black suit. Suzy turned back to Violet. "Seriously, go on. I promise, I'll be in soon." Violet smiled for Suzy's benefit, but her heart was suddenly beating incredibly fast. For a moment, she wondered if she was having a heart attack. She just needed to get her bearings. She just needed Suzy to leave her alone for a moment.

"All right," Suzy said reluctantly. "Come in soon though, okay?"

Violet nodded, trying to keep her panic from showing. Suzy hurried up the steps and Violet shut the car door behind her. Her breath was coming in shallow pants, and it occurred to her she was hyperventilating. She leaned forward and let her head hang between her knees as she'd seen done on TV and read about in books. She stayed that way for several minutes, letting the blood rush to her head as her breathing slowed down.

When Violet finally sat back up, her breathing had gone back to normal, but there was a tightness in her chest. Maybe she *was* having a heart attack. She imagined calling one of her sisters to take her to the hospital. Would they even answer their phones now? The clock on the dash read five minutes before two. She didn't know how she'd been in the car so long. There were people entering the funeral home now, three men and a woman Violet didn't recognize, all dressed in dark colors.

She could do this.

She *had* to do this.

She was surprised Suzy or Cal had not come to summon her yet, but she figured they must already be occupied with receiving condolences, like the opposite of a wedding where you received congratulations. Her father would never see her as a bride. There was no wedding to plan, and she'd never been the type to daydream about the big fluffy dress she would wear or what she would offer as favors, but the realization that he wouldn't be able to walk her down the aisle or dance with her struck her for the first time and brought on a fresh round of tears and a jellylike feeling in her legs and the pit of her stomach. She leaned her head back against the seat of the car and closed her eyes.

A knock at the window startled her. When Violet opened her eyes, the familiar yet aged face of Michael Donahue was peering in at her. He looked the same—same dark hair, same blue eyes, though his face was broader now, with the strong jaw of a man. Violet fumbled with the switch on the handle, but without the key, the electronic window wouldn't roll down. She opened the door instead, nearly knocking Michael in the face. He stepped out of the way just in time.

"Sorry," Violet apologized.

"Violet, hi." He bent into the car and gave her an awkward one-armed hug. He held one hand on the frame of the door and looked down on her as Violet struggled to get control of herself. "I'm so sorry about your dad." He looked at her more closely. "Are you okay?"

"I think I'm having a panic attack, actually." Violet attempted a smile, but her fear must have been evident because Michael frowned at her for a moment before closing her door gently and getting in the driver's side. His knees nearly touched the steering wheel, but he didn't adjust the seat, only looked at Violet with concern.

"Put your head between your legs," he ordered.

"I already did that."

"Do it again," he said, and she did. As she leaned forward to stare at the pointy black toes of her shoes, she felt his hand on her back, rubbing in smooth calming circles. "Just try to breathe normally."

Staring at her feet, the warmth of his palm on her back, Violet felt herself returning to normal, the distraction of Michael sitting so close trumping the panic. She sat back up, hoping her face wasn't beet red or her hair a tangled mess. "Sorry," she said again.

"It's okay. Do you feel a little better now?"

She nodded. "It's just the idea of seeing him in there." Violet shuddered. "His body. I don't know if I can do it." She rubbed the back of her hand across her forehead, surprised to find her face damp with perspiration.

"You can," he said. "I'll bring you in, if you'd like."

"Okay."

She let him open the door for her and help her to her feet. More people were entering the funeral home. Violet felt herself growing dizzy again, but Michael held her firmly, her elbow tucked securely in his palm, supporting her weight. Anyone watching them would have assumed he was her husband, not someone she hadn't seen since she was a teenager. Yet Violet felt stronger with him beside her, even as she knew it was Luka who should have held her up, Luka who should have stood by her side, Luka who should have calmed her when the panic threatened to consume her. And he would have, if only she had let him.

But Michael was here now, and Violet leaned into him as the overpowering smell of flowers and scented candles hit her in the entryway of the home. Violet kept her gaze down. Michael, seeming to sense her fear, held on tighter, walking her across the crowded room to where her sisters stood.

Both Cal and Suzy eyed Michael with confusion, but Violet wasn't paying attention to them. She was looking instead at the wooden coffin only a few feet away. She could see her father, his dark hair and suit, though she was still too far away to make out his features. Suzy and Cal were speaking to her, but their words didn't come through. Violet let her legs carry her closer, though she still clung to Michael, and he didn't try to push her forward to have this moment alone. He walked up with her to the coffin and stood beside her as she stared down at her father's gray face that had been painted with blush. His hands were folded across his waist in an unnatural position of rest, as if he'd just taken a nap in his fine blue suit.

Violet stared down at him, taking in the length of his inert body, taking in the details—the white satin interior of the coffin, the red handkerchief someone had tucked into his breast pocket (who, she wondered: Had Barry chosen his clothes as well?), the chain peeking out from the collar of his shirt, carrying the simple silver cross he always wore.

Her father was not here. This was not her father, this waxy shell of a man. Her father was somewhere far away, hopefully having already arrived in the heaven he'd always believed in. For the first time in her life, Violet desperately hoped all his believing had been worth something. She felt a surprising relief at having arrived at this moment and survived, followed by a dull sorrow she had missed the instant when he left.

She turned to Michael and nodded at him. "Thank you," she whispered, and he nodded back, walking her carefully over to her sisters. He passed her to Cal and Suzy, and Violet wept into the stiff fabric of Cal's dress, inhaling the faint smell of her perfume.

Violet did not cry long. When she lifted her head, she felt clean and empty, like she'd slept for a long time and woken up refreshed. She was pretty sure she was done crying. But she couldn't stay here, not for another three hours as people trouped through, wanting to share their grief. There was no way.

Cal was speaking in measured tones with a tall, thin man with a goatee, someone else Violet didn't recognize. The whole room was filled with men Violet didn't know, a few unfamiliar women mixed in as well. It was as if her father's entire life before moving to Maine had evaporated into thin air. And perhaps it had.

"I've got to get out of here," she whispered to Cal and Suzy.

Cal extricated herself from the conversation she was having. "You can't go. It's only just started."

Violet shook her head. "I'm not staying." They didn't need her anyway. Cal had risen from the dead and resumed her role as lead sister, and thank God for that, because Violet was a fraud. She couldn't stand by this coffin for the rest of the day and pretend to be a devoted daughter to the father she hardly knew. Suzy may not have been close to him, but she hadn't turned her back on him either. Maybe the story of Beckett was true, maybe it was not, but a stronger person would have stood by her father anyway. A stronger person would have let him know she still cared.

Cal let out a sigh of exasperation. Suzy stepped in. "You need to be here, Violet."

"Why? The two of you are here. You'll do better without me. I'll be fine at the funeral tomorrow, I promise. I just can't handle this whole wake thing." She gestured to the coffin without looking at it again. "I don't understand why we even needed to do it."

"Because Dad was *Catholic*," Suzy said in an uncharacteristically irritated voice. "Just because you don't get it doesn't mean it wouldn't have been important to him."

"Fine," Violet said, holding up her hands in defense. "But I'm leaving."

"I'm not driving you," Cal said.

Michael had taken a seat in a chair against the wall. He gave her a small smile when she looked over at him. "I'll find a ride," Violet said.

"Come on," Cal hissed. "Are you for real?"

"What? I'm sure he'll take me home."

"You're unbelievable," Cal whispered, ever intent on not making a scene, but she was livid, her cheeks bright with rage. "You never change."

"I don't need to explain myself to you," Violet said, then turned to Suzy. "You'll be okay?" Cal had clearly pulled herself out of whatever hole she'd fallen into. It was Suzy she was concerned about now. Suzy nodded, though she didn't say anything. "I'll see you back at the house." Violet leaned in to hug Suzy and whispered in her ear. "I'm sorry. I just can't do it."

"It's okay," Suzy whispered back, and Violet squeezed Suzy's hands before walking toward Michael.

"Can you get me out of here?" she asked.

He opened his mouth in surprise but rose quickly. "Sure." Violet followed him out of the funeral home and tried not to be ashamed by the little flutter of excitement she felt in her stomach.

Chapter Thirty

Suzy

Suzy watched Violet follow the dark-haired man out of the funeral home. She didn't recognize him, but Violet and Cal obviously knew him.

"Who is he?" she asked Cal.

"Michael Donahue. The one Violet was talking about the other day." Cal shook her head in disgust. "She should know better by now."

Suzy leaned forward to take the hand of another man and accept his condolences. She tried to focus on his words as he told her how he knew her father, as a regular at Veg, but she just nodded and mumbled, "Thank you," allowing Cal to do the work of conversing.

Though she didn't ask her to stay, Suzy had been sorry to see Violet leave. She could have used Violet's acerbic humor to get through the rest of the afternoon. Standing in her father's living room the day before, she had been reminded of the summer she stayed with him, and since then, she'd been on edge. Now she found herself scanning the thin crowd of mourners, terrified Zach would make an appearance here. It was a ridiculous fear—the likelihood that he still lived in Portland was slim and he had no connection to her father, no reason to appear at his wake. But she couldn't shake the feeling an old ghost was following her around.

On her way home from the grocery store this morning, Suzy had driven down Spruce Lane and tried to pick out the house she'd gone to that night, but the houses on the street all looked different. The neighborhood had gotten a face-lift from its dilapidated early life as a college slum, and the houses were now respectable family homes.

However, being in this town had done something to Suzy. Some shards of memory had gotten loose and were rattling around inside her, trying to take shape, to make some meaning of her story. Their sharp edges cut at tender skin Suzy had long assumed was healed over.

But what shape could the pieces ever take? What story could they tell? When she was fifteen she went to a party and something terrible happened. She never told her parents, never told the police. It wouldn't have occurred to Suzy to tell either of them. She told Cal and Violet, and at the time, she thought that was enough.

When Suzy returned to her father's house the night of Zach's party, her father was indeed lying on the couch with his drink, watching some action movie on TV.

"You're home early," he said when he saw her. He pushed himself to sitting and muted the TV. "What happened to the movie?"

"It was sold out," Suzy mumbled, grateful the only light in the living room was the flickering blue glow of the television. Certainly he would be able to see the damage done if he just looked her in the eye. But he was distracted by the special effects and swift martial arts taking place on the screen. His attention was divided. "I'm going up to bed."

"Okay. Night, honey." He unmuted the movie, and Suzy wasn't sure if she was relieved or disappointed he hadn't asked what was wrong. Not that she would have told him. As she began to climb the stairs though, he called for her.

"Suze?"

"Yeah?" She paused, her hand on the railing, her head pounding. She wanted nothing more now than to close the door and let the tears consume her. She'd managed to hold them back the whole terrible walk home for fear her father would see them and force her to tell him what was wrong. But she couldn't keep them at bay for much longer.

"Everything okay?" he asked, and he did turn to look at her, but in the dim light and from where she stood on the stairs, he couldn't see her face well. "How come you and your friend didn't go see something else?"

"Nothing else good was playing. We got an ice cream instead and decided to go home."

"Oh." He searched her face, trying to figure out if there were more questions to ask. It would have been so much easier for him if Suzy had been a boy.

"Good night," she said, as much to spare him as to escape.

"Night, honey," he said again, satisfied with her insufficient answer. Her mother never would have let it go at that, though Suzy never would have made it to the party in the first place if her mother had been here. Not that this was her father's fault. But still.

Up in her bedroom, Suzy sobbed into the pillow so her father wouldn't hear her. Then she started thinking about the next two weeks of the summer that loomed ahead. She couldn't go back to the pool, obviously. But what if she saw Zach somewhere else, in town or at the grocery store? What if she was out with her father when she saw him? Zach would probably say hello as if nothing had happened, and Suzy would have to explain to her father who he was.

She thought of calling Cal, but she knew her older sister would be full of judgment. *Why were you at the party in the first place? Why did you tell him you were older? How much did you have to drink?* Cal would pepper Suzy with questions that would make her feel more ashamed than she already did.

So she called Violet, Violet who had done her share of rule breaking and wouldn't fault her for anything. Suzy hardly remembered what she said on the phone to Violet. "I went to a party. Something happened," she'd murmured tearfully into the phone. Somehow Violet had asked the right questions and deduced the rest.

They were there the next morning to bring her home, landing on their father's doorstep just as Suzy emerged downstairs from a fretful night's sleep. They were Suzy's white knights, coming to rescue her.

"Suzy needs to come home with us," Violet told their father. Her long red hair was pulled back into a ponytail and she looked fresh-faced and confident. Cal stood beside her, dark-haired and serious. Their father looked from Violet to Cal, who nodded.

"Why?" He shook his head in confusion, turning to Suzy. "What's wrong?" If he noticed the puffiness of her face or her bloodshot eyes, he didn't remark on it.

"Nothing," Suzy said softly, though she wasn't sure anyone heard her.

"She needs to come home," Violet said again.

"But I thought you were having a nice time here," her father said. Suzy hated the look of hurt on his face. It only thickened her guilt. "Did something happen?"

Her eyes filled then and Cal stepped in. "Dad, it's a girl thing, okay?" she said gently. *A girl thing*, a coded excuse for everything from a menstrual cycle to this, but it was enough to make him back off and allow them to help Suzy pack.

In the car on the way home, Cal was furious. "We should be going to the police. There's a good chance he could go to jail. It's a *crime*, Suzy; he shouldn't be let off the hook like this." *It* was a crime. No one ever defined *it* aloud.

But Suzy had shaken her head. *No, no, no.* There was no need for anyone to know about *it*, not either of their parents, certainly not the police. Suzy just needed to go home. Homesickness, Cal and Violet explained to their mother. A bad case of homesickness. But Suzy was home now, so everything would be okay.

"I'm so sorry for your loss," an elderly woman said to her now, clutching Suzy's hand. The overpowering scent of mothballs hovered around the woman, and Suzy had to swallow hard so as not to gag. Suzy thanked her and tried to smile. Had her father ever thought about what might have happened to her that summer? What this terrible girl thing was that would require her older sisters to drive three hours north to bring her home? Or had he let the indomitable force of womanhood overshadow his own responsibility?

"Your father was a wonderful man," the old woman added. Was it true? Was he a wonderful man? This new story of his firing from Beckett had made her question that as well. If the accusations were true, what kind of a person did that make her father? A person who took what he wanted at the expense of others? A person like Zach?

She would have to believe Cal's version, whatever that was. The idea of anything else made her sick to her stomach.

Chapter Thirty-One

Cal

It was typical of Violet to leave and let Cal handle everything. For a moment the previous day, when Violet forced her out of bed and acted like the grown-up someone needed to be, Cal thought maybe her sister had changed. Maybe Violet *was* capable of thinking about people other than herself, of acting her age, of not being totally and utterly selfish. But no. It had just been a rare moment when she was forced to rise to the occasion, but now that Cal was upright, Violet was allowed to slide back into her role of perpetual child.

It was bad enough Violet had left the wake. But to leave with Michael Donahue? That was just the icing on the cake.

Michael had been in Cal's class at Beckett. Like many of the girls in their class, Cal had an enormous crush on him, but Michael had been taken since the beginning of their junior year when he started going out with Bitty. That didn't stop Cal from having a crush; it just stopped her from doing anything about it. Not that she likely would have even if he'd been single—Cal's confidence had always wavered when it came to boys. She could make a presentation to the entire senior class without batting an eye, but working up the nerve to call a boy on the phone? That was another matter entirely.

Since Violet had started at Beckett two years earlier, Cal had watched boys fall under her spell. And not just the boys in Violet's class. Not just the stoners and artsy guys Cal didn't care about. Smart boys, athletes, boys in Cal's class—they too were drawn to Violet. Cal watched them stare at her sister's overlarge breasts and red hair as Violet sashayed through the halls of Beckett. Cal hated Violet for the way she captivated these boys, the way she preyed on their desire for what she was willing to offer. There was a word for girls like Violet, and it wasn't a very nice one.

Cal and Michael ran in the same circle of the academic elite whose schedules were packed with extracurriculars as they were bound for the Ivy Leagues. They were on the yearbook committee together, and they'd spent many late afternoons sitting shoulder to shoulder in front of the computer screen. There had been a tiny part of Cal that hoped maybe, just maybe, he might like her too.

But then Cal came home early one afternoon and found Violet and Michael bent over a math book, though even then Violet could barely keep her eyes on the page. Their father should have known better than to hire a tutor like Michael for Violet.

Cal hoped Michael would be above Violet's charms, especially considering he already had a girlfriend. But the next time Cal came home early on a day Michael was over tutoring, she found the kitchen table empty and Violet's bedroom door closed. The muffled sounds coming from inside the bedroom told her all she needed to know, and Cal gathered her books and headed to the library for the remainder of the afternoon.

She'd been tempted to tell Bitty. They weren't close friends, but they were friendly. Bitty was sweet and bland, smart enough but not particularly intellectual. Even so, it didn't seem right that Michael was cheating on her. Yet as jealous as Cal was, she couldn't bring herself to betray Violet.

Then Cal realized she wasn't the only one who knew. One afternoon between periods, she saw Violet pass Michael in the hall. Michael barely acknowledged Violet, just nodded at her with his chin. Then he turned to leer at her with a cluster of guys by his locker once she'd passed. Cal seethed silently, unsure who she was angrier at, Violet or Michael. She continued to eat lunch with Bitty and Michael and the others in their crowd, pretending she had no idea what was going on. She wavered between feeling bad for Bitty and then worse for Violet when Michael splayed his hand across Bitty's knee and ignored Violet eating with a few sophomores on the other side of the quad.

During his time at Beckett, Cal's father had been beloved, but as Cal stood by his coffin, it was clear her father's life as a teacher was far behind him now and had been for some time. Michael was the only one from Beckett that Cal recognized at the wake. She wondered if Violet would be home when they got back, but she doubted it. Violet still used sex for everything—as a weapon, a pastime, an icebreaker, an escape. Surely this would be her way to grieve as well.

The room was stuffy, filled with the quiet tones of respectable conversation. Cal's feet hurt in her flats and she wished she had worn a watch. It had to be close to four by now. Looking around, Cal noticed nearly all the mourners were men. There were a few women, but the majority was men her father's age or a few years younger, trim and handsome in nicely cut slacks and dress shirts. Barry was at the center of a group of them, standing a head above the rest, though his shoulders were bowed and his head bent to talk. The group seemed to know each other well, and Cal was wondering if they might be coworkers from Veg when she noticed they were standing closer to each other than most men would be comfortable with. The backs of their hands brushed, their shoulders nearly touched, and they comforted each other with hands on forearms or at the small of their backs.

They were gay, Cal realized. She wasn't sure why this surprised her, since she'd long suspected her father and Barry of being involved in a relationship. What was more surprising was to find that her father had a community of other men up here, friends who knew who he was and accepted him, despite his inability to admit the truth to Cal.

Chapter Thirty-Two

Violet

"After you." Michael held open the door to the hotel bar. Violet had already glanced at his finger to see if he wore a ring. He did, a simple silver band on his strong clean hands. She told herself the ring meant nothing. They were just two old friends having a drink. (*Old friends?* a voice in Violet's head chanted. *Was Michael ever really a friend to you?*) She pushed the voice away and focused instead on his broad shoulders in the blue blazer, the way his hair still curled around his ears.

There had been no question about going back to the cottage. Violet wasn't going to sit around there for the next few hours while she waited for her sisters to return. So they were coming here for a drink. *Just a drink,* Violet said to herself, even while she knew it was a lie.

She couldn't help it—even now, she was attracted to him. They'd done the small talk thing in the car, and she learned he lived in a suburb of Boston and worked in finance. He hadn't mentioned the blond woman or the children she'd seen in his Facebook photo.

Though it was still late afternoon, the sky was slipping to dusk, and Violet was grateful for the cover of darkness and the dim glow of the lights in the bar. It would have been harder to do this in the bright light of day. She followed Michael to a small table in the corner and ordered a glass of white wine, not needing a repeat of last night's hard alcohol. Michael ordered a beer and when their drinks arrived, he raised his glass to her.

"To your dad," he said. Violet clinked her glass against his.

"It was good of you to come."

"I'm glad I could. Your dad was a good man. I tracked him down a few years ago on Facebook, and we've stayed in touch. Mostly just occasional e-mails and that kind of thing." Violet was surprised to hear this, but she didn't want to think about her father. That was why she left the funeral in the first place.

Michael glanced at his phone, fingers flicking the screen like a nervous tic, his attention fractured. Luka had never been like that. When she spoke to Luka, his eyes held hers like he really cared what she was saying.

"You expecting a call?" Violet asked.

"What?" Michael looked up with a sheepish grin. "No, sorry." He tucked the phone into the pocket of his coat.

"Is your wife here?" Violet was flooded with a moment of embarrassment. It was possible she'd come to Maine with him, a quick romantic getaway, and Violet was making a fool of herself down here with this little flirtation.

"No," he said in surprise. "I mean, we're separated." He fingered the silver band instinctively with his thumb. "Liz and I, we've tried, but I'm not sure it's going to work." His face clouded.

"Oh. Sorry." *Not really*, Violet thought. She was ready to get this part over with. The explanation, the guilt, the small talk. Violet already knew she wasn't here just for a drink, no matter what they were both telling themselves. She was ready to be upstairs in his room, taking off their clothes. That was always the best part. During was fun. After was awkward. And *after* after was just a jumbled mix of regret and justification. But before, when the clothes were still on but barely, when the heat between them crackled, the expectation ripe, that was the best part.

There was a power that came with sex. Violet discovered this at a young age, even before Michael, though he was the first she went all the way with. Since that distant first there had been many others. Relationships, short and long, and a slightly larger handful of one-night stands than she was proud of. Yet when she and Luka were together, she'd been faithful. She hadn't even thought about cheating. She didn't miss the thrill of the new, the intensity that was always more powerful at the beginning. She'd fallen into the easy rhythm of monogamy with an unexpected feeling of relief and gratitude.

But now that Luka had made it clear he was done with her, she was ready for the buzz of new sex and the thrill of seeing the power she could wield, even if only for a short time.

"It's okay," Michael said. "The hardest part is how it affects the kids."

Violet nodded in what she hoped was a sympathetic way, but really she didn't need to hear about the drama of his kids or his separation from his wife. That's not why she was here. She didn't think it was why he was here either, but now she wondered if maybe she'd misread things. Maybe he really had only come to pay condolences to her father.

"Kate's eight and Sam is five," he added, though Violet hadn't asked. She drained the end of her wine and signaled to the waitress for another round. Maybe another drink would loosen him up and get him to focus on her instead of his messed-up marriage. She let him go on for a few minutes about adorable Kate and headstrong Sam.

Violet wasn't entirely sure how she felt about Michael now. Part of her was still angry with him for the way he'd treated her as a teenager—having her as his dirty little secret on the side and then dropping her before things could get out of hand. Part of her had always hated him for the way he made her hate herself, even while she knew she would have taken up with him again if only he'd wanted to. But she was not the same easily hurt teenage girl she was then. She was stronger. *She* was in control now, and she would show him. But this grown-up version of Michael, with his obvious sensitive-dad persona and the gentle way he'd cared for her in the funeral home, was in contrast to the Michael she'd hoped to seduce.

Michael continued blathering on about weekend visits with the kids and how Liz thought he worked too much to have joint custody. Violet nodded sympathetically, even asked a few questions. *Let him get it out of his system now,* she thought. He'd feel less guilty later that he'd been up-front with her.

"Do you have kids?" he asked finally.

"No." Violet didn't elaborate or tell him her own sob story of Luka and her current state of couch living. She crossed her legs, let him see the slender cut of her calf in black stockings, her heel dangling from her foot. "Do you want to go up to your room?" she asked, determined to get things moving.

"Oh." Michael looked surprised, taken aback by her forwardness. "Um, I'm not sure. I mean, you were so upset earlier . . ."

"I'm fine now," she said, and she was. He was the perfect antidote to the panic and grief that had overtaken her in the car. "Isn't that why you're here?" She leaned closer across the table. In the car she'd undone the first few buttons of her blouse, and she knew he had a perfect view of her cleavage and the scalloped rim of her lacy black bra.

"Uh, well." He looked nervous. For a moment she doubted herself. But no. She wasn't willing to back off yet. She placed her hand on his knee under the table and slowly let it slide up the inside of his leg. She wasn't usually this forward, but she needed something to take the edge off the afternoon, the week, the past few months. Michael's face tightened, and he let out a quick exhale.

"Do you want to go up to your room?" she asked again. When she rubbed him through the expensive fabric of his pants, she felt his hardness. It hadn't taken him long to forget all about Liz and his kids after all. Violet felt a little drunk, though she suspected it was from Michael's easy arousal more than the wine.

"Okay," he said breathlessly. His eyes had gone glassy, and she took him by the hand and let him lead her upstairs. She was glad it was a large hotel, not a small B&B where the rooms were done up to look like a fancy version of your own home. They needed the anonymity of a standard hotel room. He unlocked the door and she followed him inside.

"Violet," he said, turning to her, but she shushed him and pulled him by the belt. His kiss tasted as she remembered it, of fresh-cut grass and some other indescribable flavor, though she could also taste the beer in a not unpleasant way. She helped him out of his jacket and unbuttoned his shirt, pulling the tucked-in tails out of the waist of his pants. He no longer had the body of a high school swimmer, the flat stomach and chiseled shoulders giving way to a slight softness over the years, but he was a man now in a way he had not been then. Violet unbuttoned her own blouse and let him cup her breasts in her bra, grateful they were as nice now as then, unsullied by breast-feeding or pregnancy. Unlike Liz's, she assumed.

Violet closed her eyes and sighed into the warm contours of his neck. This was the part she lived for, the place she craved, his hands exploring, his mouth at her throat, her chest, her stomach, her mind finally giving over to the needs of her body, blocking out thought and criticism and pain. *This* was what she needed.

Chapter Thirty-Three

Suzy

In the car on the way home, Suzy held the box with the photos that were displayed for the wake. She asked Cal what surely everyone else at the wake already knew. "Were all those men gay?"

Cal kept her eyes on the road.

"Does that mean . . ." Suzy trailed off, unsure how to finish the sentence. "Dad was out? Everyone else knew?"

"I guess." Cal looked wiped out. The corners of her eyes were inky with mascara and her skin was pale, but she'd stayed steady and strong for the whole wake.

"We'll have to talk more with Barry," Suzy said.

Cal nodded, and they drove the rest of the way in silence.

They stopped for dinner on the way home, a quick, quiet meal, and by the time they got back to the cottage, it was close to eight. There was no sign of Violet, which Cal pointed out quickly with a huff. Suzy went upstairs to take a shower, not in the mood to listen to Cal's judgment. It had been a long night and Suzy was tired. She was exasperated by Violet as well—it's not as if the wake had been easy for her or Cal either. Suzy just wasn't in the mood to bad-mouth Violet over it.

In the shower, Suzy soaped her skin and washed her hair, trying to rid herself of the cloying scent of flowers. She let her fingers roam along the curves of her waist. She was still the same size, small and slightly square in an athletic way. However, within weeks she knew her small breasts would balloon up, for the first time in her life, if she let nature take its course. Even now they were tender, like an exaggerated version of PMS.

The clock was ticking. She needed to make a decision soon, one way or the other, though maybe Cal was right that this was not the week to do it. Suzy had told her father tonight, as she stood above his coffin. Not aloud, but in her mind she had whispered to him. *I'm pregnant, Dad. I just wanted to tell you.* This simple declaration didn't have to mean anything—her father was dead after all. But Suzy knew that had he been alive, she never would have told him unless she planned on keeping it. It didn't seem fair to tell him now when his spirit hovered wherever, unless she was going to see it through.

Suzy stood under the scalding water, not yet ready to emerge from the steamy haven of the bathroom. Assuming her father was gay, which had become clear over the past few days, it was sad he'd never trusted any of them with this deeply personal piece of information. She wondered if he thought they would judge him or be angry for some reason. Suzy had never told him about Lani for much the same reason, though in her own case it had to do with her father's ambiguous brand of Catholicism. It was sometimes difficult to know which church sins he could let slide and which were unforgivable.

Ironically, her father had always been a stickler for lying. In their house, lying was a sin, though even he didn't use that word. But if one of them did dare lie (usually Violet), there would be consequences. The same for taking the Lord's name in vain, another rule he was strict about. But he was obviously willing to let go of the sin of birth control, as evidenced by the diaphragm Suzy once discovered in her mother's bedside table. Though he'd never outwardly projected hate toward anyone, she hadn't been sure of his stance on homosexuality or gay marriage. Suzy would have told him about Lani eventually, but then they broke up, and there didn't seem to be any reason to make him ponder if she was going to hell.

She stepped from the shower and wrapped herself in a towel. She was sorry now she hadn't told him. Perhaps it would have forced a conversation he'd wanted to have all along but hadn't known how to begin.

Chapter Thirty-Four
Cal

Now that Cal had finally gotten out of bed, she was beginning to feel like herself again. She'd finally plugged in her laptop and sat on the couch going through e-mails from work. Already her fingers were itching to get started on the things that would need to be done up here—cleaning out their father's house, going through his things, figuring out the division of the estate. As his lawyer, she knew the house in Portland would be passed along to the three of them, though what they would ultimately decide to do with it, she had no idea. The three of them were now part owners of Veg, though how they would manage that she wasn't sure. They'd probably end up selling to Barry, if he could afford to buy them out. She didn't care about the house or the restaurant and wasn't worried about whatever money he'd left to her, but careful planning and organization had always been Cal's way of dealing with the chaos of life, trying to gain some control over it.

Cal had always been focused on success. As a young child this meant participating in a ridiculous number of activities—swimming, gymnastics, violin lessons, dance class. As she got older it meant attaining As in every class while still keeping up her outside activities. Then the goal was to get into Yale, to do well there, eventually to get into law school and graduate at the top of her class. For the last several years the goal had been to make partner. Only lately, it was a goal she wasn't sure she actually wanted to achieve. But it seemed easier to keep pursuing it than to figure out what came next.

When her parents first split up, Cal was a sophomore in college, and while this cocooned her from much of what Violet and Suzy had to deal with, it also left her feeling out of control. She handled this by throwing herself into her studies and taking care of her father. Despite huge amounts of homework and the lure of weekends on campus, Cal traveled from New Haven to Boston nearly every other Sunday to visit her father. He lost twenty pounds that year, his face sinking against the bones of his skull, his broad shoulders collapsing like a crooked scarecrow. He barely ate, living off cereal and peanuts, his days and nights spent watching television in the dingy two-bedroom apartment he'd rented in Watertown.

Despite her meager college income, she'd go by with groceries. She'd bring fruit and vegetables, bagels and cream cheese, and fresh-ground coffee. Her father always greeted her warmly, his gray face flushing with pink as he enveloped her in an embrace. In the stale apartment, he'd quickly clear the dishes and peanut shells, picking up crumpled wrappers and piles of newspapers from the floor. She wondered if the place looked like this when Violet and Suzy came by or if he invented excuses to keep them out of the apartment.

Cal would stay for several hours, telling him about her classes, analyzing a professor's style or outlining a particularly interesting lecture. He would brew them coffee and listen, stopping to interject or ask a question, pushing her to think more deeply about the topic at hand. When Cal talked about school, he was the same father she'd always respected and admired, the same brilliant man who had made her who she was today. Cal always left inspired by her father and furious with her family for abandoning him.

His defeat was visible in the apartment's squalor and his ravaged appearance, and Cal was certain these were her father's darkest moments, the purgatory between life with their family and his new life in Maine. At the time, she'd assumed his dramatic decline was due to the swift dismantling of his career and the way everyone but Cal had turned their backs on him. In recent years, she'd come to suspect her father was wrestling with deeper secrets than any of them had ever realized.

Chapter Thirty-Five

Violet

Violet sighed and rolled over in the massive hotel bed. The sheets were starchy, and the duvet was a synthetic gold spread she didn't want touching her skin, but Michael's arms were warm and solid, and she liked the familiar warmth she found in the open space between his chest and arm. Familiar, not because she remembered this from the last time they were together, but because this was the place in a man she loved the most.

"That was nice," Michael said.

"Hmm," she sighed.

"I really wasn't expecting that though."

"Me neither." Violet smiled into the heat of his skin.

"I don't want you to think that's the reason I came up here." Michael pulled her closer so she could see his eyes. "Not that this wasn't great. But I came to pay my respects to your dad."

"I know." They were quiet for a moment, and Violet wondered if it might be possible to spend the night. She didn't feel like going back to see her sisters, but it couldn't be much past nine. It would be hard to justify a sleepover.

"I always felt bad about the way things went down with him." Michael interrupted her thoughts. Violet didn't feel like talking about her father. She'd rather raid the minibar and watch crappy TV and then fool around again in a few hours. She pulled the covers up higher, though the heater in the room was humming and the room was nicely warm. "I just never expected it to happen the way it did. None of us did. I always felt bad about my part in it," Michael continued. "It's why I tracked him down a few years ago."

Violet shifted in the bed so she could see his face. She forced herself to focus on his words. "About what? What are you talking about?"

Something flickered across his face. "Forget it. Nothing." Michael sat up and climbed out of bed, wrapping a towel around his waist. "I'm going to take a shower."

She pushed herself up in bed. "No, wait. You feel bad about your part in what?"

He was quiet for a moment, likely trying to figure out how to get out of the conversation. When he couldn't, he finally spoke. "Those accusations against your dad."

"What about them?" His cheeks were flushed, and he avoided her eyes.

Michael tipped his head to the side, his face in an unfamiliarly embarrassed expression. "They were made up."

"What do you mean?" She felt her body grow still. Even her heart seemed to hold steady.

He looked down at the ground. "None of it was true. Some guys from the team made it up." Violet felt her body grow cold. There was a ringing sound in her ears.

"Why?" Her voice was just above a whisper.

"They wanted to get rid of him. They didn't want him to coach anymore." Michael reached for Violet's hand, but she pulled it away and sat up in bed, wrapping the sheet tightly around her.

"You told them about what I told you. With Mr. Louis."

He nodded. "I didn't care—not really. None of the older guys did— he was a great coach. I was graduating. It wasn't going to affect me if he kept coaching or not. But the younger guys—they were looking at the next two or three years with him. They made up those things they said he did." He scratched his head, ran a hand along the stubble on his chin. "I don't think they realized what would happen. They figured the administration would just tell him he couldn't coach, but it took on a life of its own. No one really thought they'd fire him."

Tears sprang to her eyes. "I can't believe this," she whispered. Violet lay there silently, taking in Michael's words, putting together the pieces of the story. She thought about the group of boys walking past her that hot afternoon in the parking lot—Jason Brickman's vulgar words—how she'd taken the reaction of the other three boys as the shame of their vulnerability, not as their own guilt. The white wine she'd had in the hotel bar was at the back of her throat, sour and sharp. "How could you have let that happen? You knew it wasn't true. Why didn't you stand up for him?"

"I don't know," he said sincerely. "I was young and stupid. I didn't realize what would happen till it was too late."

Violet sat up in bed and shook her head, suddenly filled with rage. "Young and stupid? That's your excuse? They made him out to be some sick pervert." Her head was spinning in a million directions. "You destroyed his career. My parents split up when he lost his job. And I believed it!"

"I'm sorry, Violet. I'm really sorry." His face was pale, his eyes wide. "I felt terrible about it for years. It's why I reached out to him. To apologize." He blinked, and Violet saw his eyes were damp with tears. He really did feel bad, not that his remorse was worth anything at this point. Michael tried to explain. "It wasn't my intention to destroy his life. It was another time—we were teenage boys suddenly finding out that our coach was gay. We spent the majority of our time with him practically naked. He walked through the locker room while we were showering. I'm not saying he intended anything sexually, but we suddenly felt exposed. Like we'd been tricked." Michael ran his hands through his hair.

"So what was *this*?" She swept her hand across the room. "Your way of saying sorry for ruining my dad's life?"

"I didn't expect for this to happen. I didn't have a plan when I came up here," he said defensively.

She got out of bed and began to find her clothes in a pile by the floor. She pulled them on quickly, not wanting to be naked in his presence for a moment longer. Even as she got dressed, she was reminded of just a few mornings earlier with Luka, another argument after sex, another angry leaving. How did she find herself here so often?

"God, you haven't changed at all," she said to him, angrily zipping up her skirt. She needed to get out of here before she fell apart in front of him. He didn't answer, and she continued. "Forget the whole good-dad routine. You're still the same selfish prick you were in high school."

"Violet," he said, reaching for her.

"Fuck you," she snapped, picking her purse up off the floor. She slammed the door behind her, leaving him standing bewildered in his towel. She stood shaking in the hotel hallway, shoving her feet into the uncomfortable heels. It wasn't true what she'd said to him; Michael wasn't the same as he was in high school. It turned out *she* was the one who hadn't changed much.

Chapter Thirty-Six

Suzy

Suzy was sitting on the couch with Cal watching a home-improvement show on TV when Violet got in. She entered in a surprisingly quiet and restrained way—no big pronouncements or huffy sighs. Instead, Violet went straight into the kitchen with barely a hello and poured herself a glass of water. She faced the sink while she drank it down in one long swallow, as if composing herself to face them.

"We weren't sure if you were coming home." Cal was always ready to pounce on Violet.

"Well, I did," Violet muttered into her water glass.

"Nice of you to make an appearance," Cal said.

"Give her a break, Cal," Suzy said softly.

"A break? Oh, you mean like the break she got during the four-hour wake? It's not like either of us wanted to be there either. But we did it anyway."

Suzy was tempted to point out that they'd given Cal a break for the past several days, and how Cal nearly missed the wake. But she didn't.

"That's because you're perfect, Cal. No one can match you," Violet snapped. When she finally turned around, her eyes were red and swollen.

"Are you okay?" Suzy got up from the couch and went into the kitchen, putting her arm around Violet. For once Cal kept her mouth shut.

"I'm fine," Violet said, pulling away from Suzy. "I'm going to bed."

"What happened?" Cal asked.

Violet shook her head. "Nothing."

"Where have you been?" Cal asked, her voice gentler.

"Where do you think?" Violet said, though her voice lacked venom. "You already know the answer. Does hearing me say it just make you feel better about yourself?"

"Did something bad happen?" Suzy feared for Violet. She liked to think she was in control of sex, but Suzy knew just how quickly a person could lose their grip on a situation.

"No," Violet said, instantly knowing what Suzy was referring to. She opened the fridge and then closed it, crossed to the pantry and pulled out the box of crackers and a jar of peanut butter. She had the top off and the knife out before Cal noticed and sprang up from the couch.

"What are you doing?" she asked in panic.

"Um, eating?" Violet looked at Cal like she was crazy.

"Get that out of here. That can't be in the house. Why is that here?" Suzy had forgotten all about the peanut butter she'd absently bought their first morning here when she walked through the grocery store in a fog. Cal scooped the jar up from the counter and threw it into the trash, then proceeded to pull the trash bag from the bin.

"What the hell, Cal? What is wrong with you?" Violet asked incredulously.

"What's wrong with me? What's wrong with *you*? Maisy's going to be here tomorrow."

"Sorry," Suzy said. She'd forgotten all about Maisy's allergy in her hazy trip to the grocery store. "I'm really sorry, Cal. I forgot." Cal waved away the apology with her hand and then lugged the trash bag outside.

Violet turned to Suzy. "What the hell was that?"

"Maisy's allergic to peanut butter. You *know* that." Suzy got out a bottle of disinfectant and started to spray down the counter, though

Violet hadn't even eaten any of the peanut butter. Violet sighed in exasperation and gestured to the kitchen.

"Yeah, I know, but Maisy's not even here. She's in another *state*."

"It's a bad allergy," Suzy said, spraying another round of disinfectant on the counter. Cal came in and closed the door behind her. She washed her hands methodically at the kitchen sink.

"Sorry," Violet said, though she didn't sound all that sorry.

"You do realize that could kill her?" Cal asked, hands on her hips.

"Okay, I get it," Violet sighed. "A nice way to top off an already shitty night."

"Right," Cal said, calm restored now that the poison had been removed from the kitchen. "Because Suzy and I had a great night too."

"I'm sorry, okay?" she said again. This time she sounded more sincere, though Suzy wasn't sure if she was apologizing for abandoning them at the wake or for the peanut butter, or just for being herself. "Do we have anything else to eat?"

"There's some lasagna in there," Suzy offered. Violet pulled the casserole dish from the fridge and put it on the counter. She found a fork and began to eat straight from the tray.

"Do you ever use plates?" Cal asked, but she was smiling.

"It's good. Grab a fork," Violet said with her mouth full.

Suzy took a bite. It *was* good, another offering brought over by Barry from Veg's kitchen. She handed Cal a fork. "Should we heat it up or something?"

Violet shook her head. "Nah. It tastes good cold." The three of them picked at the dinner for a few minutes of companionable silence, their heads bent over the dish. Cal finally broke the quiet.

"So what happened? Where have you been?"

Violet swallowed and sighed. "I went back to Michael's hotel."

"Did you sleep with him?"

"Yes, all right? I slept with him." Violet sounded more tired than angry.

"God, Violet, isn't he married? He has kids. That's never going to end well," Cal said.

"He's separated, okay? And it already ended." Violet sat down beside Cal at the counter, and Suzy joined them. "It's not as if I was planning on marrying the guy. It was obviously a one-night stand."

"Oh, obviously," Cal said with a roll of her eyes. Sometimes Suzy wondered if Violet and Cal were capable of speaking to each other without sarcasm.

"Enough already. That's not even what I'm upset about."

"Then what?" Suzy asked.

"I don't even know where to start."

"What? Just tell us," Cal said.

"He told me something about Dad."

"What about him?" Suzy asked.

Violet looked at Cal when she answered. "About him getting fired."

Since the conversation about their father's termination from Beckett, Suzy had wanted to ask more questions, to learn the complicated truth of that difficult time in their lives, but she sensed the tension the topic created between Violet and Cal, who had a tenuous relationship under the best of circumstances. She had tried to broach the subject earlier over dinner, but Cal just waved Suzy's questions away with her fork, closing her eyes and pressing her fingers against her temple. Suzy understood they didn't want to unearth these skeletons right now, but she felt hurt to have been kept in the dark for so many years.

Violet's eyes welled up suddenly, and she pressed her palms to her face as if to push the tears back where they'd come from. "It's my fault," she murmured.

"What's your fault?" Cal asked.

Violet shook her head, her hands still clasped to her face. "Dad getting fired. And then everything else. Him and Mom splitting up. It was all my fault."

"Violet, what are you talking about?" Cal said impatiently. "Start from the beginning."

Violet took a deep breath and dropped her hands to the counter. "The accusations against Dad? Michael started those rumors. They didn't want Dad to be their coach anymore, so they made those things up. The idiots thought he just wouldn't coach anymore. They didn't realize he'd get fired." She shook her head in anger. "God, he could have gone to jail. If it happened today, there would be a trial."

"But why is that your fault?" Suzy asked, trying to make sense of the pieces of the puzzle Violet had presented. Violet chewed on her fingernail, not making eye contact with either of them.

"I told you I saw Dad with another teacher. Mr. Louis, a man." Violet swallowed. "I was confused. I told Michael. And he kind of freaked out." She shook her head in frustration. "I was stupid. I didn't think he'd say anything to anyone. And then Dad got fired. And then he and Mom split up, probably because of those accusations. It's all my fault." She buried her head in her hands.

Suzy turned to Cal, waiting to see her attack Violet like a cat waiting for its prey. But when Cal spoke, her voice was calm and measured. "What those boys did was terrible, but he didn't fight it. Not really. If he'd fought harder, he might not have lost his job."

"You're just saying that to make me feel better." Violet wiped her nose with a napkin.

Cal let out a huff of annoyance. "When do I ever say anything just to make you feel better?" Violet met Cal's eyes and then let out a laugh. Cal looked surprised, trying to figure out whether to be irritated. After a moment she started laughing as well, prompting Violet's laughs to reach a pitch of hysteria that caused Cal's giggles to grow. They hunched over, clutching their stomachs, their laughter the first bright sound in the house since they'd arrived. Suzy looked back and forth between her sisters and smiled.

Chapter Thirty-Seven

Cal

Cal buttered a slice of toast and sat down at the kitchen counter. Though Maisy wasn't around to announce in the middle of the night that she needed to use the bathroom, and Sadie wasn't here in need of nursing, Cal's internal clock had gone off all night, waking her nearly every hour. She'd arisen at five to brew coffee and wait for her mother, who had landed safely and was on her way. It was now close to seven, and Suzy and Violet would likely wake soon to make it to the church by ten. Then again, maybe not. It was entirely possible Violet would roll out of bed at nine thirty, even on the morning of her father's funeral.

Outside a car door slammed, and there was the sound of something being dragged along the sidewalk. Cal pulled her heavy wool cardigan more tightly about her and walked to the window to see who it was.

A taxicab idled off the sidewalk, and struggling up the walkway with a heavy suitcase was Cal's mother. She wore a long purple velvet coat that looked entirely impractical for the weather, and her legs were bare beneath. She tottered up the path in chunky red high heels, and her frizzy auburn hair looked even wilder than usual. Cal took a deep, fortifying breath before opening the front door. Outside, the sky was just lightening, the air icy and bitter.

"Callie!" her mother cried.

"Hi, Mom."

"Baby." Her mother arrived at the front door and grasped Cal in a tight embrace. She smelled like always, a comforting blend of rose water and lilacs, and Cal leaned into her mother's arms, surprised by the sudden comfort they brought. "Oh, honey, I'm so sorry. How are you? How are your sisters?"

"We're okay." Cal straightened up. "How was your flight?" She pulled her mother's suitcase up the steps and into the house, shutting the door behind them.

"Crowded. The airport was a zoo after all of the canceled flights." Her mother stripped off her coat and threw it over the back of the couch, glancing around the house. "This place is nice."

"Where's Walter?" Walter worked as a sociology professor at BU and had helped Violet attain her position in the creative writing department. He was kind and good to their mother, even if Cal sometimes felt she and her sisters were a subject of research. One of his areas of interest was birth order.

"Oh, he sends his condolences to everyone. He felt it would be better for me to come on my own." She pointed to Cal's mug. "Is that coffee? I'm dying for a cup."

"Sure." Cal gestured toward the kitchen and her mother followed.

"Where are your sisters?"

"Still sleeping."

"What time is the funeral?" she asked with a frown.

"Ten. Though we should be there earlier."

Cal's mother pursed her lips in disapproval. "Go wake them up. I'll make eggs."

Cal felt a little lighter as she climbed the stairs, relieved to have someone else to share the burden of the day with. Not that she couldn't share it with Suzy and Violet too, but now that Cal had finally been resurrected from bed, it was clear they were turning all of her original responsibilities back over to her. While their mother was flighty and eccentric, she was surprisingly dependable. With her here, Cal would survive the day.

She stuck her head into the bedroom Suzy and Violet were sharing, just as they had as children. Both of them were still fast asleep, the curtains pulled down to keep the bedroom dark as a cave. "Wake up. Mom's here," she announced and then waited only long enough to see them each open their eyes and register her words. When she returned downstairs, the kitchen smelled of toast, and her mother was scrambling eggs in a bowl. Cal sat down at the counter and watched her mother find her way around the unfamiliar kitchen with ease. By the time she gave the eggs a final stir in the pan, Suzy and Violet had blearily wandered into the room.

"Hi, Mom," they said, going to give her a hug.

"Oh, my girls. My poor, poor babies." She turned off the burner and held her arms around them both. Cal watched Violet and Suzy experience the same physical reaction to their mother's presence as she had—a loosening, a relaxing, a relief that she was finally here, though none of them had even realized how much they needed her presence.

Sometimes Cal wondered how her parents had ever lasted together for as long as they did. Even when they were together, they were always remarkably different. In fact, her father had become more like her mother in temperament and interests after the divorce. When they were younger, before her father's yoga or vegetarianism, it was Cal's mother who was always trying out some fad diet or health-food kick—juicing or veganism before they were trendy. Her mother was an aging hippie with a collection of long wraparound peasant skirts and Birkenstocks in three colors, though she'd added her own unique brand of fashion to the mix over the years, like the red heels and purple coat. Her father, on the other hand, spent most of his adult life in khakis and button-downs, though Cal had actually seen him wear jeans and fleeces recently. Her mother was always trying to get them to talk about their feelings, while their father was more likely to stew quietly when something was bothering him and then explode at someone when his frustration reached the boiling point. They had always been a strange balance of opposites.

They'd met on an airplane from San Francisco to Boston. Their father had spent the previous six months traveling from Boston to California with nothing but a backpack and a tent. This brief sojourn was so entirely out of character that Cal wondered if their mother had ever felt tricked by him, passing himself off as a backpacking hippie when he was anything but. He'd duped her from the start, though maybe he had been tricking himself as well.

The four of them sat down at the small table in the corner of the kitchen and began to eat. They filled their mother in on the details of the past few days—the previous night's wake, the way Barry had helped to plan everything, the program for the funeral. No one mentioned Violet's night with Michael or the revelations that had come with it. But Cal needed her mother's opinion.

"It was mostly men at the wake," she said.

"Was it?" her mother asked vaguely. Suzy and Violet glanced at Cal to see where she was going with this.

"Yeah. Mostly men from up here. And only a handful of women," Cal continued. "They all seemed really close."

"Well, that's good. I'm glad your father had good friends up here." Her mother bit into a piece of toast and dabbed her lips with a napkin, not making eye contact with anyone.

"Did you ever meet his friend Barry?" Cal pressed.

"No, honey. I've never been up here before, and I hadn't spoken to your father in a while. Since you girls have grown up, there wasn't much need for us to talk." She said this somewhat wistfully.

"What Cal is trying to say," Violet chimed in from across the table, "is that Dad was gay." Cal flashed Violet a look of annoyance. "What? Isn't that what you're getting at?" Their mother turned to look at Cal, and she nodded sheepishly.

"I know," their mother finally said.

"You knew?" Cal didn't know why she was shocked. Their mother had spent twenty-two years living with their father. If anyone had known, it would have been her. "How could you not have told us?"

Their mother sighed, pushing the empty plate away from her. "It wasn't my news to share. If he wanted you to know, he would have told you. And he never actually told me."

"So how did you know?" Suzy asked.

Their mother tipped her head. "There were signs. Not obvious ones, but after a divorce, when you look back on a marriage, there are often signs." She gave them a sad smile. "Nothing obvious, nothing definitive, but little things between us." She shook her head. "But I don't think you have any interest in hearing about our sex life."

"Ugh," Violet said, pushing back from the table.

"Exactly," their mother said. After a moment she continued. "I suspected he was having an affair. With a man from school."

"Mr. Louis," Violet said softly.

Their mother turned to her in surprise, then nodded. "Kent Louis. They became friends, going out for drinks after work, playing tennis together after school. Going camping together on the weekends." She pursed her lips and sighed. "Your father never enjoyed camping. I started to put the pieces together."

"Did you confront him? Did he admit to it?" Cal asked.

Their mother shook her head. "I did confront him, but he denied it. Acted horrified I'd even suggested it." She let out a harsh laugh. "And I think in many ways he *was* horrified I'd suggested it. If I could tell, who else might know?"

Cal looked down at her half-eaten plate of eggs and felt sick to her stomach. "Was that before or after he was fired?"

"Soon before." She picked up her coffee and held the mug in front of her face, not drinking it. "I wanted to believe him, so I pretended

I did. Then he was accused of propositioning those boys, and I didn't know what to believe."

"You thought he did it," Cal said. She managed to keep the anger from her voice.

Her mother looked at Cal, her face full of compassion. "It wasn't that simple, Callie. I didn't know what to believe. That year we split up was so hard. I felt blindsided. First suspecting the affair and then those accusations and him losing his job. Your father loved teaching. I couldn't imagine him ever doing something like that to his students." She shook her head and looked imploringly at the three of them gathered around the table. "He denied it, but he just let them push him out, didn't even go to a lawyer, though I begged him to. He said there was no point, the rumors would never go away. Which was probably true. They said they'd give him a severance package if he left quietly." She looked up, her eyes earnest. "But those accusations did something to him. He shut down; he withdrew. We were once so close. We talked about everything. But he just pulled away from me. He became completely unreachable. I finally asked him to move out."

"*You* asked *him* to move out?" Suzy asked in surprise.

Their mother nodded. "What else could I do? He didn't want to go to counseling. He wouldn't admit to anything with Kent. He wouldn't acknowledge there was a problem between us, and he wouldn't talk about what those boys said about him. I didn't even know who he was anymore. I never would have believed something like that, but I began to wonder if maybe it was true."

"It wasn't," Violet said quickly. "I just found out. Some of the boys from the swim team made it up because they thought he was gay. They didn't want him to coach anymore." Violet looked guiltily down at her plate.

"That's terrible. I'm sorry I ever doubted him." She leaned back in her chair. "He knew I doubted him. That's why he left so easily."

"I wish he'd just told us," Cal said. "We wouldn't have been upset. I mean, we would have been surprised, but we would have gotten over it."

Her mother turned to her and her expression was soft. Her eyes were red, and Cal wondered if it was from fatigue or crying. "Honey, your dad was Catholic. He grew up without a father and with a distant and emotionally manipulative mother. Religion was his home. It was at church that he felt most loved. His priest, the other altar boys, that community—they were the ones who made him feel safe." She tucked a lock of hair behind her ear and then tilted her head. "Did you know that before your father and I met he was considering becoming a priest?" Cal shook her head. "That's how important it was to him. I know none of you were brought up with religion in the same way, but for him it would have felt like turning his back on everything that mattered. It wouldn't have been easy for him."

"But nobody would have cared," Cal persisted.

"Callie, *he* cared." Her mother rested her hand upon Cal's. Its warm weight was reassuring. "It was his issue, not yours. He knew you loved him. He knew you all would have accepted him either way." Cal nodded miserably. "Your father was complicated," she added. "He was very angry with me when I told him I wanted a divorce, and he blamed me for the way it changed his relationship with the three of you. But what was I supposed to do? Continue having a pretend marriage? Act like it didn't matter to me that my husband was gay, whether he admitted it or not?" She shook her head. "So I made him leave, at a time when his life was already incredibly difficult. He felt like he was abandoning the three of you, just like his own father abandoned him, and he never really forgave me for that. I don't know if I've ever forgiven myself for it." She paused and wiped her eyes. "I wish we'd made peace before he died. I hope he made peace with himself."

They were quiet, the eggs long grown cold, the dregs of coffee lukewarm in their cups. Finally, their mother pushed herself to standing. "Enough of this. I need to take a shower before we head over there. And

Callie, where is Howie and those grandbabies of mine?" Cal's mother was the only one who got away with calling Howard "Howie."

"They're coming up today. They're meeting us at the funeral." Cal suddenly missed her family fiercely and was relieved Howard had pushed to bring both the girls today. She'd finally used the breast pump and her milk supply was building back up. She stood up from the table and began to stack the dishes, bringing them to the sink.

"I'm surprised they're not here already," her mother said. Cal didn't answer, but Violet did.

"Cal didn't get out of bed the first few days we were here." Violet came to stand beside Cal at the sink but didn't help with the dishes.

"Oh?" Her mother raised her eyes at Cal. "But you're up now."

"I am," Cal said.

"Good. Anything else I should know?"

Cal focused on the hot water and dishes.

"Yes?" her mother said, drawing out the word in such a way that Cal knew Violet had given Suzy a meaningful look.

"We'll talk later." Suzy picked up a dish towel and began to dry the plates.

Their mother nodded. "If you say so" was all she said.

Chapter Thirty-Eight

Violet

They all drove to the church together, Violet and Suzy sitting in the backseat of Cal's Subaru station wagon like children, their mother and Cal in the front seat, which was how it was for most of their childhood anyway. The only difference was Cal was driving and no one had tried to call shotgun. Somehow, no matter the driver or the destination, Cal always seemed to ride in the front seat.

They pulled into the parking lot of the church and filed out of the car silently. Suzy reached for Violet's hand and she grasped it tightly, gratefully. Outside it was freezing, the front lawn covered in snow, only a thin path paved to the entrance of the redbrick church. Standing on the steps, Howard held a pink-bundled Sadie in his arms and clutched Maisy's hand. Violet watched with an unwelcome pang of envy as Cal broke away and nearly ran to them, gathering the girls and collapsing into Howard. He circled his arm around Cal and passed her the baby, and together the four of them entered the church, Cal moving seamlessly from one family to the next.

People had already begun to enter the church and seat themselves in the polished wooden pews. Violet didn't recognize anyone, but they seemed to recognize Violet and her family, people nodding respectfully as they made their way down the aisle to the front row reserved for them. Violet was relieved Michael wasn't among those at the funeral. Whatever peace he'd needed to make with her father, he had done it the night before. Violet noticed Barry had chosen the second row, and he nodded when he saw them, his eyes already bloodshot. It only occurred to her now that no one had invited him to sit in the front row with their family.

Violet tried to remember the last time she'd been in church but found she was grasping at an array of childhood Christmases and Easters—each sermon, psalm, and hymn running together into one small collective memory. Suzy was the only one who went with their father to Sunday Mass, while Cal and Violet went to the mall or stayed home to study.

The church was wide and cavernous like the infrequently visited church of her childhood. Stained-glass windows filtered the thin light, giving the space a dim golden glow. Within a few minutes, the priest stepped out onto the pulpit, a gray-haired man they'd met over the weekend when planning the service. Father Anthony was older than her father and stood erect and calm in the traditional long white robe. *Vestments,* Violet remembered, the word rising to the surface of her consciousness, though she wasn't sure when or where she'd learned it.

"Joseph Bloom was a man of God," the priest began. Several in the church nodded, and Violet realized some of the members knew her father from his regular attendance here. The priest went on about her father's faith in God, his commitment to the people of Portland and his parish. It was clear the priest knew her father, and for this she was grateful. When Violet glanced over her shoulder, Barry's head was bowed and he wasn't looking at the priest, though she saw tears drop onto his lap. It was this sight that brought a fresh wave of grief, and she clutched Suzy's hand tighter.

Violet looked down the row at her family. Cal's face was a stark white, and she held Sadie to her body as Maisy sagged against her—all of them enveloped in Howard's bulk. There seemed to be comfort for

Cal in the presence of Howard and the girls that Violet wished she could have had today. She wished Luka were here, wished she could go back and redo the other morning when he'd offered to come.

"Joseph fed the people of Portland," the priest continued, and Violet tried to focus on his words. "He not only fed their stomachs with the delicious meals he prepared for them at Veg, but he fed their spirits. Joseph, with his business partner, Barry, created Hungry Hearts, a program that took the leftover food from Veg and donated it to the weekly supper that St. Mary's holds for the homeless of this community." The priest nodded solemnly at Barry, who nodded back. Violet wondered if the priest knew Barry was more than his business partner or if he was just as naive as the rest of them. "Joseph saw a need, and he quietly worked to fill it." He gave a sad smile. "That was Joseph. A quiet man of God who believed in working to make his community a better place."

Here, he looked up and nodded at Violet and her sisters. "Cal, Suzy, and Violet, Joseph's three daughters, you already know this about your father. Though you do not live in Portland, your father spoke of you each with pride." Suzy squeezed Violet's hand; Violet knew Suzy's guilt likely equaled her own. Violet hadn't known about the homeless program he'd started, because it was unlike her father to tell her about such things. She hadn't even realized he was a regular churchgoer these days. It wasn't something he talked about, and as someone who'd never considered religion an important part of her life, Violet couldn't fathom being shaped by it in the way her father clearly had been. It confused her. His faith had been vital to him, yet it seemed to have kept him from acknowledging who he was.

Suzy had decided to do a reading, and the priest called her up. Violet released her hand reluctantly and watched Suzy make her way to the pulpit. Suzy's hands shook as she shuffled through the papers, finding the reading she'd selected. Violet didn't pay attention to the words—like most religious works, they all blurred together for her into something incomprehensible—but she watched her sister. Suzy held her head up and spoke in a strong, clear voice. Despite her trembling hands, Violet could tell that Suzy felt at ease here in the formal rituals of the service in a way that Violet didn't. She kept her eyes on Suzy as her words rang clear across the crowded rows of mourners. Violet clasped her hands tightly together and hoped fervently that her father had forgiven them like they had forgiven him. Was hoping the same as praying? Violet wasn't sure.

After the funeral, Violet and her mother and sisters went to thank the priest.

"It was a beautiful service," their mother said, shaking his hand. "He would have been pleased."

"Thank you." Father Anthony's eyes were a watery blue, and he smelled strongly of lemon-lime shaving cream, though he wore a neatly trimmed white beard. It was strange to think of someone who had devoted his whole life to God doing something as mundane as shaving each morning. "Joseph had been coming to St. Mary's for many years. This is an aging church. Many of our parishioners are older, and we have fewer families and young people these days than we once did. But Joseph was always reaching out to our younger congregants, trying to get them more involved." He chuckled. "He once let it slip that he was a teacher in a former life, and I was always trying to get him to teach Sunday school, though he'd never take me up on it." He bowed his head in finality. "He will be deeply missed."

"Thank you," they all murmured and then moved forward through the church and out into the bright day. Violet noticed Barry had already made his way out of the church grounds and was heading down the street, not having bothered to stop to speak with the Father.

Chapter Thirty-Nine

Suzy

Suzy opened the door to Veg, holding it for her mother and Violet. Inside, the restaurant was warm and cozy, a fireplace in the corner already blazing. Barry and his employees must have been working tirelessly over the previous few days because there was a long table turned into a buffet lined with bowls of food. As usual these days, Suzy was both starving and queasy, and she piled her plate high with salads, sandwiches, and cookies. She joined the table where Violet and their mother were already sitting. Cal and her family put their coats on the table beside them and then went to get food.

"Easy there," Violet said as Suzy shoveled in a mouthful of quinoa salad.

"I'm sorry, I'm starving." Suzy avoided her mother's eyes. She would tell her, but now was not the time or place.

Barry came and stood by their table, holding a heavy blue coffee mug. Suzy had noticed all of the dishes in the restaurant appeared to be handmade, a charming touch. "Hello, ladies," he said. Seeing their mother, he extended his hand. "You must be Sandy. I'm Barry. I was a good friend of Joseph's."

Her mother smiled and shook his hand. "It's nice to meet you, Barry. Thank you so much for helping my girls. You've done a lovely job putting all this together." She gestured with her hand to the spread of food.

Barry nodded. "It was my pleasure," he said, blinking quickly.

"Please, sit down." Suzy nodded to the empty chair beside her. He lowered himself into the chair somewhat reluctantly. Servers in black pants and white shirts bustled around the restaurant, refilling the coffee carafe and putting out pitchers of lemonade and iced tea.

"The food is delicious." Violet raised her fork, which held a bite of arugula salad.

He smiled. "Thank you. Most of them are your father's recipes." Barry leaned back in his chair. "It was a lovely service."

"It was. Father Anthony did a nice job. Did you go to church with our father?" Suzy asked.

Barry shook his head. "I've never been one for organized religion, but your father went every Sunday. I might not have understood it, but it was very important to him."

"How long did you know our father?" Suzy asked.

Barry paused. "We worked together for ten years. I bought half the business from him seven years ago."

Violet narrowed her eyes and appraised him for a moment. "You were his lover, right?" she asked finally.

"Violet!" Suzy gasped, though they'd clearly all been wondering the same thing. Barry made a noise, something between a cough and a laugh, likely at Violet's choice of word to describe the relationship. Suzy turned to her sister, but Violet's eyes were on Barry. "That's totally inappropriate."

"Why? We're all thinking it. Why can't I ask?"

Suzy turned to Barry, who still hadn't answered Violet's question. "I'm sorry. This is obviously not the right time to have this conversation."

"What conversation?" Cal sat down at the table, holding a plate of food in one arm and Sadie in the other.

Barry laced his fingers around the blue mug. His hands were large and strong, the nails clean and cut short. He turned to Violet. "Actually, it's as good a time as any. Yes. We were partners. Beyond business partners."

Cal put her plate down with a heavy thud, but she didn't pick up the fork to eat.

"I'm going to leave you to talk," their mother said, rising with her plate. "I don't think you need me here for this conversation."

"I'm sorry," Barry said.

She shook her head. "No need. Joseph was a wonderful man, and I'm glad he had someone he loved. I'm very sorry for your loss." She put her hand on Barry's shoulder and squeezed gently, then strode across the room to where Howard and Maisy were still getting food.

"How long were you together?" Violet asked, turning back to Barry.

"The last seven years."

Seven years.

Suzy blinked, the number sinking in. He'd never trusted his daughters with this news, hiding it instead. And Suzy had never trusted him with her own truth, assuming he would have judged her, so certain he wouldn't have understood and would quietly disapprove of her.

And now it was too late.

"I'm sorry you had to find out this way. I wanted to tell you." Barry gestured to the crowded restaurant. "Before this, I mean. But Joseph wouldn't."

"Why not?" Suzy asked.

Barry frowned. "You heard the service. Your father was very devout." He traced his finger along the rim of the mug. "We were very happy together, but his religion complicated things."

"Was he . . . out?" Suzy asked. It occurred to her that even if she had told her father she was gay, he might not have reciprocated.

"He had friends who knew, but it was a small group, most of them friends of mine from before your father and I met. And I don't think you're really 'out' if your own family doesn't know." He leaned back in his chair. "I wanted to get married. So did he, but I told him I wasn't going to do it in secret. If we were going to get married, he needed to tell the three of you. Unfortunately, we never got that far." Barry gave a sad smile, and they were silent. Suzy imagined her father calling to invite her to his wedding to Barry. It was more than she could imagine. "I do hope that we'll be able to keep in touch though. I didn't have a chance to know any of you when your father was alive, but I'd like to now."

They murmured in agreement. Suzy hoped they all meant it. She'd like the chance to get to know this mild man their father had loved for the last years of his life.

"Did he ever tell you about his job at Beckett?" Cal asked from the end of the table. She held a sleeping Sadie against her shoulder.

Barry nodded, rubbing the knuckles of one hand. "I knew he was a teacher in another life, but he didn't talk much about it."

"Did he tell you why he left?" Cal asked. "About the accusations by the boys on the swim team?"

His jaw tightened. "He told me."

"It was all lies," Violet said. "The kids found out he was gay and were trying to get rid of him."

"He figured as much," Barry said. "He wasn't certain, but he thought that was their agenda."

"Why didn't he fight it? He left so quietly. He just let them push him out," Cal said.

Barry glanced around the table at the three of them as he spoke. "Your father knew that if he fought the charges, he would be outed. The boys would tell everyone what they suspected. To have that happen would have been devastating for your family." He gave a sad smile. "At that point, you see, your father still thought he could stay married to your mother. He was trying to save the life he had with you."

Suzy looked at Cal and Violet. Had there ever been a chance for their family to go on? The lies those boys told had fallen upon each other like a line of dominoes, each one clacking against the next until they all lay on the ground.

"Your father had a wonderful life up here, and we were very happy," Barry continued, "but I know there was a part of him that missed the life he'd left behind." He motioned across the table to the three of them. "When he talked about all of you and the life he had before he moved here, it was with a kind of nostalgia." He frowned and stared into his mug. "He lost the life he had with you, and I know he carried sadness with him over that."

"I wasn't as close to him as I wish I'd been," Violet sighed.

"Me neither," Suzy added.

Barry hesitated a beat before answering. "Was his relationship with the three of you as close as he would have liked?" He shook his head. "No. But he loved you, and he knew you each loved him too, in your own way. Your father had regrets in his life, but he never held anything against you. He even loved your mother, though possibly not in the way he wanted to." He took a sip of his coffee. "I also know he was happy here, with me, with the life we created together, despite his unwillingness or inability to be open about it. He was happy and that must count for something." He took a deep breath and looked at them intently, as if challenging them to argue. Then he wiped his eyes and stood up from the table. "I'm going to go check on the food. Make sure you try the muffins. They were your father's favorite." Suzy and her sisters watched him make his way across the bustling room and disappear into the kitchen.

Chapter Forty
Cal

Cal was in the bathroom nursing Sadie when Maisy ate the nut. Cal had wanted to ask Barry about the ingredients in the food, but then they'd started talking about his relationship with their father and it didn't seem appropriate to interrupt him to ask which of the dishes were nut-free. Howard had steered clear of all the breads and cookies, only giving Maisy a slice of vegetable lasagna and a cup of black bean soup after asking one of the servers and picking through them each with a fork.

Cal was perched on the edge of the toilet and had just switched Sadie from the left side to the right when she heard Howard through the thin wood-paneled door of the restroom. His voice was higher-pitched than usual, a clear note of panic in it as he yelled the words Cal had feared Maisy's whole life. "Cal! Cal! I need the EpiPen! Someone call 911!"

Cal responded instinctively, instantly, though recalling the moment later, the seconds took place in slow motion, her body several ticks behind her head and heart. She pulled Sadie from her breast with a slick pop, barely stopping long enough to pull down her shirt, not bothering to fasten the nursing bra. She scooped the diaper bag up off the floor and fumbled with the lock of the stall. As Cal ran, she rummaged in the bag for the pocket that held the bright-yellow pen. She retrieved it and rushed into the center of the restaurant, holding it over her head. "I've got it," she cried. "I'm here! Howard!"

An uneasy hush had fallen over the room since Cal had gone into the bathroom, though there was the sickening sound of wheezing coming from somewhere. She scanned the small crowd, trying to locate Howard and Maisy among the darkly dressed mourners.

"Right here," Howard called, and he was at the table where she'd left him with Maisy a few minutes earlier, though now his face was stricken with fear and he was hunched over their daughter. Maisy was gasping like a fish out of water, her lips flapping uselessly as they closed over air she couldn't swallow.

She's going to die, Cal thought to herself as she raced to Maisy and Howard, Sadie's fat cheek bouncing against Cal's shoulder. *She's going to die right here in front of us.*

"Take her," Cal said, roughly handing Sadie to Howard. All around her there were noises—murmurs and whispers as people tried to figure out what was going on. *Allergy, peanut, EpiPen,* the words of her daily life buzzed around the room, but Cal tuned them out, focusing only on Maisy.

Cal removed the safety tip of the plastic needle case. "It's okay, baby," she crooned to her daughter. "I have some medicine that's going to help you breathe. In just a minute you'll be okay." Cal prayed the words were true. Forcing herself to breathe calmly, she scanned the directions on the side of the plastic package, though she already knew them by heart. She'd read these directions hundreds of times in preparation for a moment like this, and she'd practiced with a fake pen in the pediatrician's office, but Cal made herself double-check. If she did it wrong, there would be no second chance.

Maisy's eyes grew wide at the sight of the thick needle and then wider in pain as Cal plunged it into her thigh through the thin black tights she'd worn under her corduroy jumper, sending the medicine into her bloodstream. Cal held on to the plastic case, even after she'd depressed the plunger, both afraid to take such a large needle out of Maisy's tender flesh and fearful that every drop of medicine hadn't yet drained. The bright-yellow plastic case stuck out of her leg like a traffic sign. *Slow children. Child dying. Mother praying.* The whole room seemed to hold its breath, waiting for Maisy. *Breathe,* Cal pleaded. *Breathe, breathe, breathe*—a mantra and a prayer.

Maisy inhaled sharply, a wet and sputtering choking sound, but an inhale nonetheless. She took sharp, uneven breaths, but it was the sweetest sound Cal could imagine. She clutched Maisy's hand, the other on her leg beside the empty syringe. Howard held Sadie in one arm, his other hand pressed against Cal's back. The four of them connected, her circle of life. There was so much love in this tiny foursome. *So much love.* This was it. Right here, this was all that mattered. She could survive the loss of anything—her job, her house, even her father, as long as she had this.

In the distance she heard a siren.

Chapter Forty-One

Violet

Violet sat on the bench outside of Veg, smoking a cigarette. She didn't smoke, not really, not since college, but every now and then on a bad day, she broke down and took out the crumpled pack of Camels she kept in the pocket of her purse. She'd had one recently, the day after she and Luka broke up, but she figured breakups, funerals, and near-death experiences entitled her to a few carcinogenic puffs.

It was even colder in Portland than in Boston, and Violet hunched into the thick collar of her wool coat in a futile effort to stay warm. Cal and Howard had gone to the hospital with Maisy, and their mother had driven behind the ambulance in Howard's car. It appeared Maisy would be fine, but Violet could see the residual panic all over Cal's face, her mouth tightly pleated. No wonder Cal was so neurotic. The front door of the restaurant opened, and Violet looked up to see Suzy zipping up her black parka.

"What are you doing out here?" Suzy asked.

Violet exhaled a plume of smoke. "Hiding."

"Me too." Violet scooted over to make room, and Suzy sank down beside her on the bench. She tipped her head to the burning cigarette. "Those are bad for you."

"You don't say." Violet held it out to her sister as an offering.

Suzy waved her hand through the smoke. "Ugh, get that thing away from me."

"Oh, I forgot," Violet said, raising an eyebrow. "You're with child."

Suzy rolled her eyes. "Shut up."

Violet took another drag, making an effort to blow the smoke out of the side of her mouth, away from Suzy. "So did you decide to keep it?"

Suzy scanned Violet's face as if waiting for a wisecrack or judgment. "I think so," she answered when none came.

Violet nodded, grinding the butt under the heel of her shoe. She hoped it would be a while before she'd need another one. "You know you really have to tell Ian. Either way."

"Do I?" Suzy asked hopefully.

Violet wasn't sure full disclosure was necessary with just anyone. If Suzy had had a one-night stand or gotten pregnant by the male version of Lani, she might have felt differently. But this was Ian, possibly the nicest guy in the world. He and Suzy had a history. Suzy was going to need help if she was going to do this, and Ian would give her that support. "Yeah. You do."

Suzy hung her head like a scolded child. "I know."

"What's he going to want?"

"To be involved. To be a dad. Whatever that means."

Violet nodded. She'd always liked Ian, though during his time with Suzy, she'd thought him simple and boring. Then Suzy started going out with Lani, and Violet suddenly missed Ian's easygoing kindness. She didn't think either of them was Suzy's soul mate, but if Suzy had to be saddled to someone for the rest of her life with a kid, Violet preferred it was Ian.

"Thank God Maisy's going to be okay," Suzy said, changing the subject.

"Yeah. Did you know she got like that?"

Suzy shrugged. "I knew about the allergy, obviously. Nut allergies can be pretty deadly. I know Cal's vigilant about what she eats. Obviously. You saw her with the peanut butter last night."

"Yeah, I know." Violet shrugged. "I just didn't realize why she was so crazy. Part of me thought Cal was just projecting her own neuroses onto Maisy." She met Suzy's eyes. "Pretty lousy of me, I guess."

Suzy shrugged, always willing to forgive. "You didn't know."

"I should have," Violet said.

"Yeah," Suzy agreed. "You should have."

Two men came out of the restaurant and said good-bye, paying their respects one more time. There were clasped hands, kind words, and awkward embraces that smelled of damp wool. When the men were gone, it was quiet again, just the two of them.

"I've been thinking a lot about the summer I came up here to stay with Dad," Suzy said carefully.

"Oh yeah?" Violet's fingers smelled of tobacco from the cigarette, and she wanted to go in and wash her hands.

Suzy nodded. "I keep thinking I'll see him up here."

"Dad? Me too. Everywhere I look, I see someone who looks like him." Violet dropped her hands back into her lap.

"No, Zach." Suzy's eyes were on the ground, her face somehow hard and vulnerable at the same time.

"Who?" Violet asked.

Suzy looked at her in frustration. "The guy."

It took Violet a moment to understand. Once she knew what Suzy meant, she didn't know what to say. "Oh," Violet said dumbly.

They never talked about that summer or the emergency rescue mission she and Cal had performed. Violet rarely thought about it, but occasionally she wondered if they should have told their parents what happened. Perhaps she and Cal had been naive to think all they needed to do was bring Suzy home. It was awful what had happened to Suzy, but with the exception of Cal, they were all teenagers. In the life of a teenager, an awful thing happened and then ended. It was with time and adulthood that you realized how such a thing could shape your life, how it could alter who you became as a person.

"I know it's crazy," Suzy continued. "I mean, he probably doesn't even live anywhere near here anymore. And it's not as if I think about what happened all the time anymore." She twisted her gloved hands in her lap and hunched further down into her coat. "For a while I did."

"Really?" Violet didn't know why she was surprised. After the car ride back from Maine, once she and Cal had gotten Suzy home, Suzy seemed okay. She never mentioned it again, not to Violet, at least. A few times Violet had tried to broach the subject in an "everything okay?" kind of way, which Suzy had just shrugged off. After a while, Violet had just forgotten about it. Not actually forgotten, but pushed it aside as something that had happened in the past. It was easier to assume Suzy was okay. But of course she wasn't, Violet realized now. Suzy hadn't changed exactly. She was still herself—caring and honest and good. But she was tougher too. Like she'd grown a protective shell, something hard and glossy that kept her from getting hurt but also kept anyone from getting too close.

Suzy nodded. "I couldn't get it out of my head. What happened. What I could have done differently."

"Oh, Suzy," Violet said, heartbroken. "You didn't do anything wrong."

She swallowed, pursing her lips together. Her eyes glittered with tears. "I went to confession once. But I couldn't go in. I didn't know what to say. I just sat on one of the pews for ages, trying to find the words."

"But it wasn't your fault," Violet said violently. "You had nothing to confess to! You didn't do anything wrong."

Suzy tipped her head at Violet, her eyebrows furrowed in confusion. "I did *everything* wrong," she burst out. "I lied to Dad about where I was going. I lied about how old I was. I went to a college party. *Alone.* I drank. I was *guilty.*" Suzy shook her head. "But I couldn't confess, because then the priest would have had to agree.

He'd have sent me home with my penance, and that was more than I could bear."

"Oh, Suzy." Violet lifted Suzy's hand into her own and squeezed her fingers gently. "You didn't do anything wrong. You have to believe that. You were fifteen. You acted like a fifteen-year-old! What he did was wrong." Violet squeezed Suzy's fingers again. "He *raped* you," she said softly. Violet had never articulated the thought, in her mind or aloud. Saying it now, even quietly, sent a chill through her. How could they not have told someone? "He raped you," Violet said again, clearer this time.

Suzy nodded miserably. "I know." She burrowed in the pocket of her coat and withdrew a crumpled tissue, which she wiped against her nose.

"We should have told Mom. Or even Dad," Violet said.

Suzy shook her head. "I didn't want you to. I wanted to just pretend it hadn't happened."

"But we should have done it anyway. And I should have asked you about it. I should have listened more."

Suzy gave a slow nod. "Maybe."

"God, I'm such an asshole. First Cal and Maisy, and now you with this." Violet tucked her hair behind her ears. "I had no idea how much it affected you. Which is totally stupid and thoughtless of me." Suzy didn't disagree, only shifted in her seat. "It is, isn't it?"

Suzy sighed. "Oh, Vi. I don't know. You have a tendency to be a little self-absorbed."

"I do?" Violet didn't mean to be self-absorbed. Sometimes it was just hard for her to see things from someone else's perspective.

"Well, yeah." Suzy's tone made it seem obvious, like this was an assessment of Violet everyone was aware of but her. Suzy waved her hand back and forth between them. "Even this conversation is self-absorbed."

"It is? How?"

Suzy rolled her eyes. "A minute ago we were talking about me being raped when I was fifteen and how it's basically something I've been dealing with since then. And now we're talking about how it affects you." She raised her eyebrows. "Do you see?"

"Yeah. I do." Violet hung her head. "I'm sorry." She vowed she would be better. She *needed* to be better, to find ways to show her love for the people that mattered instead of just assuming they knew and taking them for granted. If she could take away anything from her father's death, it would be this.

Suzy shrugged in resignation. "It's okay. Just pay attention to it."

Violet nodded. Suzy was right, of course.

"Should we head back in?" Suzy asked.

"Are you okay? Do you want to talk about this anymore?" Violet asked.

"No, I'm all right." Suzy smiled. "But thanks for asking."

Chapter Forty-Two

Suzy

Though it was barely five o'clock, outside it was already dark. She and Violet had returned from the restaurant and gone immediately to their shared bedroom, where they'd each taken a nap. Suzy had fallen into a blackout sleep, waking nearly two hours later to find her cheek resting in a warm puddle of drool and Violet's bed already empty.

Suzy made her way downstairs into the kitchen to start dinner. She'd make a pasta and salad for dinner, though she wasn't sure who would be eating with them. Cal still wasn't home. She chopped a red pepper into thin slices and sprinkled them evenly upon the salad greens. The front door opened and in swept their mother with a gust of icy air.

"Bloody hell, it's freezing out there." She stomped her shoes off on the mat. Since she'd flown in, Suzy had noticed their mother had picked up a number of British expressions. She wouldn't have been surprised if she were speaking in an English accent by the time the year was over.

"How's Maisy?" Suzy asked.

Her mother still wore her funeral outfit, and she stepped out of her black heels, padding over to the stove in stockings to put on the kettle. "She's fine, thank God. They kept her a few hours for observation, but they just released her. Cal went back to the hotel with them for the night." She found a box of tea bags in the cupboard and dropped one into a mug. She held the box up to Suzy. Suzy nodded.

"Poor Callie," her mother continued. "She was beside herself. Going on and on about how it was her fault it happened. That she should have been paying better attention."

"She *was* paying attention. She's always paying attention," Suzy said.

"I know. Who puts nuts in chili anyway?" Her mother reached for one of the pepper strips and munched on it thoughtfully. "Having children is terrifying enough without having to think about them accidentally poisoning themselves at lunchtime."

Suzy picked up a cucumber and began to peel its skin. "About that"— she started and then, having come up with no easy segue—"I'm pregnant."

Her mother's eyes widened and her mouth fell open, but only for a second and then she rearranged her expression into one of mild concern. "And what are your thoughts about this?" she asked, keeping her tone so light that Suzy could have kissed her.

"I'm keeping it." Suzy realized for the first time that it was true. Even when she'd told Violet earlier in the day, she hadn't been sure. But somehow now, telling her mother, it became real.

"Oh, sweetie." Her mother came around the counter and embraced her. "I'm so happy." She brushed Suzy's hair back with her fingers, her face just inches from Suzy's. Of the three of them, Suzy looked the most like their mother, with the same unruly brownish-orange hair, the same round freckled face. Looking at her mother could sometimes be like looking at a time-lapse video, the lines and creases of her future mapped out on her mother's fair skin. She held Suzy at arm's length. "And how are you?" she asked.

"I'm scared," Suzy said, her breath catching in her throat. "And I'm sad Dad's not here." Her mother nodded, her mouth tucked in sympathy, her strong hands still holding Suzy by the arms. "But I'm happy, I think," she said, though her voice rose up in a question.

Her mother patted her cheek gently. "Your dad would be happy too." And Suzy knew it was true.

Chapter Forty-Three

Cal

Cal tiptoed across the hotel room and stripped off the clothes she'd worn to the funeral. She felt her whole body relax as the grip of panty hose was removed. Pulling on a T-shirt of Howard's from his open suitcase, she sank onto the bed beside him. The doors to the other bedroom were open, where Sadie slept in the roll-away crib, Maisy in a twin bed. Cal's eyes were so tired they felt full of sand.

"Is she asleep?" Howard dropped the newspaper to his lap. Cal glanced down at the front page. The headline was about a fatal fever ravaging several countries in Africa. Death was everywhere, lurking in a kiss good-bye, a fallen tear, or a misplaced nut.

Cal nodded. "She was afraid she was going to stop breathing in the middle of the night."

"Poor babe." They spoke in whispers, worried the girls would stir. "What did you tell her?"

Cal lay down on top of the covers. "I told her nothing could happen while she was asleep. That we're going to be even more careful about what she eats. That we'll always have the EpiPen with us in case anything like that ever happens again, but we'll make sure it doesn't."

Howard nodded. She could sense him itching to return to the paper. They were both exhausted. Between the funeral and the hospital, the day had wrung them out. Howard lifted the paper half up. "I'm quitting my job," Cal added before she lost her nerve.

"What?" Howard dropped the paper back down on the bed and looked at her incredulously.

Cal nodded. "I am."

"Cal, why? What does that have to do with anything?" he asked, wrinkling his brow in confusion.

"It's too much," Cal burst out, sitting up in bed. "I can't juggle it all. I've tried, I really have, but I just can't do it."

Howard's expression softened. He looked even more tired than she did. "Callie, Maisy having an allergic reaction had nothing to do with you working. It was an accident. If it's anyone's fault, it's mine. I was the one getting her lunch. I should have spoken to the chef."

"I was distracted," Cal said.

"It was your father's funeral," Howard said, frowning. "I think you were entitled to be distracted."

"It's not just today." Cal shook her head, frustrated she wasn't getting her point across the way she wanted to. It wasn't just today. "I'm stressed out all the time. Even when I have time to relax, I *can't* relax. It's not fair to anyone. I'm miserable, and I'm making all of you miserable too. Something has to give, or we won't survive it." Howard didn't agree or disagree. He was quiet as they both digested her words.

"But you love your job," he said finally.

"That's just it, I don't." She felt like laughing. It was so preposterous how hard she worked at something she didn't even enjoy. "Maybe I did once. But I don't think I ever really did. I think I just wanted to be good at it. And instead, I'm missing everything happening here, right in front of me." She reached for his hand, rubbed her thumb along his palm.

"What about money?" Howard pinched the bridge of his nose with his thumb and forefinger, closing his eyes for a moment.

"We'll figure it out. We won't have to pay for day care, so that will be a big savings. And it won't be forever. Just for the next few years. It will give me a chance to think about what kind of work I actually want to do." She looked at him hopefully.

"This is really what you want?" he asked, searching her face.

She nodded. Admitting it was terrifying.

"Cal, I don't know what to say."

"Say it's a good idea," she pleaded.

He let out a breath. "Well, it would make things easier. Just the day-to-day of it all." He peered at her with a half smile. "You're going to go crazy being home all day."

"I know it's not going to be easy. I'm used to working. It will be a huge change, and I know it will be hard. But it has to be better than what we're doing now."

"Where did this come from?" Howard asked. "I didn't even realize you were thinking about this."

"I wasn't. And then today, Maisy almost died." She swallowed, the reality of these words still stunning her. "And I was looking at her trying to breathe, terrified we were going to lose her, and in the back of my mind I was thinking about the other morning, when we found out about my dad. Do you remember? I was yelling at her about getting dressed. It was just a stupid argument, but I was so angry." Cal took a deep breath, her frustration over something so small bubbling up like a rash. "And it had nothing to do with her. I'm just stretched to the point of breaking."

"I know," Howard said softly.

"And meanwhile, we have these two beautiful girls growing up right before our eyes, and I'm missing it because I'm worried about making it out of the house on time." She hadn't realized it, but she'd begun to cry remembering Maisy's face as she struggled for breath. Howard wiped her cheeks with the tips of his fingers.

"Okay," he said.

"Okay?"

"Okay," he repeated. "Now come to bed."

Cal curled into the space beside him, sliding in under the covers. She burrowed closer into him when he turned off the light. He'd been right here all along. From the room next door, Sadie gurgled in her sleep. Cal kissed Howard softly, and his familiar taste and smell were like coming home after a long trip away.

Chapter Forty-Four

Violet

Violet stood in the middle of the bedroom in just her towel, peering at the contents of her suitcase. There were several skirts and tights, a pair of wool slacks, a silk blouse with tiny buttons—none of which she felt like wearing. She wanted something shapeless and warm, though she hadn't thought to pack anything like that. The coziest thing she had was a wool turtleneck, though the collar made her itch. She padded over to Suzy's suitcase and found a pair of worn flannel pajama pants and a zip-up sweatshirt. Violet was several inches taller than Suzy and a good deal heavier, but the clothes were so oversized, they still fit. Violet rarely wore anything more casual than black jeans, but the clothes were like being wrapped in a soft blanket, and for once Violet understood Suzy's compulsion to dress comfortably and casually.

Violet toweled her hair dry and dropped the damp towel on the floor, then bent to retrieve it to hang it over the closet door. She'd slept for over an hour and then stood beneath the scalding hot water for ages. She finally felt renewed, as if she'd washed the stains of the past week from her skin, though she knew it wasn't so simple.

She sat on the bed, knees pulled up to her chest, phone in hand. Her heart pounded like when she was a teenager trying to work up the courage to call a boy. Though usually they called her. Finally, she took a deep breath and pulled up Luka's number. She listened to it ring and waited for it to click over to voicemail, unsure whether she would leave a message. Just as she was contemplating hanging up, he answered.

"Hey." His voice was low and gruff.

"Hi." Violet swallowed, suddenly uncertain what to say now that he'd answered. "I wasn't sure if you were going to pick up."

"I wasn't sure either."

Violet was silent for a moment, not sure how to continue. "Is she there?" she asked after a moment.

"Who?"

"Elena." She had a sudden image of him in bed with her while they spoke.

He let out a sigh of frustration. "No." And then, "Why are you calling, Violet?"

She thought for a moment, trying to summon an honest answer, one that wouldn't make him more annoyed with her than he already was. "When you offered to come up here, I should have said yes." He was quiet. He wasn't going to make this easy for her. Why should he? She'd never made anything easy for him. "This week would have been so much less awful if you'd been here."

"I wanted to be there for you." His voice was hard.

"I know. I should have let you." Violet focused on her chipping toenail polish. With her thumbnail she scratched the purple paint from her big toe, leaving the pale pink of her nail peeking through speckles of old polish.

"Violet, why did you break up with me?" Luka asked.

"I shouldn't have, I was stupid."

"Why did you break up with me?" he repeated.

"I thought we wanted different things," she said, her voice tiny on the phone.

"That's not true." He wasn't letting her off the hook. There was no getting out of this. "Tell me the truth. I already know it. I just want to hear you say it."

Violet waited, trying to find the words that were true but that would be least hurtful. "I didn't think you were the one I'd end up with," she said at last, taking her fingers away from her toes and holding the phone with both hands, as if protecting him from her words. "It sounds so dumb, but when I thought about whom I would spend the rest of my life with, I didn't imagine someone like you." Her face burned with the shame of this admission, though she knew he'd suspected as much all along. She pressed her lips together so tightly they ached.

"Yeah. That's what I figured," Luka said in a clipped tone. He was getting ready to hang up, she could hear it in his voice, and Violet pushed on, determined not to end things like this.

"I know that sounds terrible and shallow and just awful. And I am, I know. But the thing is, all this time I imagined I'd end up with someone different—an artist or a professor or whatever I *thought* I wanted—I was so blind to what we had." She squeezed her hand into a fist, flexed it, and squeezed again. "No one understands me like you do, Luka. No one has ever cared about me the way you do." She thought of Michael's empty eyes as he pressed down upon her, the same empty eyes of nearly every man she'd ever been with. "And maybe we're different, but I've finally realized that's not bad. In fact, it's actually what makes us so good."

On the other end, Luka was silent. Downstairs, her mother and Suzy were talking, quiet murmurs in the kitchen, the sound of dishes being arranged. Violet pressed on.

"I know you're angry with me, and you have every right to be. I know you're seeing Elena now, and maybe you've moved on. But I saw the way you looked at me the other night, and I don't really believe you let me come home with you just because you felt sorry for me." She swallowed down a lump in her throat, terrified she was wrong.

"Violet, what do you want from me?" Luka asked, and his voice held so much—anger, hurt, exhaustion. But somewhere in there, she was sure there was love too. Hope fluttered in her chest like a hummingbird trying to break free. She got up from the bed and stood by the single window that overlooked the ocean. The frigid air drifted up from the seams of the frame. In the distance, a rusted buoy bobbed in the waves.

"I want it all," Violet pleaded. "I want to come home. I want to be with you. I want to start all over, or where we left off. I want to marry you, if you still want that." Violet leaned her forehead against the cold pane of glass and closed her eyes. "Because we were good together, Luka. We really were."

"I don't know if I can do that," he said.

"Please. *Please.*" She had never begged a man before, but she would have gotten down on her knees if it meant Luka would take her back. Beneath her closed lids, she pictured him lying on the bed in their old room. His long, loose limbs splayed across the quilt, a bottle of Orangina on the bedside table. He drank bottles of the stuff, even though she tried to tell him it was full of sugar. She missed him so much her throat ached. *Please, please, please,* she whispered silently. She kept her eyes clenched shut. Maybe this was praying after all.

"I don't know," he said finally.

"You don't have to decide anything right now; we can talk when I get back." The silence stretched between them, endless and deafening.

"Okay," Luka said.

"Okay?" Violet opened her eyes, not sure what he was agreeing to, not daring to hope for too much.

"Call me when you get back in town."

"I will. Right away."

"When will you be back?"

"I don't know. In the next few days, I think. We'll have to come back here at some point to go through my dad's stuff." They hadn't talked about it yet, but there was still so much to be done. Packing up his clothes, going through the house, deciding what they were going to do with the house. Talk more with Barry. But none of this would get done this week. That would be another trip.

"Fine. Just call me when you get back, I guess." The emotion from just a few moments ago was gone. She'd put him off again, without even realizing it. If he was going to give her another chance, she needed to learn to give him more.

"Tomorrow," Violet said quickly. "I'll come home tomorrow."

She could almost see him rolling his eyes. Too little too late, as always. "Violet, do what you need to do up there. We'll talk when you get back."

"I'll be home tomorrow. Can I see you? Please?"

Luka let out a huff of air, a laugh of exasperation. "Okay. Call me when you get in tomorrow."

"I will. As soon as I get in."

"I can't promise anything, Violet. I don't know if I can go back."

"I know. Just don't decide anything yet. Please. Just be open to giving us another chance."

"Okay," he relented. A pause stretched between them. "I'll talk to you tomorrow, then."

"Luka?"

"Yeah."

"I love you." The silence on the line was unbearable. He didn't answer. "I just needed to tell you," she continued when he didn't say anything. "And I'm sorry. I'm so sorry."

"Okay. All right," he said gruffly.

"I'll call you tomorrow." She was ready to hang up when she heard him speak again.

"I love you too, Vi," he said, and then the line went silent.

Chapter Forty-Five

Suzy

Suzy poured flour into a bowl and added two cups of milk. She added eggs, baking powder, and salt, breaking the little clumps of flour against the side of the bowl, whisking the mixture until it formed a smooth white batter. With one hand she stirred; with the other she sipped lemon tea. Coffee was the first thing she'd given up for this pregnancy, though she suspected it would not be the last.

Violet and Cal were going home today; they would drive Violet's car back to Boston, and Cal was leaving her car for Suzy and their mother. They would stay on for a few more days and then return to Boston over the weekend. She wanted to explore Portland, see Barry, and have a meal at Veg. It occurred to her that she was now part owner. Later today Suzy planned to call her doctor's office to schedule a prenatal appointment. Over the next few days she'd figure out a way to tell Ian. She was glad to have her mother here with her. In a family of three girls, it was rare to have her mother all to herself.

Suzy dug through the pots and pans in the cupboard and was pleased to find a griddle, the same kind her father had used to make pancakes when she was a child. She put it over the burner and lit the flame, pouring a pool of golden oil in the center of the pan. When Suzy was seven, her father had let her flip the pancakes for the first time, kneeling on a stool to reach the stove. Once, a drop of oil had jumped from the pan and stung her on the wrist like an angry bee. Her father had held her wrist tenderly under cold water for several minutes, and when he withdrew it from the stream, the pain had magically faded.

With a wooden spoon, Suzy scooped circles of batter onto the griddle and waited patiently for bubbles to appear. From upstairs she heard the sound of a suitcase scraping along the wood floor and then being dragged down the stairs, the wheels hitting each step with a loud thump. A moment later Violet appeared, hauling her suitcase behind her.

"Smells good. What are you making?" She was freshly showered and wore a black wrap dress and knee-high brown boots, her long red hair braided neatly down her back. Last night Violet had emerged from the bedroom wearing Suzy's oversized pajamas. Seeing Violet in clothing so casual and sloppy was almost like seeing her naked, and Suzy was relieved to see she was back to her own self. Likely she'd discarded Suzy's clothes in a heap on the floor somewhere upstairs.

"Pancakes."

Violet stared at the empty coffeepot. "Is there coffee?" she asked, as if Suzy might have hidden it somewhere else.

Suzy held up her own mug. "Nope. Lemon herbal tea."

"Ugh." Violet made a face and filled the carafe with cold water. "Why?"

"I don't know. Supposedly caffeine isn't good during pregnancy." Suzy flipped the first round of pancakes and was pleased to see they were perfectly golden.

"Says who?"

"The Internet."

"Ah."

Suzy slid the pancakes onto a plate and poured more oil in the pan. The next batches were always harder to get right; since the griddle was so hot, it was easy to burn the surface without cooking the pancakes all the way through. She lowered the heat and ladled out more circles of batter.

"Morning, dearies." Their mother came into the kitchen in a floor-length pink robe and went straight to the cupboard, pulling down a heavy black mug. She too made a beeline for the coffeepot. Violet was haphazardly dumping tablespoonfuls of grounds into the filter. Suzy wondered if Violet had ever made coffee for herself or if there was always someone around to do it for her.

"No coffee?" her mother asked.

"Apparently, Suzy's giving it up," Violet said.

"Is she?" Her mother rubbed her hand along Suzy's back. "When I was pregnant with each of you I still drank coffee."

"So you know!" Violet burst out. "I wasn't sure if she'd told you yet."

"She told me. And I think it's wonderful." Her mother brushed the hair out of Suzy's face and kissed her on the cheek.

"Hello!" The front door opened and in came Cal. For the first time in days she didn't look like a walking zombie. Her skin had lost its pallor and the deep circles beneath her eyes had either faded or she'd managed to artfully cover them with makeup. Even if that was the case, the fact she'd bothered to put makeup on was an improvement from just days earlier. "It smells good. What are you making?"

"Pancakes. Does someone want to get plates out?"

"I will." Her mother turned to Cal and kissed her lightly on the cheek. "Hi, sweetheart. How's Maisy?"

"She's fine. Back to herself today. Howard and the girls just left. Vi, I told him we'd be leaving soon too."

"Well, we're not going anywhere till I've had some coffee." Violet flipped on the switch, having finally wrangled the grounds, water, and filter into submission. The smell of it brewing was tempting, though Suzy was pretty sure it would taste terrible—weak and watery or bitter and dark.

Suzy slid the next batch onto the plate and poured a final splash of oil onto the griddle. When she worked at Ciao they had a Sunday brunch. Each week, Lani would create an elaborate pancake special—coconut with cinnamon, cranberry-orange, lemon and sour cream, banana–chocolate chip. They were decadent and delicious, though Suzy suspected they left the diners with a stomachache for the remainder of the day. Her father's pancakes, on the other hand, were simple. Buckwheat, buttermilk, or blueberry was about as fancy as he ever got, but Suzy would always leave the table feeling satisfied rather than stuffed.

"Suzy's giving up coffee," Violet told Cal, raising her eyebrows.

"Oh yeah?" Cal's voice was neutral.

"Yup. For the baby," Violet answered.

Cal turned to Suzy and though her eyes were trained on the griddle, she didn't miss the way Cal's face lit up in joy. "You're keeping it?" Suzy nodded, and Cal threw her arms around her shoulders, squeezing hard. "Oh, Suzy, I'm so happy to hear that."

"I know, I know." Suzy smiled and then shrugged Cal off. "Careful, I don't want these to burn. Someone get silverware. Breakfast is ready."

Within a few minutes they were all gathered around the table. Somehow, they'd all taken the same places as they did in the house in Cambridge—Violet and Cal seated beside each other and across from Suzy, their mother at the head of the table. As a child, Suzy had sat in the seat to her father's right. While the rest of the family buzzed about, her father and Suzy would eat quietly, appreciating the flavor of butter and maple. It would be a Saturday morning, and the whole weekend lay ahead of them. Occasionally, her father would catch Suzy's eye and wink at her.

This morning, there was a general jostling for syrup and butter and slices of melon. Everyone agreed Violet's coffee was terrible, and Cal went to put on another pot. They talked about Maisy, how terrifying yesterday had been for everyone, and then they remembered the funeral, the warm way the priest had spoken of their father, the many people who had come to pay their respects. They did not talk about Barry, though Suzy knew this was out of some strange deference to their mother, despite the many years of divorce that lay before this startling revelation.

Suzy let her hands rest on her still-flat belly. How long before her body began to change? The seat to her left was empty, but in some ways their father was more present here today than he'd been in any of their lives, with the exception of Cal, for many years. Suzy wasn't sure what God she believed in these days, but she knew it was no accident she felt closer to her father today than she had just a week ago.

Suzy thought of Ian, of his easy smile and the patient way he spoke to everyone, his steady predictability. He would be a good father. Across the table, Violet and Cal were arguing over the drive back—how long it would take, who would drive, at what time the traffic would be at its worst. Suzy could almost feel her father there, the way he would roll his eyes at Suzy, a small smile playing on his lips just for her. Suzy smiled, holding his presence in the room as she stared at the sticky remnants of maple syrup on her plate.

And just as when she was a child, the fleeting moment of intimacy ended. Cal began to clear the table, and Violet fussed around the living room to make sure she hadn't left anything behind. The room echoed with the clinking of silverware and the clack of their mother loading the dishwasher. Suzy gave a final glance to her father's empty seat before she rose to join the women.

Acknowledgments

Many people helped *The Bloom Girls* see the light of day.

I owe a great debt to my extraordinary agent, Marlene Stringer. Your professionalism, commitment, and hard work made my dream a reality. Thank you.

To my brilliant editors, Charlotte Herscher and Jodi Warshaw: From our first conversation, I felt confident placing myself in your capable hands. Your gentle yet astute observations helped shape this into a tighter and more cohesive novel.

To my writing colleagues, Cynthia Riggs, Catherine Finch, Amy Reece, Mathea Morais, Lisa Belcastro, Ruth Weiner, and Katherine Ventre: your steady encouragement offered renewal and a welcome harbor from writing's isolation.

To Sarah Smith, a true writing companion and friend, for patiently listening while I went on and on about my characters as if they were real people.

To Bob Moore and the Martha's Vineyard Public Charter School for creative writing professional development.

To Jonathan Simpson: for your keen legal eye and willingness to lend advice, despite quite a few other obligations.

To Marya Cohen: For thirty-three years of unwavering friendship, for always, *always* being there to listen to my worries, no matter how small. Your generosity of spirit amazes me.

To Holly Thomas and Amelia Angella: for your enthusiasm, reassurance, and constancy over the years.

To my mother, Pam Cavanagh, for being my cautious yet tireless cheerleader in any venture I undertake, for working so hard to make the lives of those you love easier, and for convincing me I could be both a writer and a teacher. To my father, Tom Cavanagh, for being a critical writing mentor and editor since I was able to compose a complete sentence, for filling our house with books, and instilling in me the value of stories. And to both of you, for teaching me the importance of optimism.

To my daughters, Nevah and Olivia, who are always in my writing in some form or another and who simultaneously empty me out and fill me up. You are everything.

And finally, to Reuben, for dreaming big, pushing me to believe in myself, and always making space in our busy world for writing. Without your love and support, I probably would have stopped a long time ago.

About the Author

Photo © 2016 Eli Dagostino

A teacher as well as a writer, Emily Cavanagh lives with her husband, two daughters, and an Australian shepherd on Martha's Vineyard island. Her work has been published in *Red Rock Review*, *Grain Magazine*, *Transfer Magazine*, and *Martha's Vineyard Arts & Ideas*. Read more about Emily's work and life at www.emilycavanaghauthor.com.